AIRBORNE, AIRBORNE, WHERE YOU BEEN?
'ROUND THE WORLD, AND I'M GOIN' AGAIN.

"Their hands were tied behind them during the torture. Death came as a result of loss of blood in both cases. No vital organs were intentionally damaged. I don't know how long it took, but undoubtedly over an hour. I suspect the victims were aware most of the time. Large amounts of amphetamines were in the remaining blood."

"They were intentionally kept awake?" Wayne asked, unbelieving.

Hayman nodded. "Like a wide-eyed teamster, pedal-to-the-metal, popping bennies at 3 A.M. I imagine there was a lot of screaming, but no one was around to hear it."

"I hear it in my dreams," Boyles said.

Other Avon Books by
William Lovejoy

SEAGHOST

WILLIAM H. LOVEJOY

AVON BOOKS ◆ NEW YORK

RIPCORD is an original publication of Avon Books. This work has never
before appeared in book form. This work is a novel. Any similarity to
actual persons or events is purely coincidental.

AVON BOOKS
A division of
The Hearst Corporation
1350 Avenue of the Americas
New York, New York 10019

Copyright © 1992 by William H. Lovejoy
Published by arrangement with the author
Library of Congress Catalog Card Number: 91-92085
ISBN: 0-380-76447-4

First Avon Books Printing: January 1992

AVON TRADEMARK REG. U.S. PAT. OFF. AND IN OTHER COUNTRIES, MARCA
REGISTRADA, HECHO EN U.S.A.

Printed in the U.S.A.

RA 10 9 8 7 6 5 4 3 2 1

Dedicated to the memory of my gruff and lovable friend
Bob Nolan,

and offering strength, hope, and love to
Sally, Tim, Tom, and Suzy

ONE

AT THE END, the body hung suspended from a gnarled beam, caught in a harness fashioned from leather straps. Like the livery of a favorite Pekinese.

The once proud head, with its full mane of thick blond hair, was canted at an awkward angle, wide chin resting near the left collarbone. The hair was matted and limp, the face ashen, the mouth a frozen rictus caught up in its own horror. Both eyelids were gone. The overly large, round, and fading dark blue eyes had been forced to bear witness.

Sloping at a steep angle from the thick neck, the shoulders were massive and strong, sinewed with muscle, and the thick arms hung straight down, fingers curled into claws fighting a departed pain. There were white depressions around the wrists where the thongs had been tied. The two hands had six fingers left between them. The forefingers and the thumbs were gone. Four fingers still had fingernails.

Golden curls of hair on the big chest were streaked with the blackened remnants of blood from scores of eighth-inch-deep slashes which had carefully avoided the broad band of leather tightened under the rib cage and the two thinner, vertical bands which went up over the shoulders. Dried rivulets of blood were patterned down the torso, disappearing into the pubic thatch or continuing

1

down the heavily muscled thighs and calves to drip off toes pointed at the manure-crusted earth. Body fluids had been sucked up by the porous ground, leaving a barely discernible stain. A gory heap on the primitive floor was what remained of the genitalia.

Nine feet away, facing the body of George Henry Andropoulous, hung the body of Mrs. George Henry Andropoulous, in much the same condition, except for the broom handle.

The couple hung like abandoned puppets from the central beam in the corridor of the barn. Empty stalls along each side contained the ghosts of long-gone dairy cattle. Moonlight spilled through the large gaps in the roof, spreading a blue light over the interior of the loft and corridor, crisscrossed by the shadow of eroded rafters.

Rusty hinges held the rotted doors closed, as if against the chill of the night. The small corral which abutted the building was missing many of its cross poles—hands without fingers, a stark silhouette played against a moon-washed landscape. An ancient, open-faced equipment shed with a rusted, corrugated tin roof leaned precariously into the light wind. The rock foundation of a four-room house was buried in the parched earth a hundred yards away. Its soul had fled in flames years before.

The spring thaw in the higher elevations had released the perfume of manzanita, sumac, and golden currant; here, the scent was tainted.

To the east, the pink tinge of dawn spread fiery tendrils over the piñon and the ponderosa pine and the white peaks of the Sangre de Cristos.

TWO

SEVENTEEN YEARS FROM the beginning, it was a different harness, of wide webbing, fitting snugly over shoulders whose muscles were not fully developed, with wide, buckled straps across the chest and looped through the crotch. The packs hung heavily in front and back.

There was fear then, too, though it was subdued and mildly displaced by the methodical discourse of the instructors. The leap from the C–130 Hercules was less than voluntary, propelled by the jump master's shouted, "NOW! GO! GO! GO!"

One thousand one.

Now arch the back, hold the head high. Elbows bent below the body, palms flat, legs spread wide, bent at the knees. A frog in flight, balanced on the precarious pressure of atmosphere.

One thousand two.

God!

One thousand three.

All right!

One thousand four.

The static cord jerks.

There is the promised pop of the pilot chute, then the whispering slither of the canopy sleeve and suspension lines dragging from the pack. Brace the back in eager expectation.

The canopy cracks open, billows, becomes momentarily concave from its domed top as downward speed is cut drastically. The tug on the harness, biting, as his body swings into a vertical position.

And elation. My God, the elation!

Carlos Rivera leaned against the front fender of his white Chevy Blazer, studying the barn, waiting.

Four of his deputies crisscrossed the yard slowly, their tan Stetsons inclined toward the ground as they scanned the immediate world for . . . something, anything, among the weeds or lodged in the dried ruts of earth. The sun was high in the brassy blue sky and spatters of light bounced from the chrome and glass of the vehicles parked randomly outside the yellow tape.

Deputy Luisa Rodriguez, called Lu by most of her colleagues, his chief investigative assistant, stood by another Chevy Blazer adorned with a rack of siren and strobe lights. It was parked catty-wampus across the narrow two-rut lane a quarter mile away, and he could tell Luisa was having trouble with Janet Willow from *The New Mexican*, whose car was blocked by the four-wheel-drive vehicle. She was gesturing madly in the direction of Luisa, then the barn, then Rivera with wild swings of her arms. A blue van, emblazoned with an Albuquerque radio station's call letters, dipped through the barrow pit from the county road and drew up behind Willow's car. The driver got out and joined Willow in debate with Luisa.

How do they find out so fast? Rivera thought.

He sighed and felt beleaguered.

Carlos Rivera appeared bigger than he really was. At five-ten, he had a disproportionately large head and chest, bulging biceps under the short sleeves of the khaki cotton drill shirt, and a stomach beginning to strain against the same shirt. That distressed him and caused him to add repetitions to the morning exercise regimen. To no apparent benefit, as far as he could tell.

He had worn a droopy mustache while he was captain of the investigations division in the Santa Fe County sheriff's department, but when Sheriff Dawes dropped dead of a heart attack eight months before and Rivera had been appointed acting sheriff for the remainder of the term, the mustache had gone into the bathroom sink. There was a new and distasteful concern for his public image, an encroachment upon his privacy and independence. The commissioners' appointment had been as unexpected as the brand-new feeling of being constantly in the eye of a scrutinizing public, one that watched Hispanics in authority with utmost care. Carlos Rivera was confident of his competence as a law-enforcement officer and a homicide investigator, but much less so of his talent as a politician. Five agonizing months had gone into the decision to announce himself as a candidate for the permanent position.

Now this. With three weeks to go until the ballots were cast.

He had taken one look at the maggots crawling over the rotting bodies, gagged at the sweet stench, and backed out of the barn. After several swallows to regain his composure and keep the bile down, he turned back to the eleven and twelve year olds still clutching their .22 single shot rifles to their skinny chests, as if they expected them to be taken away. Luisa Rodriguez had led them fifty yards away from the barn and stood beside them, diminutive and pretty and sober faced. Her nicely molded hips supported a cotton drill skirt and a heavy gunbelt. The nine millimeter Beretta grip protruding from the holster looked too big for her small hands, but she held her own on the range. She gripped her Stetson in her hand, and she appeared concerned, her dark eyes guarding the boys.

Rivera squatted in front of them, speaking in English because he believed that in a multicultural environment, it was well to develop the less familiar language. "Well, it's Juan and Roberto, huh?"

"*Sí* . . . yes."

"And how did you happen to be out here this morning? Hunting rabbits?"

The taller boy was not stupid, and he figured out where this policeman was going with his question and spoke, "The school bus, it was too fast. We missed it."

"And your mother, she knows of this?"

Shadow in the eyes. "We thought not to worry her, *capitan*."

"I'm sure you did. Do you often come here?"

Violent nodding.

"To hunt rabbits and play in the barn?"

More nodding.

"Did you come last weekend?"

Juan answered, "*Sí*. On Sunday."

"What time was that, Juan?"

He shrugged. "I do not know. In the afternoon."

That helped to fix the time. "On Sunday, the barn was as always, empty?"

Affirmative nod.

"So you came to the barn this morning. Then what?"

Juan responded. "The door is usually open, but we had to open it. It was hard to do. When we saw the . . . the . . . Roberto, he got sick." He pointed to the pool of vomit alongside the doorway, perhaps taking some pride in his manly ability to keep his breakfast down. "Then we ran down the road to Delgados' "—he swung and pointed across the shallow valley—"because of the telephone they have. Senorita Rodriguez, she pick us up there."

"You did the right thing by calling us, Juan and Roberto. I thank you."

Rivera stood, motioned to Rodriguez, and they moved away from the boys. "Luisa, I want you to take them into the medical clinic. Talk to Dr. Pamela Ostrander, the psychiatrist, and explain what happened. Tell her I'd like to have her talk to them for a while, maybe see if there's any trauma. As soon as you're gone, I'll have somebody pick up the mother and meet you there. I don't want the reporters getting to them, so take care.''

"I've got it, Carlos." There was no cheer in her face today, no ready smile.

After Luisa had driven out with the boys, Rivera had turned on his radio and called for more deputies, the forensics team, and the medical examiner. That was at 9:30.

He had been waiting since then. Waiting for an answer to sadism? Was there an answer he could understand?

Carlos Rivera had been a cop for long enough to know that the answers did not present themselves for inspection on call. They had to be pulled out of people, and they did not come out easily. It was like hammering away at solid rock for a glimmer of gold.

Just before eleven, he heard his number called and leaned through the window of the truck to grab the microphone. "Eagle One."

Dispatch told him to switch over to channel two, for Eagle Eleven.

That would be Deputy Vern Ketch. Rivera had to open the door to reach the radio and change frequencies. He sat on the edge of the seat, his legs hanging outside, and the stifling heat of the interior caressed him.

"Eagle One to Eagle Eleven."

"Yeah, Sheriff. I'm at the hospital with a DOA."

Not another one. "What have you got, Vern?"

"White male, late fifties, looks like a heart attack. He expired out at the Timbers Motel sometime last night. The paramedics caught the call, but I heard it on the scanner and stopped for a look."

"Something unusual?"

"In the death? I don't think so, but I thought you ought to know about it because the dead man is Senator DeLamma. Ralph DeLamma." The radio crackled with static.

"DeLamma? He's the one from . . . I don't remember. Some northeastern state."

"Right, Sheriff. A honcho on the Senate Appropriations Committee. I remember because he was the one trying to screw up the drug enforcement funding last year."

"Yeah, that's right. Okay, Vern. Treat it as a VIP. Help in any way you can. Notifications. Better call the media people, show we're working with them. Edgerton over at the FBI, too, I suppose, with a US senator. If you run into any problems, let me know."

"Gotcha. Eleven out."

As he tossed the mike back into the bucket seat, the gas-masked ambulance attendants emerged from the barn, dragging two rubber-tired stretchers topped with black rubber body bags. The gurneys broke through the hardened crust of soil and bogged down. The attendants had to plow ground, getting the bodies to the orange and white ambulance. Rivera found himself studying the ruts in the parched, ecru earth.

Down the hill by Luisa's Blazer, the media people were using up film as fast as their autowinders would turn it.

The ME followed the gurneys out of the barn, shedding his own mask. He spotted Rivera and walked toward him.

Unlike Rivera, Dr. Gerald Hayman had come to terms with the round little paunch that sagged over the Coors belt buckle on his engraved belt. Like a large soft watermelon, it jiggled under his cotton dress shirt as if he were completely unaware of it. Hayman was otherwise long and lean, his hips so thin that the beige slacks kept inching downward. He wore scuffed Wellington boots in a brown leather that matched his similarly scuffed medical bag, no tie, and a sagging suit coat that matched the slacks. He was originally from back east, Pennsylvania, and his skin had never acclimated to New Mexico. His face always appeared bright red in the sun.

Switching the bag from left hand to right, he eased out of his coat as he neared Rivera, then laid his bag, mask, and coat on the hood of the truck. Hayman's hair was an oatmeal beige and gray, and it was constantly in a state of disarray; he had little time for the more mundane tasks in life.

Rivera smelled the stale odor of the dead on him. He shook a couple Marlboros from his pack, offering one to the doctor, then lighting both with an old silver Zippo with etched letters that had almost eroded:

101st AIRBORNE DIVISION
PHAN RANG, RVN
AUG 65–AUG 66

"I've seen a number of examples of man's inhumanity to man, Carl."

Like the two boys earlier, Rivera just nodded.

"But never anything like this. Nothing like this. It just doesn't happen in New Mexico these days."

Hayman took two deep drags of the cigarette, then tossed it away, as if the taste bothered him.

Rivera wrinkled his nose at the odor emanating from Hayman's suit. "I couldn't stay in there long enough to make any guesses, Jerry."

"It's terrible, Carl. I think they were kept alive for a long time. There are needle punctures on the arms. I won't know until the chemistry is done, but intuition tells me they were pumped full of stimulants, to keep them alert and aware of what was going on."

"How long?"

"Have they been dead? Couple days. I'll be more precise on that by tomorrow. Have you got any water?"

"Some coffee." Rivera reached through the open window and picked up a Thermos from the front seat. Unscrewing the cap, he poured it full of lukewarm coffee.

The doctor sipped, swished it around in his mouth, then spit onto the ground. Then he took a drink while they watched the ambulance drive away. "My guess is that the two perpetrators—"

"Two?"

"One of your forensics people in there said there were two different shoe tracks. I'm guessing they worked on the woman first, in front of the man, but he didn't give them anything. I don't think he'd have been as mutilated if he had talked while they were cutting her up and abusing her. Initial exam shows there was a lot of vaginal soft tissue damage from the broomstick. Her ears and nipples were sliced off. The cuts are so clean, I'd suspect a scalpel."

"You think they were after information?"

"What else?" Hayman's eyes looked over at him from under shaggy gray brows.

"There's the possibility of simple sadism, isn't there?" Simple motives were easier.

The ME harumphed. "Simple? I suppose so. Unlikely, in my opinion. This was done slowly."

"How about ID?"

"The male was one-eighty to one-ninety pounds, light blond hair, blue eyes, thirty-five to forty-five, but in excellent physical shape. It'll take a while to determine if there were earlier scars. The female was around one hundred and ten pounds, brown hair, hazel eyes, maybe ten years younger. That's it for now."

"Dental?"

"No teeth. They were broken out."

"Will we be able to get prints, Jerry?"

"Thumbs and forefingers are also gone. Taken away."

Steven Wayne had done some research beyond what had blared in the newspapers and across the anchor desks before he left Albuquerque. After a couple of telephone calls, he had some idea of the professional and political arenas into which he had been summoned.

Not summoned. Invited.

Normally, Tom Edgerton, the agent resident in Santa Fe, would have received the invitation, but he had escorted Senator Ralph DeLamma's body back east and then taken a couple weeks of vacation time while he was on that end of a bureau-paid airplane ticket. So Wayne drove up to the capital.

The government sedan did not have the same agility and pure sense of power of his own altered Trans Am, but it felt good to be on the highway again, away from the confines of his desk with its texture of memos and files and paper, paper, paper. He ignored the air-conditioning and rolled the front windows down and turned the radio up. His tanned left elbow rested on the window ledge. The warm wind whipping the short sleeves of his shirt reminded him of similar drives on graveled country roads, listening to KOMA out of Oklahoma City on the erratic radio of a '54 Chevy, on summer days when he had nowhere to go but to the county line and back. That was a western Kansas that was no more, a quarter century into history, and as outdated as the vacuum tubes that had reproduced Chuck Berry, Richie Valens, and the Big Bopper over a single ratty speaker.

Wayne had a law degree and eighteen years wrapped up in his career, and he was feeling his forties, though not showing them quite yet. His body was agile and looked lean in his conservative dark suits. Some people sensed a potential for rapid and exact violence under the surface, and while it had been present when needed in the past, it was generally expelled on a racquetball court. His dark hair was neatly trimmed to be slightly longer than policy—he reacted adversely and usually subtly to bureaucratic regulations—with a stubborn curly forelock which often hung over his forehead. His green eyes were set wide under dark straight eyebrows that echoed the normal set of his lips. His nose was thin, and his tan disguised the few wrinkles at his eyes and the corners of his mouth. Except for the missing upper tip of his left ear, he was bureau average, exactly the kind of American the ghost of J. Edgar approved.

Kind of depressing to look so middle-of-the-road, Wayne had often thought.

Wayne would never have considered himself a complex man, nor one who was particularly emotional. At unexpected moments, however, his throat would clutch and his eyes would squint against unwanted wetness. Tammy Wynette singing "Amazing Grace." Candid photos of John F. Kennedy. Though Wayne was a lifelong Republican, born of staunch Kansas Republicans, it was Jack Kennedy who had inspired him and interested him in government service. He took pride in his work, and it was sometimes exhibited in an arrogant swagger in his walk, shoulders high and back. It was a subconscious trait.

Already in mid April, the heat waves could be seen shimmering in the rearview mirror as Wayne slowed from the steady sixty-five—it was a government car with federal license tags—he had been driving and left the Interstate for the four-lane Cerrillos Road leading into Santa Fe. Traffic in and out of the city was steady and heavy. Exhaust fumes hung low in the heat and stung his nostrils. He drove slowly through town, cutting around the Plaza and downtown area by taking Sandoval Street and Palace Avenue. He found the county building, and parked in a rare opening on Lincoln. The Federal Courthouse dominated the end of the street ahead of him.

Locking the car, he pulled on his coat, jaywalked the street, crossed the sidewalk, grass strips, and parking lot, and entered the county building. A receptionist pointed out the meeting room for him, and he walked down the echoing corridor to its door. Wayne was so accustomed to institutional linoleum and paint that the drab colors did not even register with him. Uniformed deputies and women in civilian dress passed back and forth through the corridor. In a room at the far end, a loud drunk enumerated his rights.

He knocked once and opened the door.

There was a big wooden table, surfaced in scratches and scars, papers, and a couple of briefcases, surrounded by upholstered chairs, three of which were occupied. The three men looked up at him.

"Steve Wayne. I'm the Special-Agent-in-Charge at Albuquerque."

The swarthy man in the short-sleeved summer khakis stood up and came around the table, extending a hand. "Carl Rivera, Agent Wayne."

Wayne shook the hand and found it firm and dry, warm. The sheriff spoke with only a trace of a Spanish accent.

"Please come in," the sheriff told him, waving in the direction of the others. "Dr. Jerry Hayman, the medical examiner. District Attorney Keith Boyles."

Wayne shook hands with the other two men, then found a seat. Hayman was an unkempt, skinny man, except for the bowling ball stomach. His suit coat was tossed over the back of the chair next to him. It was difficult to feel confidence in him, though Wayne's telephone source had suggested the man was more than competent. Boyles was a fat man, sweating in the refrigerated air, but his well-tailored three-piece suit helped discourage the impression of sloppiness. He had neatly trimmed thinning hair, a round face, a slightly puckered mouth, and eyebrows that arched like prone question marks.

Rivera regained his chair and said, "I'm glad you could join us, Mr. Wayne."

"Steve'll do. Did you ask Tom Edgerton to sit in?"

"Yes, but he was scheduled for a trip to Washington. Besides, he pointed out that what we've got is not a federal crime. Not yet, anyway. That's why I really appreciate your sitting in."

"Well, I'm not sure what I can do, either, but I'll be glad to listen."

"Fine. Thank you. We've been reviewing our progress since yesterday, and we'd like to share with you what we have. You have read the papers, of course?"

"Yes. This Janet Willow who broke the story is calling it the Razor Murders. Plus, I'd suspect she's also the one who brought on the attention shown by last night's national network news. She made extensive use of the terms 'torture,' 'maimed,' and 'mutilated,' though there was no detail.''

Hayman cleared his throat and leaned forward to put his elbows on the table. ''I'm afraid she got that much out of one of my rather gullible assistants. Before I managed to put a lid on it. The wounds could have been caused by a razor, but I doubt it.''

''She had pictures of a barn and a telephoto shot of the two body bags.''

''Photographers like body bags,'' the DA said.

''That's true,'' Wayne agreed.

''Show him the pictures, Jerry,'' Rivera said.

Wayne accepted the stack of eight by tens from the medical examiner and went through them slowly. The police photographer had covered every possible angle. It took some willpower not to gag.

''Jesus Christ!''

''My reaction, also,'' the sheriff told him softly.

Wayne had seen some gruesome murder scenes, but this one turned the stomach, threatened the Big Mac he had eaten on the drive up. He had to force himself to finish the series, finally tapping the photos against the table to square the corners and handing them back to Hayman.

''The newspaper article didn't say anything about them being hung up,'' he said.

''I'm trying to keep that quiet. A key detail if we ever get to any kind of interrogation. And so far, we've kept the reporters away from the kids who found the bodies, and I'd like that to continue. Also, I'd like to keep to ourselves the exact mutilations. The way it was, Steve, there were two pulleys up on that central beam in the barn, used for hauling bales of hay into the loft, I imagine. They were used to pull the bodies up.''

''After the torture?''

''Before,'' Hayman said. He got up and paced around

the table, hitching up his pants by hooking his fingers under an engraved western belt that read JERRY across the back. The belt buckle suggested the brand responsible for his paunch.

"The body fluids and excretions were directly under the hanging positions. Blood, urine, feces. The leather harnesses were saturated with blood. Their hands were tied behind them with leather thongs during the torture. We found the thongs. Death, by the way, came as a result of loss of blood in both cases. No vital organs were intentionally damaged. I don't know how long it took, but undoubtedly over an hour, and I suspect the victims were aware most of the time. Large amounts of amphetamines of a couple varieties were in the remaining blood and the tissue around needle punctures."

"They were intentionally kept awake?" Wayne asked, unbelieving.

"Like a wide-eyed teamster, pedal to the metal, popping bennies at three A.M. I imagine there was a lot of screaming, but no one was around to hear it."

"I hear it in my dreams," Boyles said.

"Have you pinpointed any time lines?" Wayne asked.

"I'm hanging it on the night of the eighth, Monday, around midnight, but giving it six hours leeway, before or after. That's as close as I can come with the state of decomposition, the lividity, and the temperatures involved."

"Any identification?"

Hayman kept pacing while he explained the teeth, fingers, and thumbs. "Every clue we have, along with tissue and chemical samples, has been forwarded to state and FBI laboratories for further analysis. I sent out the samples by special courier last night. We've asked for help from your identification division, also."

Boyles said, "Today's *New Mexican* will run photos of sketches we've had drawn, to see if anyone in the area might know them. There are no missing persons reports out with similar descriptions."

"Nothing else?" Wayne asked.

"She had worn a ring on the left ring finger, probably a wedding band, but it was missing," Rivera said.

"No clothing?"

"None. Out back of the barn, we found the ashes of a small fire. The clothing may have been burned. We're analyzing the ashes," the sheriff explained.

Wayne shifted his position. The arm of the chair pressed the short-barreled Smith and Wesson .38, holstered high on his belt, into his left side. He was getting close to the reasons for his invitation, and he was a trifle uncomfortable. "How about motive? Anybody discussed that?"

The district attorney stretched his neck, mopping around the tight collar of his shirt with a handkerchief. "I, for one, have talked about little else, Steve. And I, for one, have come up with very little."

"Drugs?" he suggested.

Rivera sighed. "Unlikely. I'm not saying we don't have our share of drug problems. I'm saying this would be a pretty farfetched reaction to a double cross on a drug deal."

"Object lesson?" Wayne asked.

"Crossed my mind," Rivera admitted. "And I'm sure that is one aspect. Otherwise, the bodies would have been buried somewhere. No, you're right. Somebody, somewhere, is supposed to learn a valuable lesson."

Hayman returned to his chair. "The way it was done, it was intended to extract information. Of that, I am pretty damned positive. And no drug dealer, I don't give a damn how macho he thinks he is, is going to hold out for that long, and endure that much pain, over some suitcase full of coke."

Steve Wayne did not think so either, but he did not confirm the ME's opinion.

The DA came to the point. "Where we're at, the day after the discovery, is point zero. Carl may come up with more in the days ahead, but everything points to this thing being much larger than Santa Fe County. The implications, to me, suggest some kind of national activity." He stressed the word "national."

From the stoic set of Rivera's face, Wayne was certain the sheriff did not necessarily agree. But he would have succumbed to the public outrage generated by Willow's articles and the pressures building among city, county, and very probably, since this was the state capital, state officials. Plus, on May 2, the voters would decide whether or not Boyles and Rivera should stay on the job. Boyles, with two previous terms, had an advantage in that regard, but Rivera was on the ballot for the first time. An unsolved vicious crime did not induce confidence in an appointed incumbent.

"You'd like the Bureau to intervene?"

"We can use all the help we can get," Boyles said generously. He smiled.

When an election was not so imminent, the locals liked to keep investigations, trials, convictions, and positive public relations in their own hip pockets.

Wayne said, "But there's no evidence that the victims were brought across state lines? No federal property involved, like Los Alamos? No suggestion of a federal crime? It's very seldom that we get involved in murder."

"No federal angle yet," Boyles said. "But you've got to admit that something like this stinks to hell and gone of espionage and spies and all that. Maybe they were trying to get something out of the labs at Alamos? We think you ought to at least take a look."

Wayne asked, "You mind if I say I think you're reaching a bit?"

The DA grinned. "I don't mind. Hell, Steve, we've got one of those homicides that may never be solved. I'd just as soon have the FBI not solve it."

Before Wayne could respond, Boyles checked his watch and jumped up. Lively for an obese man. "I've got to run to another meeting. Steve, I'm glad you could join us."

The medical examiner rose also. "I'll walk with you, Keith. Nice to meet you," he told Wayne.

Steve stood and shook hands again and said, "I'll talk it over with my superiors and get back to you."

"I appreciate that," Boyles said. "Carl will give you a copy of our file. Hope you'll keep it to yourself?"

"Of course."

The two men left, Hayman hitching his pants up, and Wayne wondered if he was free to go. Rivera remained seated, and when Wayne turned back to him, said, "You like a cup of coffee, Steve?"

He wanted to talk some more, and Wayne was always willing to listen—one of his best traits was patience. "Why not?"

Rivera went into the hallway and returned a few minutes later with two steaming and aromatic Styrofoam cups. He passed one across the battered table. "What do you think?"

"Being honest, and all that?"

"I'm a big boy."

"At this point, I don't think you have a chance in hell of shifting out from under the jurisdiction. And, like Boyles said, it's the kind of case that takes months or years to solve, if it's ever solved. I think your reelection may be in jeopardy."

Rivera grinned at him, his expressive eyes joining in. "Election. First time. But I guess I wouldn't be all that unhappy about going back to captain if I had to. The pressures are a damned sight easier to handle."

The sheriff fingered a cigarette from a crumpled pack and drew a lighter from his pocket.

Wayne decided he could like this man. "So you're mainly going along with the people in power?"

The lawman spun the wheel and lit his cigarette. "You know another way to do it? Tell me it's different in the Bureau. If I had the time, I think I could work this one out all by myself."

It was the same kind of confidence Wayne had felt

himself in several dozen tough cases over the years. "You've got something the others don't have?"

Rivera snapped the lighter shut, laid it flat, and flicked it with a snap of his finger. It slid across the rough table. Wayne picked it up, studied its dented and scratched sides. "101st Airborne?"

"The minute I looked in that barn, I was struck by the rigging on those people. It was made especially for the job. But damned if I didn't have some kind of flashback. I remember a night jump out of Benning, and one of our people got hung up in a tree. Looked the same way, hanging there, all scratched up from the tree limbs he'd hit, and blood dripping."

"He hurt?" Steve asked.

"Not badly, not then. But he took a Claymore head-on in 'Nam."

"This . . . this similarity gives you a clue?"

"Gut instinct only, *mi amigo*. Not a goddamned shred of evidence yet. But I think we have us a paratrooper involved in this thing somewhere."

By the time Wayne had driven back to Albuquerque, composed a telex, and sent it off to Washington, it was 3:30, and he was fully intrigued by the case. It was 5:30 in Washington, and he did not expect an answer until tomorrow or the next day.

There were three other agents assigned to him. One had the day off and the other two were testifying in federal court. His secretary was taking a break with the four women in the clerical pool. He adjusted the venetian blinds against the western sun, settled into his chair, and began to reread the stack of reports in the Santa Fe file.

At 4:10, his secretary appeared in the doorway.

"Yes, Carmen?"

"Telex for you, Steve. Marked urgent."

"Thanks."

He grabbed the flimsy sheet of paper, noting the deputy director source in the lead. It was simple:

NO BUR JURISDICTION APPARENT IN SF COUNTY HOMI-
CIDES STOP AUTH TO ASSIST INVEST DENIED AT THIS
TIME STOP

THREE

Airborne, Airborne, where you been?
 'Round the world, and I'm goin' again.
Well, what you gonna do when you get back?
 Goin' around again with a full field pack.

'NAM WAS THE start of the helicopter era, and the ground pounders were inserted into the hostile fire zones and extracted from them by chopper. Worse, there weren't any front lines. There were no demarcations on some map to jump behind, and some were afraid that it signaled the end of the proud commando traditions inherent in the 101st and 82nd Airborne Divisions.

Though qualified jumpers continued to receive jump pay on their monthly vouchers for the twelve-month periods of their Vietnam tours, many of them missed the regular qualifying jumps required with Stateside duty.

There was another form of compensation. Straight-legs gave them sideways glances, checking out the jump badges above the breast pockets, the stylized eagles on the left shoulders. "Envy, man. Jealousy of the highest fuckin' order. Ain't no one around as good as me."

Dress is right and cover down,
 Forty inches all around.

First squad is lookin' good,
Oughta be in Hollywood.

The special notice and the extra bucks on payday were okay, but the leap into near oblivion was better. It was hard to achieve the same high on pride or greenbacks or military scrip or RVN piaster that could be achieved by floating in space.

So some of them took steps to rectify the US Army's typical oversight.

Lew and six avid troopers in the first squad of his platoon made six jumps on their own, onto foreign soil, which was kind of special in itself. They utilized government avgas for the aircraft and recovery vehicles and gear carefully appropriated from the reserve supply stores. They jumped twice from C–130s, once from a C–123 Provider piloted by a half-drunk—or half-sober— Aussie lieutenant, once from a Caribou, and twice from Huey slicks.

Sweet thought it was a real kick in the ass.

Carlos Rivera thought of two angles of attack while he was struggling with his thirty-first push-up. Since it was better to think about his investigation, he skipped the next four push-ups and all of the sit-ups, groaned his way to his feet, and padded naked into the bathroom. Myra was already in the shower, and he stepped over the edge of the tub and slipped in behind her. The steam swirled around her. He wrapped his big arms around her and fondled her breasts.

"You're getting pretty randy in your old age," she said.

He felt her nipples harden against his palms. "Uh huh."

"Don't you have a job to go to?"

Sliding a slippery hand downward, across the slight bulge of her belly, he pushed his fingers through her damp pubic hair. "Uh huh."

She was tiny against him, five-two and ninety-five pounds. Her black hair was shiny, dotted with beads of water, smelling sweet and fresh, and he buried his face in it. Myra worked her own hand around behind her, slipping it between their bodies, and Rivera decided his new angles of investigative attack, like his exercises, could wait for a little while.

Carol was up by six, making a breakfast of coffee, orange juice, and one egg apiece for them. Wayne had known her for seven months, and they had been living together for two. So far, it was working well. Probably because J. Edgar was no longer around to disapprove of the arrangement.

She was five years younger than Wayne, divorced as he was, and made a comfortable living for herself as an account executive for a relatively large Albuquerque advertising agency. Sometimes irritatingly independent, she insisted on sharing the rental, phone, utility, and grocery bills for the top floor apartment he had lived in since being transferred from Montgomery two years before.

Carol Curtis was also known as Cece. She had dark red hair cropped at the earlobes, sober and direct green eyes, alabaster skin sprinkled with tiny freckles on her slim nose and on her shoulders, and an expressive mouth that reposed, lower lip full, in a half pout. He was fond of watching her at night, asleep. When she was on her back, she snored. Little chugging gasps culminating in tiny snorts. Wayne was undecided about whether or not he could tease her about that, and had not yet done so.

He also liked to watch her move about the four rooms of the apartment in the nude, which she did often and without apparent modesty. She was tall and slim, with gently flaring hips and tiny dimples at either side of her lower spine. The smooth turn of the calf of her left leg was marred with a four-inch scar that looked much like a depressed zipper. She had slipped crossing a barbed wire fence on the family ranch in northern New Mexico when she was thirteen. Her breasts were overly full for her physique with what he told her was the "sexy sag" of middle age. They swung gently, heavily, when she took the upper position.

She was logical and organized, occasionally nagged him for his piles of dirty clothing, and followed some strict timetables. At 6:10, Wayne knew he was behind schedule and slid out of bed. He donned an old terry cloth robe, belting it around him. He crossed from the master bedroom, which was slowly taking on some feminine touches—in bedspread and drapes—and went into the kitchen. "Mornin', Cece."

She was naked at the stove, and she half turned, holding the frying pan firmly. She could always manage a smile in the morning. "It's about time."

"Please don't burn anything."

"I haven't yet."

She slid an egg onto each of two plates, carried them to the table, and sat while he poured coffee. There was a jar of orange marmalade and two slices of toast on a plate. Cece had a thing about proper diet.

The routine was still difficult for him, watching her breasts across the table. He had once accused her of being a tease, and she had quickly denied the accusation, saying she was always ready to fulfill any provocation.

"Full day?" he asked.

"The Rupert account I told you about? The toughie? I'm going to spend all morning with the old boy. I'll get him to split with a few thousand, yet."

He was certain she would.

"How about you?" she asked.

"I'm flying to Alamogordo at eight. Top secret, and all that." She was very good about not probing for detail when he told her a case was classified. On top of which, she did not like hearing about criminal detail. Cece thought cops should leave their jobs in the office at five o'clock, and though she did not really complain earnestly at the magnitude of his overtime, she mentioned it from time to time.

And the two card tables in the spare bedroom were littered with sketches, proposals, and flip charts from the McComb-Davis Agency which she pored over on some nights. He thought it prudent not to mention parallels.

"I suppose you'll be late?"

"Probably. Carmen made the reservations, but the flight back is at ten tonight, I believe."

"You don't know?"

"That's why I have Carmen."

Wayne finished his egg, thought about a piece of toast, and decided against it. "I'd better make a call while I've got the time."

He slid his chair back across the linoleum patterned to look like red brick and grabbed the phone from its wall mount. Information got him the home number, which rang once. A small voice spoke to him, "Hello?"

"Hello. Is Sheriff Rivera there?"

"Daddy. He's busy, I think." Giggle.

"Could you take a message?"

"Sure! I'll find the paper." Clunk.

Wayne waited two minutes, then heard: "I've got the paper! I'll find the pencil." The phone clunked again on the table, and he had to grin.

The pencil must have been elusive because, after another two minutes, a deeper voice took over. "This is Sheriff Rivera."

"Steve Wayne. Sorry to bother you at home."

"Why should you be the only one who's sorry? Glad to hear from you."

"I'm not calling with good news, I'm afraid."

"Depends on the perspective. Your bosses don't want you in it?"

"Not now. But between us, I'd be happy to help in any way I can. Quietly, of course."

"Your curiosity is raised, huh?"

"It's up there, somewhere near the top of the heap.

Keep in mind, Carl, that I own a large heap.''

"Okay. I appreciate it. I had an idea earlier this morning on the paratrooper angle. I'm going to try to get a listing of jumpers who went to 'Nam.''

"Yeah? The 101st was shipped to Vietnam in . . . ?''

" '65. They were out by '73. Outside of the 173rd Airborne Brigade, they were the primary airborne outfit assigned to Vietnam. Of course, this guy could have been a jumper early, then had himself transferred to a non-airborne unit. It's a long shot, I know.''

"Hold on a second, Carl. I don't want to get confused. We're talking about the victim being a jumper or the perpetrator?''

"One or the other, maybe both. The perp may have thought it was a fitting end for the victim. To start with, I want to get a list of names of every Vietnam veteran with jump training, keying on the period between '65 and '73.''

"Going to be a long damned list, Carl. That's eight or nine years, and with one-year tours, there was a hell of a turnover. And no assurances that your suspects or the victim were ever overseas, or if they were in Vietnam, that it was with an airborne unit.''

"I know, but it's a start. You ever done any police work that wasn't boring as hell?''

"All right,'' Wayne conceded. "Your contact at Bureau Identification Division should be Bob Maranzino. Get hold of him personally and drop my name. He'll expedite matters with the Pentagon.''

"Thanks. I'm also going to go through the Screamin' Eagles Association. I still belong, and they should have some computer printouts that might be helpful, even though the membership doesn't include everyone who was once active with the one-oh-one. The Pentagon records will only have the last address, given at discharge, unless the guy went into the reserves somewhere. The Association is more up-to-date.''

"Good luck. Keep me posted, will you?''

"Happy to."

When he hung up, Cece wrinkled her nose at him. "Starting work awfully early, aren't we?"

He looked around for a weapon and settled on the orange marmalade. Dipped two fingers into the jar.

"Oh no!" she shrieked, leaped out of the chair, and ran for the bedroom.

Wayne pursued.

FOUR

ON THEIR SECOND unauthorized jump, on a day when there was a break in the monsoon weather but still a high wind, Lew and his charges obscenely put down the Aussie lieutenant's slurred cautions, threw their empty and crushed Shlitz cans out first, then leapt after them from the side doors of the Provider at 12,000 feet.

Right into VC land.

A clerk from the headquarters platoon was waiting at the planned grassy LZ with a six-by to retrieve them, but the wind blew them off course, and they drifted a mile across a stand of rubber trees and came down on a ville of fourteen tin and wood shanties they had not known existed.

Scared the shit out of themselves. And the villagers. Unexpected company dropping in.

People scurrying around like lab mice. No where to go, no where to run. Dig up the arsenals.

Hanging nearly defenseless from the shrouds, they became the targets of a half dozen barking AK–47s.

Andy was the first to return fire, unslinging his M–16 and directing fully automatic fire down into the hamlet. "Shoot at me, you son of a bitch! Here you go!"

Rattle of 5.56 mike-mike.

The others joined in, and the seven troops landed in the shit-smelling alleys—Pilo and C.B. crashing through

28

fragile tin roofs—spreading a withering spray of 5.56 millimeter slugs in every direction, ejecting empty magazines and slapping in new magazines as fast as they could.

Deep voices yelling choppy American phrases, to keep track of each other. "Andy, you at? . . . Here, babe . . . Your left! . . . Hit the deck, Lew! . . Fry that fucker, Sweet!"

Hearing the screams, chittery trills of all-consuming fear. Was it begging?

Stepping through the wreckage, swiveling eyes, finding a movement, pulling off a guarantee round, getting high on it. Jet of blood, glazed eyes, spasms.

So high, the tremors ran through the muscles.

Except for a few abrasions, they all came out of it unscathed.

There were nine fatalities among the Vietnamese, including two black-toothed, betel juice—stained old women and one kid, maybe five, six years old. Six confirmed VC males. One hell of a large cache of penicillin, cloth bandages, RPGs, frag grenades, 7.62 rounds, Kalashnikovs, a Mannlicher, and a couple of old Springfield 30–06s in a hole under a reed mat in one hut.

It was an afternoon and an episode difficult not to brag about.

Though they were otherwise good friends socially and professionally, on unsecured telephones just in case there were unwanted listeners, the caller was known as Boxer. "You squash this thing?"

"Absolutely," Rebel told him. "There'll be no sophisticated assistance. What can you expect of some hokie New Mexican sheriff? Especially with the little he's got to go on."

"I hope so," Boxer said with some degree of sincerity. "The repercussions would be wide and cannot be tolerated just now. Or ever, for that matter."

"There'll be no repercussions. Except that you owe me a big one."

"Acknowledged."

"One question, Boxer. How in hell did you let your group get so out of hand?"

"I didn't have a choice in the matter. You know they're contract players. They are very effective, but they handle their own internal squabbles."

"Well, somebody in your shop ought to sit on them with a very big butt."

"I have already sent that message," Boxer said.

Wayne followed the sheriff back to the property room and waited while he signed a log and checked out a large plastic bag tagged with a date and case number.

His flight from Alamogordo had not arrived back in Albuquerque until after eleven and that, coupled with the long meetings with the team members from DC who were investigating the disappearance of some rather complicated and classified lab equipment, had left him exhausted. Still, he had awakened early with a headache and a bad case of curiosity, and he had decided to spend his Saturday morning in Santa Fe.

He drove up in his silver-blue Trans Am, listening to a country station out of Albuquerque and to the muted throb of the glass-packed dual exhaust, playing Kansas Kid, the hot-rodder. Cece had declined the outing, suggesting that his curiosity was entirely too morbid and the desert sun too hot, if he was going to remove the T-tops. Which he did.

Someday, he swore to himself, he was going to buy himself a real convertible.

Tugging on his forelock, Wayne sat at an old table in a side room under glaring fluorescent lights while Rivera opened the plastic bag, then laid the harness on the table. The heavy leather was discolored and stiff with the blood it had absorbed. There were two one-inch-wide vertical straps that passed over the shoulders, attached solidly to the front side of the chest strap, and connected with adjustable buckles on the back side. The cross strap, which went around the chest, was two inches wide, thick, and also had an adjustable buckle at the back. Near the apex of the vertical straps were two D rings.

Rivera took a seat and shoved the rigging toward him. "The two D rings? There was a short yoke made of nylon rope, maybe eighteen inches long, with a snap fastener on each end that clipped on the rings. The yoke was connected to the hoisting cable."

"They were made to be adjustable," Wayne observed, handling the harness with some distaste, turning it over, looking for any marking that might identify a source. The texture was smooth on the outside, porous on the inside; the color originally a light brown, but now a crinkly, ugly black.

"The male's was adjustable from forty to forty-six inches. It was a tight fit, because he had a forty-six-inch chest. The female's was a little loose because the cross strap dug into the bottom of her breasts."

"Suggesting?"

"Suggesting that whoever made them up was less sure of her chest size."

Wayne scrutinized the stitching that attached the buckles, the D rings, and the vertical straps to the cross strap. "Heavy-duty thread and a big sewing machine."

"It's a reinforced nylon thread like that used in the construction and repair of parachute rigging."

He looked up at Rivera as the man lit a cigarette. "You've verified that?"

"Forensics is checking it out, but I know. I've done some rigging, and I've packed more than a few chutes myself. The leather can be picked up at practically any crafts shop. If they had used some standard webbing, it would have been helpful."

"Still, you think they had access to a place where parachutes are repaired?" Wayne shoved the harness across the table, and Rivera put it back in the bag.

"Damned right, they did. Oh, it could have been an upholstery shop where it was put together, but whoever constructed it was thinking parachute harness. I still think it was a specialty shop. Skydiving club, maybe."

"Could be anywhere in the world."

"Something of a drawback, I admit." The sheriff grinned at him.

"Pretty serious one."

"Yet, if it came from outside state borders, that would bring the FBI into it."

"Interstate transportation of a harness? There'd be some raised eyebrows over that."

"Transportation of a device specifically designed to be used in the commission of a capital crime."

"Hmmm. That would have some researchers flipping the pages of dictionaries and law books."

"C'mon, I'll buy you a donut."

Rivera returned the evidence to the property room, and they went out the back door to a lot where sheriff's department sedans and Blazers were parked. After they climbed into Rivera's vehicle, the sheriff started it, called a code number into his central dispatch, then pulled out into the street. A few blocks away, on Paseo de Peralta, they went through a drive-in for two capped cups of coffee and a box filled with a half dozen donuts.

"Want to see the site?"

"Yes," Wayne told him and pried the lids off the Styrofoam cups, passing one to the driver.

Rivera pulled back onto Paseo de Peralta—named for the Spanish explorer who had founded the city, an intrepid man of foresight to some and a savage tyrant to others. The erection of a statue depicting the founding father was proving controversial to those from both camps. The truck bumped through a chuckhole in the asphalt, spilling some coffee. The street was a ring road around the city, and Rivera followed it westward until he could turn off on Bishop's Lodge Road, heading north. They climbed upward a bit onto a plateau. The scrub oak was thick and green and tall. Wayne could see the flat roofs of quite a few houses barely showing above it.

"How old's your boy?"

"Jeff? He's six, and I've got a little girl eight. Tracy."

Wayne noted the names were not traditionally Hispanic. Someday, maybe the cultures would finally meld together. There was both good and bad in that, and he suspected it was a long way off. Hoped it was. He did not want to see the Indian and Mexican traditions blurred.

"He had a hell of a time finding a pencil."

Rivera grinned at him, chewing on a donut. "You know how they are at that age? Pad and pencil were right under the telephone book. You have a family?"

"I was married for a few years, but it didn't click with all my transfers. No kids."

"Too bad, but cops and robbers is tough on family life," Rivera said.

Too tough. Patricia, with whom he occasionally thought he was still in love, had endured three moves, late nights, and unexplained absences for seven years, and then called a halt to it. A relatively amicable halt. He had been assigned to Washington, DC at the time, and it had proved to be a fatal environment for an Ohio girl. The crime statistics were too real for her. She was remarried now to an attorney with sense enough to specialize in real estate. They lived in Cleveland—which at one time Wayne had thought more dangerous than DC— and had three children. From time to time, when he was alone in a new town, sitting in a strange lounge, he missed her terribly, a deep ache in the heart. And he wondered how things could have been done differently. He did not have any answers.

Transfers were not a subject he had raised with Cece, and he felt somewhat traitorous toward her whenever he thought about Pat. And yet, while he and Cece had established a comfortable domestic routine and had both professed great affection and even love for each other, the future for them had been ignored, a subject labeled with an understood taboo. There was an underlying fear that delicate balances would achieve overload if either of them mentioned next Christmas, or next Easter.

After a long northward drive, then a shunt a few miles to the west along narrow dirt roads that had been graveled some time in the last decade, Rivera pulled off the road down into a shallow barrow ditch, and stopped. He got out and untied a yellow tape stretched between the gap in a broken-down barbed wire fence. A white cardboard sign tacked to a rotting post supporting four strands of barbed wire forbid trespassing on the scene of a crime. The sheriff got back in and drove another half mile to where more yellow tape attached to wire stakes had been stretched completely around the abandoned farmyard. He slapped the shift lever into park, and they both got out, Rivera bringing a flashlight with him.

"Desolate," Wayne said. To the east, he could see the range of mountains. This narrow valley was dotted with piñon, scrub brush, yucca, and a few stands of ponderosa pine. Chunks of low-lying cacti. There was a shallow creek with stands of aspen off to the west. Purple and white and red wildflowers were sprinkled about, but they would disappear as summer beat them down.

"Maybe a little, but I'd never leave it. Not again," Rivera said.

Wayne smiled at him. "I've only been here two years, but it's growing on me."

"You have to get out in the desert and the mountains, Steve. Albuquerque's getting too big. The *yanqui*'s are going to develop it into total mush before long."

They stepped over the tape and went right to the barn, which Wayne suspected was a century old, give or take a decade. The door was open, and when Wayne stepped into the sun-dappled darkness, he felt as if he had been there before. Having seen the pictures and the forensic and medical examiner's reports, it all looked strangely familiar.

Most of the shingles and a few of the boards of the

roof were missing or broken, and the sunlight came through the irregular openings in multiple bright shafts, making vision difficult. It took several minutes for his eyes to adjust. Looking up, he saw the two pulleys bolted to the peak beam. Directly below them, the earth, a combination of soil and cracked cow manure, was discolored. In the places of loose soil, if there had been footprints, they were now obliterated by the passage of other feet. "You did get shoe prints, the report said."

"Two men. One in well-worn running shoes, the other in dress shoes, both of them size ten. The heel print of the dress shoes suggests Florsheim. The other pair checked out as Adidas. We didn't get enough prints to check for a stride, to estimate height."

"Weight?"

"Both of them over one-sixty. Probably under one-eighty."

"What about car tracks?"

"It was a single vehicle with passenger car tires. Firestone. We're checking on rentals."

Wayne stepped over to where the woman had been hung. "Has Hayman made any deductions about the weapon?"

"From the wounds, he thinks either an old-fashioned straight razor, the kind with the folding handle, or a surgeon's scalpel. In addition, there was a heavy pair of nippers used on the fingers. I think he's inclined toward the scalpel."

"Suggesting somebody with medical training."

"That's the way I took it, but he says no. While the cuts were clean, they did not demonstrate the finesse, as he put it, of a surgeon."

"You believe him?"

"Implicitly. Jerry's not flashy, Steve. Just very able. And he's got good instincts."

Rivera stood near the door while Wayne wandered slowly around.

"Anything out of the fire?"

"A few fabric threads, buttons, bra snaps, and two zippers, but not much else. Their clothes were burned. The zippers were from Levi jeans."

"They wouldn't want to be stopped on the road, even by accident, with anything incriminating in the car."

"Which means," Rivera said, "the thumbs may be in the area, too. But it's a hell of a lot of area, and there are a few predators around."

Wayne could imagine some coyote or rodent discovering a juicy thumb. He had to struggle to push the image out of his mind.

Over the stalls, which ran down each side of the barn, were lofts, one on each side. They were constructed simply, two-by-twelve planks laid over a slim number of two-by-six joists.

"Your people check up there?"

The sheriff looked up. "I'm sure they did." But he sounded uncertain. "Wouldn't hurt to check again."

Short lengths of two-by-fours were nailed to the stalls on one end of the barn, providing rudimentary ladders. While Rivera climbed one side, Wayne worked his way up the other, glad he had worn his weekend jeans.

There was not much to be seen. The floor was littered with old straw and bird droppings. It was scuffed where earlier searchers had trod. The aroma was musty and mildewed. If he had hayfever, he would be hacking by now. A rusty pitchfork with a broken handle was tossed into one corner and two sagging, rotted hay bales were in the other. He walked the length of the loft, looking at the floor, but could see little in the dim light.

"Toss me your light, will you?"

From the other side of the barn, Rivera threw his flashlight, and Wayne caught it. It was a six-cell job, with a powerful beam, and he played it back and forth over the floor in a careful search pattern. He shoved the bales to one side. Nothing.

Working his way back toward the ladder, he almost missed it.

A dull gleam between two planks, reflecting in the beam of the light.

Moving the flashlight back, he found the glint and padded up to it, bending down.

"Got something?" Rivera called to him.

"Maybe." He lowered himself to his knees on a bed of old straw, held the light at an angle, and peered into the gap between the planks. Laying on the narrow ledge of the underlying joist was a gold ring.

He tried to reach it, but could not get his fingers into the gap.

"There's a wedding band here, Carl, but I can't get at it. You want to get down in the stall, I'll knock it loose with a pen?"

He fished a ballpoint from his pocket, and after Rivera was underneath him, holding his Stetson inverted, he used the pen to dislodge the ring. It dropped through the gap, trailing a cloud of dust and bits of straw.

Clambering down the ladder, he nearly fell when one of the rungs broke. Rivera had dumped the ring out of his hat onto a handkerchief and was standing in the light of the doorway.

He held it up, and let Wayne read the inscription inside the ring: Andy and Andrea—2/17/79.

Rivera had a big grin on his face.

They were trapped as soon as they drove back into the parking lot behind the sheriff's office.

Wayne opened his door, slid down from the high seat, and slammed the door shut. A teenybopper emerged from behind tall evergreen shrubs and confronted him.

"Hey, you're cute!" she said.

She looked like a teenybopper. Short blonde hair in a frizzy halo about her cherubic, pert-nosed face. Big, big, sincere brown eyes. She wore scuffed brown cowboy boots with runover walking heels, faded Levi's, and a man's white shirt that was way too big for her. The shirt hung outside the jeans and revealed that she was flat-chested.

Despite the first impression she gave, Wayne's experience had made him adept at reading character, defining faces, and establishing identifiable traits. An educated estimate would put her near thirty. She was either hanging on to youth with a white-knuckled grip or she did not care much about appearances. Probably the latter. She was other-minded.

"Likewise," he told her.

"What's your name?"

"Steve. What's yours?"

"What's your last name?"

Persistent imp, he thought, but his built-in threat alarm was buzzing.

Rivera came around the hood of the truck and stood on the sidewalk. "Let me introduce Miss Janet Willow. Janet, Steve Wayne."

"What do you do, Steve?"

"I'm a friend of the sheriff's."

"I'll find out anyway."

"Special Agent, FBI, but I'm just visiting."

"Oh, I'm sure," she said, turning to Rivera. "What's new on the Razor Murders? Got a suspect?"

"No developments for discussion just yet, Janet."

She pouted, then asked, "How about the campaign? How come you don't have posters out, radio spots, and newsletters like Blessing?"

Rivera grinned at her. "I'm a simple man. I'll let the people decide by what I do, not by hype."

"You're making a very large mistake," she said.

She was a judgmental type, Wayne thought, but happened to agree with her. As far as Wayne was concerned, almost all of politics was hype.

Rivera did not respond to her instant analysis, and she trod off down the sidewalk, headed toward the Plaza. She walked hard on the heels of her boots, a somewhat masculine and very determined stride.

"God must love reporters," Wayne said. "They get away with a hell of a lot."

"They do that," Rivera agreed, "and Janet is in there with the best of them, trampling over everything in sight in order to get her story. Don't take her wrong though, Steve. She's ambitious and pushy, but she's always been fair. Can't recall a time when she's embellished the facts or speculated beyond logic. The police beat can be boring compared, say, to political reporting in this town, but she makes the most of it."

"She's not a political reporter, then?"

"Only as far as the race for sheriff goes. I suspect she convinced her editor that it was part of the police beat."

They turned toward the door of the sheriff's office and started up the walk.

Wayne asked, "What party are you running with anyway?"

"My own," Rivera said. "Independent. You know what old Brother Dave Gardner, the comedian, once said?"

"What's that?"

" 'If I were bound by either party, I might forget America.' "

Delwin Blessing was an effete man, a natty dresser, always prepared to be onstage. The narrow and subdued stripes in each of his gray or blue suits were intended to visually enhance his height, raising him above his five feet eight inches. He treated his temples weekly to add gray to the umber hair, to give him more maturity and more wisdom. He wore a carefully cultured mustache for the same reason.

Blessing considered himself an above-average strategist, and a top-of-the-line politician, though he was just at the beginning of what appeared to him as a long career with ever-increasing responsibility and recognition. He had served one term as a city councilman, losing the second term by a scant seventeen votes. He had not cried over it. He had considered it a learning experience, a needed therapy for overconfidence, and had set his sights on another elected office.

An attorney with a private practice, he might have aimed for the district attorney's position, except that he was astute enough to know that unseating Keith Boyles would be a nearly insurmountable task. Instead, he decided to go after the post of county sheriff, running as a Republican.

Since he had faced no contenders in the primary, it was a wise choice, and he told his advisors, "We've got to take advantage of this Razor thing. Rivera's made no progress at all, and the pressure's building on him. Let's be sure to raise the issue in every public outing."

"We push too hard, Del, we might push him right into solving the damned thing," Aaron Clark said. Clark was county chairman for the GOP.

"That's not likely to happen," Delwin Blessing assured the man.

"The other thing to think about, I suppose," said Humphrey Moore, retired from the *New Mexican*, "is that you could get elected to office with that case unsolved. What would you do about it?"

"Goddamn," Blessing said. He had not considered it. "You don't think anybody would ask?"

"I wouldn't be a damned bit surprised. You might just work yourself up a little theory, Del. Just in case you run into Janet somewhere. Or she runs into you."

FIVE

WHEN THE CO, a wimpy-looking jerk named Conrad, investigated the rumors that arose after the boasting of the first squad of the First Platoon, Lew was given a mild oral reprimand—nothing was entered into his personnel file—by a company commander who rather admired the derring-do. An actual combat jump in the 'Nam! And division headquarters, after all, was always happy to report an increase in the enemy body count to MACV.

Lew told the guys in the squad they would have to cool it for a while. "And keep your mouths clamped tight. You've got to learn to shut up."

Later, Lew and his troopers, having proven themselves, were asked to volunteer for four more jumps. Called into the CO's hootch, Lew met with a one-oh-one colonel named Sanders and some guy in civvies from Saigon, who was never introduced, but Lew assumed he was CIA. The missions were not given the sanction of official channels, a procedure which always resulted in the VC or the NVA hearing about the operation before jump-off time.

In the four raids, fifty-six Vietcong or North Vietnamese army regulars were killed or wounded. The wounded mysteriously died later. Sweet took a round in the foot, Brooklyn lost a chunk out of his ass, and Country was shot in the forearm, breaking a bone, and went back to the World first, to a little bump in the road north of Memphis.

The best by far was the September jump. They called it the September jump. HALO. High altitude, low open-ing. 0530 hours, the first streaks of dawn breaking over the top of the jungle. Overcast in the west. Enough light to see the slit of a clearing in the triple-canopied Cam-bodian jungle, and not enough for the hostiles to pick them out of the sky. The assholes were sleeping or staring at the ground, anyway.

Black nylon for the chutes. The CIA guy dug them up especially for them. Brooklyn really went for those fancy black ones because he considered himself a classy dresser and an expert on appearances. Big city guy.

They dropped off the open ramp of the C–130 Hercules at 18,000 feet, wearing oxygen masks. Free-fall, side by side, a team. Planing their bodies toward the clearing.

Wind in the ears.

Down.

And down.

Wanting to laugh aloud.

Shed the masks.

Pop the chutes at less than a thousand feet above the clearing.

Unsling the M–16s.

Lock and load. The snick of the receivers loud in the hot air of morning.

All seven of them touched down within seconds of one another, steel-soled boots not making a sound in the dew-drenched undergrowth, rolling off shoulders, rising again, black chutes billowing in the breeze and then collapsing in the shadow gray of the clearing.

Back to back, they circled up like a wagon train, crouched, watching outward.

NVA major smoking a fag, staring into the jungle. A dozen slopes in uniform and half a dozen coolies—for the hard labor—sprawled out on mats and blankets. Under the leafy protection of the canopy, there were stacks and stacks of crates, cardboard boxes, and fuel drums.

"Waste 'em," Lew said.

Waste them, they did. The assault rifles opened up in a shocking thunder that stunned those who lived long enough to wake and sit up.

Blood and guts everywhere.

A few survived the initial burst of automatic fire. Pilo yelling. Andy flying on adrenaline. C.B. screaming, "God bless you, heathen!"

The NVA major, grunting and groaning and bitching in Vietnamese from ten or twelve slugs in the stomach— "That's a bunch of hurt, man!"—rolled wide, white eyes at Lew as he knelt beside the guy. Lew looked him over, pulled the Colt from his holster, and stuck it in the ape's mouth.

Guy quit thinking about his stomach.

Lew pulled the trigger, and the .45 round took off the back of the major's skull.

C.B. grabbed a wounded coolie, probably Cambodian, tossed him belly down over a drum of low-octane gasoline lying on its side, and holed the drum with a few 5.56 rounds. Tossed a match.

Flash! Blue-red flames licking high, lighting the predawn jungle.

"Asshole's gotta be Hindu or Buddhist," C.B. said. "This'll be good for him."

C.B. thought he knew all about religions.

The Cambodian sucker's probably still screaming.

Sweet got himself some Cambodian pussy, everybody standing around, watching the action. Then iced her with a scalpel he'd stolen from the Eighth Army Field Hospital.

"How 'bout that, little girl?" Sweet asked the corpse. "Best you ever had?"

A fucking scalpel. Damned Sweet, hung like a Mexican donkey. Liked to flaunt it, twirl it around in the showers, thinking he made others jealous.

They blew the cache of arms and gasoline with a couple blocks of C–4 plastic explosive, then hiked out of there, headed for the extraction point.

Laughing a little along the way.

They all lived to tell about it, but never did.

The Sunday edition of *The New Mexican* contained a front page article bylined by Janet Willow that also made the Albuquerque papers and the wires. The Razor Murders had captured enough attention nationally to merit updates which were buried somewhere in the first section of the major city dailies. Certainly, there was more interest generated by the grisly dual murders than had been devoted to the untimely death of the vocal and often obnoxious Senator Ralph DeLamma.

When Wayne scanned through the columns, lying in bed with Cece, he was disturbed by Willow's veiled suggestion that federal investigators had been brought into the homicide case. That was more speculation on her part than had been credited to her by Rivera. Conversely, he *was* hoping to help out a little, though not officially.

"Damn."

"S'matter?" Cece was sitting cross-legged, leaning into the balled-up beige and blue and pink comforter, papers spread across her lap. She was analyzing the major advertisements, making strange marks around the graphics and text with a red felt-tip pen.

He told her about his meeting with Janet Willow.

"She interviewed you?"

"No. We just bumped into her."

"She use your name in the story?"

"No."

"Then what are you worried about?"

"Ten bucks says I get a call from the deputy director first thing in the morning."

Continuing to study her ads, she said, "When have you worried much about what your bosses think?"

"Not often," he admitted. "But the tone of that telex I got from the deputy director was different."

He began to wonder why it was different.

"Cute?" she asked.

"The deputy director? No."

Cece looked up from her paper. "The reporter, dummy."

"No tits to speak of." He reached out to demonstrate his preference.

Boxer was upset. "You told me you had it contained."

Rebel was not exactly happy himself. "The papers are misleading. The Bureau is not becoming involved in Santa Fe. I don't know what Wayne's been doing, but it will be stopped immediately."

"It damned well better be."

"Don't threaten," Rebel told his old friend. "It's not becoming. You know, it might help if I knew what the hell happened out there."

Rebel knew about the operational objective, of course, but he knew very little about the unit itself. He had never been told more than the code name of the operational unit, even back in Vietnam, and he had never before had reason to want to know more.

"You're better off having deniability," Boxer told him, which was true.

"I see."

"Believe me, it's better for you."

"I suppose so." He hated making the next admission. "There is one more thing."

"Ah, shit! What now?" The bass voice became even more raspy.

"I'm sure Wayne was just trying to be helpful, but his name was used in a nonchannel way to get some information through Ident to that sheriff down there."

"Information? What kind of information?"

"I'm not sure myself what it means. It came from the

Pentagon, and it was a computer listing of army personnel with parachute training.''

"What! What units?"

"173rd Airborne Brigade and 101st Airborne Division. I think it was cross-referenced by duty in Vietnam.''

Boxer's minute-long silence was ominous. ''You're sure of that?''

"I'm sure. It's important?''

"How in the hell would they figure . . . ? Look, I'll get back to you."

From the abrupt buzzing of the dial tone, Rebel thought that Boxer had slammed the phone down.

He took the call on the scrambled second line into his home in Malibu. The number dialed had no relationship with his beach house. The phone was located in a rented garage on a back alley in Culver City, and all calls to that number were shuffled through an electronic relay, then scrambled for the last leg of the electronic journey.

The scrambler gave voices an echo-chamber quality. Tinny, like two cans on a string.

"This is Boxer."

"STRAC."

"You have a definite problem. It arises out of your rather stupid move in the Southwest.''

The man who identified himself as STRAC resented the reference to stupidity, but ignored it in order to get the rest of the information. "What problem?''

"That podunk sheriff just got a complete listing of all jumpers assigned to the 173rd Brigade and the one-oh-one in Vietnam.''

Son . . . of . . . a . . . bitch! How did he come up with that? Shit. It'd have to be ESP.

He kept his voice calm, his normal commanding baritone. "That must be a hell of a list.''

"I don't know what kind of a list it is, but you can be damned sure your name's on it. That sheriff's not so damned stupid.''

"I'll take care of it."

"You'd better act soon, and with more finesse than you've been showing lately."

On Monday, Wayne got a mid-morning call from Deputy Director Mark Ellington. He did not like Ellington very much. Like many of the administrators in power, Ellington had spent much of his career under J. Edgar, and Wayne considered the man's philosophy to be rather narrow and his patriotism overly exalted.

Wayne was himself patriotic—more so than the average American, he thought—but he hoped his mind was also open to differences of opinion.

"Special Agent Wayne, sir."

"Wayne, I read some disturbing news reports over the weekend."

"Sir?"

"The newspapers and the television reports suggest the Bureau is becoming involved in those Santa Fe homicides. Didn't you receive a telex on that?"

"Yes, sir, I did, and no, sir, I have not indicated in any manner that the Bureau is involved. What we're dealing with is a local reporter with creative writing instincts."

Was that a little white lie? He had not actually denied FBI involvement to Willow, only told her that he was visiting Rivera as a friend.

"I see," Ellington said, as if he did. "Well, I suppose I might have expected that. The press does get carried away with itself sometimes, does it not?"

"Yes, sir."

"That sheriff—what's his name, Rivera? Is he making any progress?"

How to answer that? The little threat alarm in the back of Wayne's head was buzzing again, as it had with Janet Willow. For some strange reason, Washington wanted to be indifferent to this case, yet still know all about it. Or was it something else? Was he being tested on his involvement? He decided that the truth, as usual, was the best response.

"I'm not sure where he stands today. Last week, he wanted to follow some lead he had on military personnel and asked me the best way to go about it. I gave him Maranzino's name. I didn't think I could do less."

"Yes, well, I see. I suppose that's right. What's going on with your other cases?"

Wayne briefed him quickly on the eleven cases currently under way.

"And Alamogordo?"

"We've got a suspect pinpointed. Shouldn't be too much longer before it's wrapped up."

"Good. Well, keep me informed if there are developments in the Santa Fe thing that suggest a federal arena."

"Yes, sir." Wayne hung up and wondered how, if he was supposed to stay away from the case, he was also supposed to keep up on developments.

On Monday, Rivera received the computer printouts from the Pentagon, by way of the FBI, and another set from the Screamin' Eagles Association.

He had sent Luisa Rodriguez with the ring, from which no clear prints had been lifted, on a tour of jewelers, trying to determine the manufacturer. If they could identify the company that had made the ring, they might be closer to finding where it had been sold. And then closer to whomever had purchased it in January or February of 1979.

The Screamin' Eagles Association listing was far shorter than the army's, so he chose the army roster first.

For his first runthrough of the Pentagon printout, which contained, he estimated, nineteen or twenty thousand names, he used his single clue to a name, Andy. It could be a first name or a middle name or a last name. It could be part of a name. Worse, it could be an unrelated nickname—military people were big on nicknames—and not

even listed. From his own time in, he remembered Animal, Teach, Swats, Bucky, Phip, Way Gone, and a
dozen similar tags, none of them necessarily associated
with a man's true name.

Jerry Hayman had not further defined the age of the
victim, so he could not even use the listed birthdates as
a culling aid beyond isolating those who would be over
forty-five today, the top limit estimated by Hayman.

Rivera refilled his coffee cup, cracked a fresh pack of
cigarettes, flipped the stack of paper to the beginning,
and began his first scan through the listing. He used a
black ballpoint pen to circle any name that might even
be close to spawning Andy and lined out any name with
a birthdate that made the man older than forty-six. He
decided to give the ME a year's leeway.

Steve Wayne's office had a window that overlooked
Gold Street. The downtown street names in Albuquerque
were taken from the elements—gold, silver, lead. If he
pressed his cheek against the window and looked east,
he could see the cars whizzing past on Interstate 25,
fourteen blocks away. He could not see it from his window, but the east-west Interstate 40 was twenty-two
blocks north. He was located that close to a major crossroads of the country.

He did not think about it much.

He did like the downtown area, with its slipping grasp
on the architecture of the past. The new city–county
police building, between Roma and Marquette avenues,
was a nice blend of high-tech construction incorporating
the best that adobe design had to offer. The city streets
were narrow and crowded, but a hell of a lot friendlier
than those of Washington, DC or New York or
Baltimore.

Wayne's office was not large or ornate. He had a desk,
a swiveling, brown Naugahyde-covered desk chair, two
straight-backed visitor's chairs, and a catch-all table
shoved into the corner. The desk and table were topped

with Formica that was supposed to give him the warm feeling of walnut. He had foregone the President's and the Director's framed photographs and hung four water-color studies of old Navajo men. He thought that there was a great deal more life, experience, and wisdom in the wrinkled and weatherworn faces of the Navajo men than in the public relations facades of the President and the Director.

On Wednesday, Carmen brought a large Federal Express box into Wayne's office and opened it for him. The box contained five pounds of photocopied computer printouts. He rifled through them briefly and saw hundreds of names circled with heavy black ink. Hundreds more had single black lines drawn through them.

Using a ruler, no less.

Wayne appreciated the sheriff's neatness.

He read the short note resting on top of the stack: "Ring made by Creighton Associates. Lu's checking their home office for outlets."

He wondered who Lu was.

Wayne considered calling Rivera, then passed on it. It was still a local case, even if the sheriff kept sending him updated information. He would have to play this one vicariously and avoid the chance of running into the hotshot blonde with the big mouth. Certainly, he had enough to do anyway, and he went back to his desk to organize notes for the Justice Department attorney who was to open the trial on the Albuquerque National robbery next Tuesday.

"Should I log it, Steve?" Carmen asked.

"Let's skip it for now. It's not our case." Besides, given Ellington's frame of mind, Wayne would just as soon not have much paper from Santa Fe hanging around the office. At least, none that was considered official enough to record in a black and white log book.

One time, in rookie days, he had worked on a civil rights case in Missouri in which two people had been.

killed. The Justice Department was pursuing violation of
civil rights charges against five men who might have
been involved. Wayne had packed his notebooks with
details from the crime scene, the interrogation of witnesses, and his own creative insights.

On the witness stand, the defense attorneys had bad-
gered him for two full days, watching him as he leafed
through his notebooks to respond to requests for detail.

On and on. Forever and ever.

Pressing, demanding, wanting to know what was on
every page. Castigating him for his speculations. He
finally slapped a notebook down on the witness box railing and said, ''Fuck it! You read it.''

The SAC had had a long talk with him about the
Bureau's penchant for decorum. And Wayne quit writing
down any more than was absolutely necessary.

On Thursday, Delwin Blessing received a phone call
at home, in the study furnished primarily in antique oak
pieces that had been his father's. The elder Blessing had
been a county judge, and Blessing had always been proud
of him.

He did not think that he had ever heard the voice on
the other end of the line before.

''Mr. Blessing, we've been following your campaign
with intense interest.''

''Oh? Is that right?''

''Definitely. We think that you have impressive qual-
ifications and would be an asset to the office and to the
community.''

''Well, that's flattering. Thank you.''

''A question, however, if I may?''

''Certainly.''

''How do you stand on issues of national security?''

Caution was suggested. ''In what way?''

''Should a case arise in which the public airing of
details is to the detriment of the United States, how would
you handle it?''

There was no doubt in Blessing's mind. He was a patriot, first and foremost.

Never say the damning word, "cover-up."

"Certainly, I would defer to the wisdom of national agencies."

"That is surely a diplomatic approach," the voice said. "What if I were to tell you that I represented such a national agency?"

CIA? My God! Here, in Santa Fe?

"Yes?"

"And suggest that your campaign ignore what is being referred to as the Razor Murders?"

"The murders? What do you mean?"

"Just what I'm saying to you."

"My God! You mean to tell me there's a national security implication?"

"Quite so. The details are best left vague, and then forgotten. Your public statements are keeping the issue prominent, and that is not helpful. Naturally, our agency believes in one hand shaking another."

Favor for a favor?

"What do you mean?"

"That if your public relations people were to forget this case, you might be surprised by the help your campaign receives."

With two weeks to go to election day, Blessing could use all of the help he could muster. Especially cash help. The radio spots and newspaper pages were quickly depleting his campaign treasury. No matter the lack of progress Rivera was making on the murder case, Blessing's campaign volunteers were still reporting a lot of support for the man throughout the city and the county.

"Why, certainly, I'd be happy to cooperate. I'll tell my people to shy away from the Razor Murders."

"And after you're elected?"

"Naturally, I'll continue whatever is in the best interest of my country."

"That's wonderful news, Mr. Blessing, just wonderful. By the way, we'll send you a duplicate tape recording of this conversation for your own files. Have a good day."

SIX

THE REUNION AT Lew's seaside house in the summer of 1970, after everyone had been discharged from the US Army, was subdued. They bitched about the way the politicians had fucked up the war. They shot pool at the table in the living room overlooking the surf and the bikinis, drank five cases of Bud the first night, smoked some grass, and compared medals.

Six of them had received the Army Commendation Medal. "You get that hummer for being present when your name's called," Andy said.

All had received Bronze Stars for valor—earned during the September jump—though C.B. and Pilo received second citations of the medal because they fought their way out of a particularly incendiary part of the village.

"Shit," Country said, "all of us had to fight our way out of that sewer."

"Yeah," Pilo said, "but me and C.B. fought better. The brass recognized that."

"Fuckin' A. Talent's recognized," C.B. agreed.

Sweet, Brooklyn, and Country had Purple Hearts. Sweet didn't limp anymore, Country's arm ached in bad weather, and Brooklyn dropped his pants to show everyone the depression in his left buttock.

"What's your girlfriend say about that, Brooklyn?"

"Told her this little girl from Queens got all excited and took a bite out of me."

"And she believed that shit?"

"She didn't say she didn't."

Andy, Sweet, and Lew had been decorated with the Silver Star for gallantry in action. Andy got his in December after Country was med-evac'd out and they were one short for a jump outside of An Khe. Andy got separated from the others during the jump and landed a half klick east of the main assault party. Working his way back across the dry, rolling ground of the high plateau region, he ran into a VC heavy machine gun emplacement. The three gunners were waiting silently. One of them was spitting betel juice over the side of the foxhole. Guaranteed ambush for Lew's patrol. Andy went down on his stomach and slithered his way in close. He took them out with one grenade, and then dropped into the foxhole full of blood and gore and waited there, grinning until Lew and the others showed up.

"Just like I used to do it back in Bozeman," he had told them. Andy had played army a lot when he was a kid, out in the gullies on the run-down family ranch, the one that was finally foreclosed by the bank. Andy, in fact, was the only one who had enthusiastically enlisted in the Army. Brooklyn was forced and the others were drafted. Lew didn't count, because he was ROTC.

Sweet and Lew picked up their Silver Stars for being circumspect, for a change. It was a night raid over into Laos, a brief foray on an underground hospital. While the others provided cover, Sweet and Lew slithered into a dank and claustrophobic tunnel. They killed a doctor, his two assistants, and two patients; and Sweet cut the throat of a dog. Probably Sunday dinner. There was an NVA colonel and an old and grizzled NVA sergeant type, and though they had been wounded earlier, they could still walk. Lew decided to bring them back, and the CIA guy was so ecstatic about the interrogation possibilities, he pushed old man Conrad to recommend them for the medals.

Lew was the only one who had received the Distinguished Service Cross, for taking on that major, one-on-one, during the September jump, but they all agreed that officers always got the best deal.

Lew's medals were framed behind glass and hung on the wall over his desk. The ribbons representing the medals were lined up inside the frame, just below the medals. Along with the National Defense ribbon, the Vietnam Service ribbon, and the Republic of Vietnam's thank-goddamn-you ribbon, it was a colorful lineup.

Each of the enlisted men had received a Good Conduct Medal.

Wayne and Cece drove the sixty miles to Santa Fe on Friday evening. She wore a summery white cocktail dress with a square-cut bodice that displayed a little cleavage and a lot of freckles.

She sat, leaning back into the space between the passenger seat and the door, and smirked at him. Her green eyes laughed.

"What're you so satisfied about?"

"I can't believe we're socializing with people that *you* know."

"I know people," he insisted, aware that she was correct. Usually, they went to dinners or parties hosted by people she had met through her work in advertising. For the most part, they were nice enough people, though sometimes bland, but there were a few that Wayne found insufferable. Some of the radio and TV personalities and a few of the men on the creative side of her agency were overimpressed with themselves.

"Sure you do," she said. "Half of them are cops or attorneys, and the other half are felons. Their only topics of conversation revolve around courthouses and what got them into courthouses."

"Those are the men. I know some women."

"Of course you do," she said, a bit icily.

Wayne grinned at her and steered the conversation into her advertising triumphs of the week. It was safer.

They arrived in Santa Fe early, at 6:30, and Wayne found a place for the Trans Am two blocks south of the Plaza, on Alameda. They got out and walked back to take Old Santa Fe Trail north. A couple blocks to the south was the dome of the state capitol. Wayne knew, had heard somewhere, that it had been constructed in the shape of the Zia sun symbol.

Holding hands with Cece as they walked, Wayne felt pretty content. White, fluffy cumulus clouds in the west had blocked the sun, and the evening was balmy. The streets were crowded with tourists, but everyone was amiable, smiling at them as they passed. Or perhaps smiling at the beautiful redhead, wondering how she had hooked up with the guy who was so obviously an IBM salesman.

Cece squeezed his hand. "You're treading on history, you know that?"

"I knew something was bothering me."

"The Santa Fe Trail ends in the Plaza, at the Palace of the Governors. The eastern end is behind us, in Franklin, Missouri."

"Pretty far behind, I'll bet."

"In 1821, the trip took seventy days."

"And speaking of pretty behinds—"

"Shush. I'm giving you a history lesson. On our right is the Loretto Chapel, finished in, I think, 1878. The Plaza itself dates from the beginning of the Seventeenth Century. The San Miguel Mission was built the first time in 1610, and behind it is the oldest house in the United States. It was built in 1740."

"No running water?"

"Are you going to keep interrupting me all evening?" she asked.

"No. I apologize."

In fact, Wayne was appreciative of the Indian and

Spanish culture and tradition that surrounded him. In the few times he had visited the city, he had come to like the way the old and the new flowed together and the way the city fathers struggled to maintain the balance.

On the outskirts of town, he saw the threats posed by commercial developers, but the architecture of the city proper, under the protection of ordinances and covenants, hung on to the past. To their east, along the twisty Canyon Road, was a residential neighborhood with parts of some houses dating to 1753. It had evolved into an artists' colony and was now zoned for homes, studios, and galleries. Trouble was, the real estate on Canyon Road was some of the most expensive in the nation. Struggling artists need not apply.

When they reached the Plaza, they circled it clockwise, flowing with the tourists, and Wayne listened attentively to Cece's tour guide spiel. She was knowledgeable, having grown up on a ranch one hundred and some miles to the west of Santa Fe.

Sometimes, he felt more a tourist than he wanted to feel. He would like to be as comfortable with the Indian, Mexican, and pioneer history as Cece was. He tried to imagine her in her high school days, hopping off the school bus in jeans, boots, and a plaid shirt, climbing aboard some pony to perform ranchlike things. Nah. The pretty redhead was too sophisticated for that.

The Palace of the Governors, on the north side of the Plaza, was now a museum, and the other sides of the square housed restaurants, galleries, and souvenir shops. They peeked into the galleries and some of the shops, and Wayne was glad that Cece was not a browser or addicted to buying everything in sight that was either quaint or stamped "Santa Fe."

They ended up on the southeast corner of the Plaza just before 7:30, crossed the street dodging cars and people, and entered the La Fonda Hotel. It was a rambling adobe structure with a gift shop and a restaurant on the ground floor.

Carlos and Myra Rivera were waiting for them in the lobby. Myra Rivera was a bubbly and tiny woman with a bright, quick smile, dark hair, and ebony, flashing eyes. She had a voluptuous figure, lots of curves, and it was difficult to picture her as the mother of two. She shook Wayne's hand warmly and firmly, and he liked her right away.

Rivera led the way to the restaurant entrance, was immediately recognized by the maître d', and the four of them were guided to a corner table. The dining room was packed, testifying to its popularity. The conversational buzz was steady.

"This isn't exactly an out-of-the-public-eye place, Carl."

"True, *amigo*, but the food's great."

"Are we supposed to be in hiding?" Cece asked.

"Only from a certain reporter."

"The flat-chested one?"

Myra laughed at that, but said, "Her heart's in the right place, Cece. She's just . . . eager."

"'Zealous' is the word I would use," Wayne said.

"How about 'intrepid'?" Rivera asked.

The waiter appeared at Rivera's side. "Good evening, Sheriff."

"Hello, Manuel. Let's start it off with a round of margaritas."

"Right away."

They ordered their dinners when the full-to-the-brim, stemmed glasses arrived. Cece, who had better discipline, ordered a chili relleno and a cheese enchilada. Wayne realized he was starved and requested a beef taco, two rellenos, a rosbif burrito, and an enchilada.

"And Manuel, have them dump sour cream and guacamole over everything."

"*Sí, señor.*"

Cece gave him a particularly dirty look.

"I won't eat anything tomorrow, okay?"

"That's what you say now."

After Manuel left, Rivera asked, "You have a chance to look at those printouts, Steve?"

"Actually, I haven't—"

"Uh-uh!" Myra exclaimed. "When I checked the program for tonight, there wasn't any shoptalk listed."

Rivera grinned ruefully. "Myra and I have this little agreement. It says she doesn't like cop talk and won't put up with it. It also says I don't have a vote."

"That's wonderful, Myra!" Cece told her. "I'm going to write up the same agreement." Turning to Wayne, she said, "And you're going to sign it."

"Hey! I've been pretty good."

"Always strive to be better."

The dinner was excellent, and Wayne was stuffed when it was over. The company was even better, and he enjoyed himself during the conversation over brandy afterward.

Rivera was a low-key, easygoing type. They found some football, automobile, and political topics in common that did not arouse the ire of the women. Political subjects were the fodder of a capital city, and Santa Fe was no different from any other capital in that regard. They talked about bills currently under legislative consideration and the personalities and special interests involved with them. Rivera thought that abortion, environmental issues, and cultural protections would be hot topics in the next session.

And Cece and Myra seemed to get along well, too. Wayne overheard pieces of conversation related to advertising, United Way efforts, the ERA, and ancestral geography. As a foursome, they discussed movies, books, and the Santa Fe Opera. It was a good evening, but they ended it at eleven. Rivera had to work in the morning.

There was a minor debate over the tab, but Rivera insisted that Wayne and Cece were his guests. Wayne let him win and dropped bills on the table for Manuel's tip.

Parting outside the main entrance of the hotel, Cece said, "We're going to have to do this again, but you'll have to come to our town."

"We'll plan on it," Myra said.

Wayne was surprised at the invitation. Cece had never wanted to meet someone he knew a second time.

On the trip south with the windows down, the speed control set at fifty, and the perfume of the desert drifting into the car, Cece lodged herself on the console and snuggled against him. Travelers in a hurry passed them easily.

"Nice people," she said.

"I think so."

"No pretenses."

"What?"

"They're not hiding behind some facade of wealth or power or simulated knowledge, like so many people I know. What you sees is what you gets."

Wayne began to question his famous ability to perceive people. Until then, he had not realized just why he liked Carlos Rivera.

Some people, he just liked instinctively. But there were those he liked, but later found out he never really knew very well. It had been instinctive with Gary Poole. He and Poole went through the training session at Quantico together and had similar backgrounds. Both of them had graduated from midwestern universities, Kansas and Iowa, and both had attended law school at the University of Chicago, though a couple years apart.

They became even faster friends, sharing the rent on a small apartment in Washington when they were assigned to familiarization stints with the FBI's Identification, Records, Forensics, and other sections. They kept in touch even after Poole went into counterintelligence and Wayne elected to pursue the more domestic forms of criminal activity.

Poole was his best man when Wayne married Pat, and Wayne stood up for him when Poole married Elinor.

And then Poole left the bureau for the Central Intelligence Agency, and although Christmas letters were still exchanged, Gary Poole's assignments abroad created a widening gulf.

Wayne had not even known that Poole was back in the States until he ran into him in Miami and found a changed man. Wayne was tracing a lead out of New Orleans involving a Costa Rican national, the murder of an Army reservist, missing Louisiana National Guard weapons, and a sizable stash of dollars that he suspected had drug links. The trail led to a bungalow in the Cuban ghetto in Miami, and Wayne and three other agents were staging for a raid a block away when a black Buick pulled up next to their parked cars.

The passenger window rolled down, and Poole stuck his head out. "Hello, Steve."

"Hey, Gary! What the hell you doing here?"

"Stopping you."

"Stopping me? From what?"

"You have to leave Gonzales alone."

"Bullshit! That son of a bitch killed a man."

"Inadvertent. We'll take care of it."

"I'll take care of it, goddamn it!"

Poole's eyes were different. Flint. His mouth was a hard line. "He works for me, and he's not yours to take care of. Shove off, Wayne."

Wayne shoved off. Jerked the car away from the curb, whipped a U-turn, and accelerated down the street. He took out the white picket fence fronting the bungalow as he spun the sedan in from the street, over the curb, and into the front yard. He and his partner smashed the front door, caught Gonzales going out a back bedroom window in his skivvies, and tossed him in the car. Poole's Buick followed them all the way down to the federal building, honking its horn madly, but he refused to stop.

Wayne hauled Gonzales inside to process him. But he was on the street within twenty minutes, without one form having been filled in. Wayne had a long talk with the SAC, who did not say anything about pressure from other agencies, then packed his bags for Montgomery, Alabama.

Wayne was careful about who became his friend. He was also leery of bureaucratic power.

He thought about it on the road back to Albuquerque, Cece's head resting on his shoulder.

She snored.

"Hey! You want to move the office work you said you'd never bring home?" Myra stood over him with an armload of dishes, silver, and glasses.

Rivera grinned at her. "Sorry, love." He scooped the stack of paper up, dropped it in his briefcase, and took the case over to the coffee table. He could smell the onions cooking with the liver. He liked liver, but Jeff and Tracy had been wrinkling their noses all evening and making snide comments from where they were sprawled on the living room floor, reading the comic pages. They had carefully set the sports section aside for him. Rivera was currently following the NFL draft.

Myra set the table. "You have to work tomorrow?"

"Would you believe I'm taking Sunday off? But I did agree to talk at some breakfast a few of the businessmen are having. Politics over cold scrambled eggs."

"We could run up to Taos for a while?"

Her parents lived there. "Sure. Plan for about ten o'clock."

Myra went back to the kitchen, and Rivera heard a rapping on the front screen door. He opened the front door and went out to the enclosed porch. The absorption of details was second nature with him, and he noted that no car was parked at the curb. The man standing on the top step outside the screen door was a stranger in his early forties with short-cropped brown hair, a rugged and lined face, and a once-broken nose. The top three buttons of his shirt were unfastened, revealing tanned flesh. In the evening light, Rivera could not see his eyes. "Yes?"

The screen door pulled open, and the man raised his arm. He was holding a blued Walther automatic. Rivera was scared of guns, and respected them, but this one was more chilling for it had the long cylinder of a silencer screwed to its muzzle. "Just stand there, Sheriff."

He stood still, realizing that his own .357 Magnum was on the top shelf in the front closet, safe from children's curiousity behind a locked door.

The man signaled with his left hand, and two shadows slipped from either corner of the house, converging on the door. "All right. Get back inside. Now."

God, the kids! He backed through the doorway, keeping his hands carefully in sight. "What do you want?"

"I want you to shut up for the time being." He had a mildly deep, resonant voice.

The other two mounted the steps and followed them in. Same age range. One was bald with a fringe of grayish-brown hair, the other had lanky hair hanging over his ears. Both of them were armed with pistols. All three looked fit and hard. All were casually dressed—slacks, sport shirts, light biege jackets. The bald man had rimless glasses. The one with the dirty hair was wearing Adidas running shoes and the sight of the shoes made his heart pound. He checked the first man's shoes. Low-cut loafers. Could be Florsheims.

Rivera stopped in the middle of the living room. Jeff and Tracy jumped up, their eyes wide with fear or disbelief, and he gathered them together against his legs.

The bald one went quickly to the kitchen door, and he heard Myra yelp in surprise.

"In here, lady. Now! Move it!"

"What? Who?"

Rivera struggled to keep his own voice calm. "Do what he says, Myra. Please."

She came into the living room, and Carlos put his arm around her. The kids, big-eyed, hugged his knees.

Grinning, the one with the stringy blond hair and the running shoes spotted the briefcase and leaned over the coffee table to check it. He held up the two printouts. "Looky right here, Lew. Shit, there's even one from the Association."

He flipped through the pages. "Got my name right. Yours too, C.B."

"Can it, Sweet," the one called Lew said.

The one with the printouts actually pouted.

"What do you want?" Rivera asked.

"We got it," the one in charge told him. "Unless there's more we should know. What else you got?"

"About what?" Rivera had never been as frightened in his life, but it was not for his own life. He hoped a strong tone would reassure Myra. Tracy started to cry, and her mother bent and wrapped her arms around her.

The leader motioned to the printouts with his silenced pistol. "Along those lines."

"Nothing. That's it."

"What made you think of jumpers?"

"The rigging. I was one-oh-one."

"No shit? What else?"

"Nothing."

"You sure?" He pointed the pistol at Jeff's head.

"I'm positive."

The gun went *Phut!*

The investigation in Alamogordo had wound up late on Saturday night. Wayne had not planned a trip to the south, but the team from Washington had found what they wanted and called him in.

A technician with a penchant for lovely ladies and fast times had the right kind of access and the right kind of need for cash generated by selling fancy lab equipment. They made the arrest after the man returned to his home at midnight, and Wayne missed the last flight back to Albuquerque. He spent the night at a motel with a hard bed, thin towels, and lukewarm water.

He did not sleep well, but did not get up until eight since his flight was at 9:45. Dressing slowly, watching the morning newscast, he was utterly shocked when the anchor man went to state news. He sat stunned for a moment before grabbing the phone and placing a call to Santa Fe.

His orally delivered credentials got him past the switchboard and a secretary. A self-conscious female voice told him, "Acting Sheriff Rodriguez."

"This is Steve Wayne, FBI. What happened up there?"

"I remember Carlos talking about you, Mr. Wayne. But I can't tell you very much. There was a fire which totally destroyed the house. Carlos and his family were inside, we suspect, because we found four bodies. The state police are leading the investigation."

Rodriguez sounded as devastated as Wayne felt.

Wayne's flight back was a depressing one. He had felt a kinship with the county sheriff, an understanding of the man's competence, and an appreciation for his modesty. Without having met them, he knew he would have liked the children, too. He remembered his short conversation with Jeff Rivera. Myra Rivera's bright eyes and smile kept popping up in his mind.

After the plane landed at Albuquerque International, he drove the government's Chevy sedan from the airport to his apartment off Candelaria and told Cece about it. His throat kept constricting, and she was aware of his grief.

"My God, Steve! That's terrible! Myra?"

"And the kids."

She closed her eyes, and the tears came.

"What's more terrible, honey, is that I think it was no accident."

"It was intentional?"

"I'm not really sure—just a feeling I have."

It was a rotten, damned evening. Every time he looked at Cece, she burst into tears.

*   *   *

Monday was not any better. He did not go into the office, but hung around the apartment making phone calls that all proved fruitless.

He paced about the apartment, too sick to eat lunch, too restless to sit. He opened a can of beer, but it went flat before he was halfway through it.

Cece came out of the bedroom, dressed in one of her sales-closing outfits—modest enough, but with the hint of visual cleavage delights, if she would just lean over far enough, which she never did. She had explained her tactics to him once.

Wayne raised an eyebrow.

"The Silver Trust account. I told you. Bart and I are making the presentation, and I can't put it off."

She had told him, and it had slipped his mind. "I forgot. Good luck."

Cece came over and kissed him lightly. "I guess I could call Bart and beg off."

"No, you go ahead. I'm all right."

She cocked an eyebrow at him, but he nodded his reassurance, and she left to find her five-year-old Mercedes diesel. Wayne dumped his stale beer, got a fresh *Dos Equis* from the refrigerator, and slipped a cassette into the recorder. The Eagles did not help.

Finally, he made another call to a residential number in Santa Fe and was referred to another number. "Medical Examiner."

"Dr. Hayman? This is Steve Wayne."

"Ah, yes. *Com'esta?*"

"Not good at all. I liked the man."

Deep sigh on the other end, and Wayne recalled the uncombed hair and the red face. "And some of us loved him. He was a good man, and he had a nice family. I've had a shitty couple of days, you know?"

"I understand. Can you tell me anything?"

"The State Attorney's office has oversight on this one. I need to talk to them before I say anything."

"Between us? It won't go further."

A long, long silence. "All right. I'll hold you to that. Hearsay, first. I heard a fireman, not one with authority, say the house had been well doused with flammable substances. Arson, certainly."

"And cover-up?"

"That, too. There was very little to the remains, skeletons. All four were together in the living room. Holding onto each other, I think." Hayman's voice broke, a half sob. "All four had been shot once in the head."

"Bastards!" Wayne blurted. "Execution?"

"Yes. Those poor damned kids. Myra and my wife were good friends." Hayman was barely containing himself.

"You estimate a caliber?"

"Big one. A forty-five, maybe a nine millimeter. They're still sifting for slugs."

"Thanks. If there's anything I can . . ."

"Yeah. I'll let you know."

Steven Wayne's telephone number was unlisted, but Janet Willow had connections, and she came up with the number. He had barely hung up on his conversation with Hayman when the phone rang.

"This's Janet Willow, *New Mexican*. What's your reaction?"

"How did you get my number?"

"Do you think it was murder?"

"You'll have to talk to the people investigating it."

"I've talked to them."

"And they said?"

"Have you talked to anyone in Santa Fe?" she droned on.

"Santa Fe, New Mexico?"

"Do you think Sheriff Rivera's murder is connected to the Razor Murders?"

"I'm not sure I think anything."

"Do you think there's a conspiracy involved here?"

"Lady, anything in the world is possible. Somebody killed them, and somebody is going to pay."

The fire at Rivera's house scared Delwin Blessing to death, and all he could think about was that voice on the phone assuring him of help in his campaign.

He could not sleep; he could not eat; he could not think beyond the exact words that were on that tape. His name was on it, but not the other party's. He had only assumed that the CIA was on the other end. And for damned sure, he had agreed to suppress the Razor Murders in exchange for assistance in his campaign for the post of county sheriff.

His election was assured, as was some unknown thumb always pressing against his shoulder, directing him.

At the moment, Blessing did not want to be sheriff. Hell, he did not even know *how* to be sheriff.

The Tuesday papers quoted him via wire stories filed by Janet Willow: "Steven Wayne, FBI Special-Agent-in-Charge of the Albuquerque office, said that a conspiracy involving the Razor Murders and the alleged murders of Sheriff Carlos Rivera and his family in Santa Fe is possible. He had no comment regarding an imminent investigation by the FBI."

On Wednesday, the personnel department in Washington called him to say, "Mr. Wayne, at the end of the month, you are to report to the Sacramento office as the new SAC."

"What?"

"Yes. Agent Darmouth has retired."

"I've only been here two years."

"And I only follow orders. Don't we all?"

SEVEN

LEW HAD HAD a good idea while they were still in-country.

In 'Nam, during the cleanup after a combat mission, they always appropriated piaster, gems, and greenbacks found in pockets, tin cans, and under cane sleeping mats. They hit a jewelry shop one time and loaded up on blue star sapphires, diamonds, and jade. Not all of it, of course, so anybody wearing mighty brass and possibly in charge of the operation might notice, but a bunch. Some of those Viet merchants were really ripping off the troops in black market commodities, stacking up US dollars in nice high piles.

They divided it. Ten percent off the top to Lew—for overhead and making arrangements with the CIA guy, 50 percent spread among those directly involved in the operation, and 40 percent meted out to the whole group.

Lew had told them, "Don't blow it."

"Hell, Lew, we got it, we worked for it, let's have us a time. Guy over in the Third's got some sweet grass."

"No way. I don't care what you do with whatever you get when the eagle shits, but if you start spending more than you're supposed to have, the wrong somebody's going to notice and get suspicious. I don't want anyone here sitting down at the Provost Marshall's, spouting off about his friends."

There was a little resentment, and Sweet did spend some of his share. He had a hell of a time hanging onto money, maybe because he'd grown up in west LA and kept getting beat up for his lunch money. But he only spent a little of the operation income, doled out some scrip at the PX in Cholon for a Sansui amplifier and tuner, tape decks, turntable, and monster speakers. The tape decks and turntable didn't work worth a damn on the erratic electricity that made its way into their hootch from the generators, and he finally shipped it all home.

Pilo spent some of his, too, but it wasn't very traceable. It all went to a little girl who called herself Jackie, said she was part Montagnard, and was built like she ought to be in *Playboy*. Had to be some French blood in her line.

After a while, the amount had added up, and Lew devised a plan. There were restrictions on money orders shipped to the US—no more than a man made in a month. At DEROS—Date of Estimated Rotation from Overseas—everybody standing in line at Tan Son Nhut, looking at that beautiful bird with the golden tail, the customs people checked for excess cash.

The R&R flights to Hong Kong and Bangkok on old DC–6s were pretty loose, though, and Lew divided the booty and shipped part of it with any one of them who was due for R&R. In Hong Kong and Bangkok, they found the money changers and jewelers and cashed in piaster and—would you believe?—French francs and both finished and uncut gems, taking the exchange in US dollars. They wired the currency to savings accounts at different banks in LA that Lew had had them set up.

All told, it amounted to $156,821. Not too shabby for a few months in the 'Nam.

With that capital divided among them and Small Business Administration loans, Lew thought they should start a chain of sport skydiving centers, buying existing businesses where they had to do so. Each of them would own and operate one of seven centers in a string stretching from San Diego to San Luis Obisbo, and it would allow each of them to do what they were best at doing.

Besides which, they could often get together and jump as a team.

That was something they were also good at, teamwork.

Lew was always good at making arrangements. Ones he made later guaranteed the initial investment would keep on growing.

". . . WAS KINDA DARK IN THERE, AND WE DIDN'T SEE THEM RIGHT AWAY, YOU KNOW, BUT THE SMELL WAS SO AWFUL, AND [HIS BROTHER], HE GOT SICK, AND HE THREW UP ALL OVER THE GROUND. THE TWO OF THEM, THEY WERE HANGING THERE, LIKE IN THESE LEATHER STRAP THINGS, AND THE MAN, HE DIDN'T HAVE NO . . . [HAD BEEN EMASCULATED]. THERE WAS BLOOD EVERYWHERE. IT WAS BLOOD, I THINK. IT WAS PRETTY BLACK."

THE TWO YOUNG BROTHERS WHO DISCOVERED THE BODIES DESCRIBED FOR THIS REPORTER DETAILS OF THE GRISLY DOUBLE MURDER WHICH HAVE BEEN DENIED THE PUBLIC BY THE MEDICAL EXAMINER, THE DISTRICT ATTORNEY'S OFFICE, AND THE SHERIFF'S DEPARTMENT.

MR. DELWIN BLESSING, NOW RUNNING UNOPPOSED FOR SHERIFF, DECLINED TO COMMENT ABOUT EITHER HIS PLANS FOR THE INVESTIGATION OR HIS ATTITUDE TOWARD OPEN RECORDS. IN REGARD TO A CONNECTION BETWEEN THE RAZOR MURDERS AND THE DEATHS OF ACTING SHERIFF CARLOS RIVERA AND HIS FAMILY, BLESSING CALLED ANY RELATIONSHIP "PURE SPECULATION."

ALL OF THE LAW ENFORCEMENT AGENCIES APPEAR TO BE AT A STANDSTILL CURRENTLY, AND NO . . .

Janet Willow paused to slurp the last of her cold coffee and to light a cigarette. She smoked and reread what she had written so far, marking places for improvement or change. She had to keep the tone objective, yet somehow she also had to light a fire under all those dormant asses out there. Somewhere within her was the conviction that she could force the solution if she could keep the pressure building on the bureaucrats. That meant outraging the readership enough to keep those calls and letters coming in.

She wished she had gotten more out of Blessing, but the man had turned icy on the subject, and she suspected he was not going to be the most effective of law enforcement officers. He did not seem to have the vaguest notion about how to conduct an investigation. He had told her once that the job of sheriff was one of management, knowing how to pick the expertise to run the various divisions, not necessarily holding law enforcement credentials. She thought about working that in, but decided to save it for later, when he proved inept.

Finding the Contrarez brothers had been pure luck. The older boy, Juan, could not resist telling the story at school, and Janet picked up the trail from her nephew. When she arrived on the Contrarez porch, the mother, Juanita, came unglued, shouting and yelling. Janet persisted, though, and worked her way into the tiny living room, shooting questions at the two boys amid the English and Spanish profanities and threats from the mother. The youngest one, Roberto, was entirely introspective and frightened, but Juan had produced noteworthy details.

She would have gotten more if that interfering bitch, Pam Ostrander, had not shown up. As soon as *she* stormed into the house, claiming all kinds of doctor-patient confidentialities and forthcoming lawsuits, Juan had clamped his mouth, and it was over.

Still, the good Dr. Ostrander could not be everywhere at once, and it might be possible to reach Juan during school hours sometime.

There was another consideration. Should she save this

article for next Sunday's edition, when she was more likely to be picked up by the wires, or go ahead and waste it on Wednesday? She elected Wednesday. Much as she might like to make a larger story out of it, it was still fresh news and should go out as soon as possible. People had a right to know, and career considerations came second.

Willow knew she was a good reporter. She had performed the drudge work—society, community activities, obits—without complaint, and she had been working the police, hospital, and court circuit for three years. She had begun to think the top edges of her rut were getting awfully high when the "Razor Murders" broke. Finally, it was a chance to show what she could really do with a hot story. Then, with that recognition, move on to a political column perhaps, or even better, what she really wanted someday, a free-floating syndicated column.

But the story had to stay hot. If it dribbled away into unsolved nothingness, her rut was going to get deeper.

Snatching the phone, she tapped out Luisa Rodriguez's number again. It had been busy for hours.

At last, a ring.

"Hello?"

"Luisa, Janet Willow."

Janet and Luisa had gone to high school together. They had not been the best of friends, but still, they had known each other pretty well. They had also been at the University of New Mexico together, though in different fields, and had seen each other infrequently on campus.

"What can I do for you, Janet?" Her voice sounded way down, depressed.

"How do you like being sheriff?"

"I don't. But you'd better not print that."

"Two things, Lu. I need some sidebar info on you."

"Like what?"

"Education, experience." She already had the lead— Santa Fe's first female sheriff. Come to think of it, it was going to be more than a sidebar. The commissioners had shown some guts, naming Luisa.

"Oh. Okay." Rodriguez listed a lot of things Janet had not expected. Her degree was in law enforcement, but she had a few dozen seminars dealing with evidence, homicide, forensics, investigation, and the like.

"How long have you been with SFSD?"

"I'm starting my eleventh year here, Janet. I worked for the Los Angeles Sheriff's Department my first year out of school."

"You going to run for sheriff?"

"You've got to be kidding, Janet."

"You don't want Blessing to run unopposed, do you? It's a democratic society."

"It's way past the time for registration," Rodriguez said.

"So you'd have run, if you had had time to register?"

"No. Carlos was running."

"The situation has changed. Carlos is dead."

A long silence. "I know that, Janet."

Yeah. Well, come down to it, Willow missed him, too. He had been one of the good guys.

"All right," she said. "Lu, I'm running a story tomorrow, and I want to get your reaction."

"No comment."

"What? No comment on what?"

"Dr. Ostrander called me."

"Carlos never told us the bodies were hanging, Lu. Why hold that back?"

"This is an ongoing investigation, Janet. You may speculate all you wish, but the sheriff's department has made its statement."

"Hey, Luisa, this is the classic impasse between the press and the cops. I thought maybe we knew each other well enough to—"

"Publication of the grisly details may satisfy a small minority of your readers, Janet, but it could also hamper any future interrogation of suspects."

"Aw, come on!"

"I mean that. No comment."

"Well, hell."

But Willow kind of respected her for taking the stance. Maybe she was as tough as Carlos, after all.

He had only heard the voice once before, but the voice-print was etched in his mind, and as soon as the man spoke, Blessing actually dribbled in his crotch, staining the new gray flannel slacks.

"You know, Del, ol' boy, that reporter you've got in that hick town, the one making like a combined Woodward and Bernstein, her big mouth sure isn't helping your campaign much."

"Uh, my campaign . . . ?"

"You could still lose."

Jesus! There was only one way he could lose. Blessing struggled to avoid squeaking when he spoke. "What can I do? Damn, it's First Amendment stuff. There's freedom of the press and all that, and I can't—"

"Just shut her up, Del, ol' boy. A big man like you can handle that."

"You don't know that woman! She's—"

Blessing finally realized he was talking to a dial tone. He hung up the phone and sat in his silent study among the relics of his father and tried to imagine how, in one short week, he had been reduced to this kind of fear by a man he had conversed with twice in his life.

Thursday night, Wayne decided he had to discuss the situation with Cece. Finally, they would have to talk about next Christmas. They were in the living room watching one of the few programs besides newscasts either of them bothered with on television, a public broadcast series on the Constitution.

A cold front was moving across central New Mexico, bringing a balmy evening with it. Wayne had shut down the air-conditioning and opened all of the windows in the apartment.

He was in his armchair, and Cece was sitting on the floor, dressed in shorts and a halter top, leaning back against his knees. Steve was leaning forward, massaging her long neck muscles, absentmindedly counting freckles. "Cece?"

"Huh?"

"I've got an important announcement."

She threw her head back, peering upside down at him. "More important than the Constitution?"

"To me, yes."

She found the remote control on the carpet and turned off the TV, then scooted around to face him. "I've been waiting since you turned glum on me yesterday. Announce away."

No easy way. "I've been transferred."

There was a flicker of disappointment in her big green eyes, but her mouth remained stoic. "When?"

"End of the month."

"That's only six days away. Where?"

"Sacramento."

"Now the big one. Why?"

Why? The question struck him as funny, and he had to grin. He had never asked why before. Perhaps because he had always known. A little screwup here and there, a little shocker for the bureaucracy, an offended assistant to an assistant director, then they put Wayne on the train, get him out of town.

"Why Sacramento?"

She wrapped her arms around her raised knees. "No, dummy. Why a transfer? I know we've been evading the issue, but I was under some silly impression that we had another two or three years before the question would come up. I thought there was some kind of government policy in effect which limited transfers and saved the taxpayer all those expensive moving costs."

Wayne shrugged. "The SAC in Sacramento is retiring.

I'm supposed to take his position, and I suppose they'll elevate Norman in my office to the SAC here.''

"They want to promote Norman, tell them to send Norman to Sacramento.''

"That's a bit too logical," he said.

"The FBI and logic are incompatible?''

"No, but sometimes the logic isn't apparent.''

"Tell me.''

How to start? "The Bureau is like any massive organization. It employs all kinds of people. Some are good, and some are bad, and some are in-between. There are formal lines of authority, and there are some informal things going on, too.''

"What kind of people are you?''

"I'm probably an in-betweener," Wayne said, though he felt he was one of the good ones. "I take my orders, and I try to toe the line on both the regulations and the informal understandings. Most of the time. But, Cece, I'm not a particularly adept rule follower. By now, I suppose it's a reputation I have in the Bureau. The brass have only to look at all the reassignments in my folder.''

"What happened that sent you here?" she asked, her intuition grasping that *something* had happened. "It have anything to do with your ear?''

Wayne automatically fingered the top of his left ear. The plastic surgery had reformed it somewhat, but it was about half an inch shorter than his right ear. "Not directly.''

"But indirectly?''

"Back when I was in Montgomery, I was frequently assigned work with an agent named Fernandez. Nice guy, sharp. Everyone called him Fern. He and I once busted into a motel room after a bank robbery. There were two perps, and they opened up with handguns right away. The first slug caught my ear and ricocheted off my skull. Put me out of it right away. I mean, I blacked out. Fern took care of the two perps.''

"Jesus!''

"I owed him. And the problem was, Fern was born and raised in Puerto Rico. San Juan."

"Oh. I read something—"

"Yeah. After a while, it became apparent to me that Fern was getting all the shit details. If it was dangerous, Fern went in first, on orders from the SAC. Fern finally filed a discrimination complaint, and dumb old me, I backed him up. Testified at his hearing. I always open my mouth at times when I'm expected to be more circumspect. . . ." Wayne's voice trailed off as he remembered.

"And what came out of it?" Cece prompted.

"The SAC's still there, Fern resigned, and I received a lecture, then got shipped out to Albuquerque."

"But you were promoted."

"That was entirely an accident. I was supposed to be just another agent in the office, but two months after I got here, the SAC was diagnosed with multiple myeloma. I had the experience and the seniority, and somebody rather reluctantly put me in charge."

She pursed her lips. It looked like she was pouting, sitting there on the floor with her arms wrapped around her knees.

"The real problem is," he said, "that I have a history of similar screwups. Pissing off the wrong people just a short time before I get transferred. It's a recurrent theme in my professional life."

"Why do you do it?"

"Do what?"

"Piss people off."

"Because I don't do things their way."

"Is their way the wrong way?"

"Sometimes it is, Cece. Sometimes, common sense tells me what's right. I tend to follow instinct."

"Why do you put up with it? With the bureaucracy?"

"Maybe because I understand the organization."

"That's bullshit!"

"Maybe because I think I make a difference from time

to time. Even when I'm working on instinct.''

"That's better. That I can buy. That's why I love you. So what are you . . . what are we going to do?''

"I suppose we ought to be realistic, Cece.''

Cece lowered her forehead to her knees for a moment, one of the rare positions in which she looked tiny and vulnerable. When she looked up at him again, there was a large tear welling in the corner of her left eye. "That means finally talking about us.''

"Yes.''

"How strong is the attraction?''

"How strong is the love,'' he said. "You know there is love, though I'm often deficient with the words?''

She smiled grimly. "I know. Reciprocal, my dear. What it comes down to, though, is my job or yours.''

"I suppose so, yes. I've got eighteen years in, and it's difficult to throw away the pension.''

"I've got more than a few years devoted to building up contacts, to knowing the right people, to developing my clients,'' she told him, then effortlessly rose to her feet. "You want a brandy?''

"Please.'' He followed her to the kitchen and got out the snifters while she found the bottle and poured. They sat opposite each other at the table, and Wayne found himself wondering what breakfasts would be like without her—he certainly would not force her into a decision to give up her job here and start over in California.

"I need a few days to think about it. It would be difficult to leave. I love this country. Damn it, I was born here! It's mine.''

"Sure.'' He reached across the table to take her hand, remembering Carlos expressing the same affection for the New Mexican landscape. And it was more than the landscape. There was a mystique to it. Spirits of the Navajo hanging around. Land of Enchantment.

He felt it.

She squeezed lightly and gave him another of the grim smiles. "You want to go back to 'why'?''

He frowned. "Okay. Why?"

"It's your flat-chested reporter in Santa Fe. What's her name? Willow?"

Somewhere on the fringe of his logic-building processes, the same idea had occurred to him. "I suppose so. Hell, I know it. My name or my title keeps showing up in the paper and on the news wires when it isn't supposed to be there. Washington isn't happy about that."

"Now, ask why, again," Cece insisted.

That was the most difficult question, the one he had consciously avoided. Like any other agent, or most of them, Wayne had become disciplined over the years to doing exactly what Washington told him to do. Or almost exactly. The times he got in trouble were the times he followed his head—common sense overruling stated policy or lines of authority. But the discipline had been reinforced for him every time he stepped over one of those invisible lines.

"Simply by appearances, I've remained involved in a case that I've been told to stay away from. I'm being subtly chastised."

"Don't stop there. Keep going."

"Keep going?"

"Uh huh. Like back to Watergate."

"Cover-up? Aw, Cece, that's nonsense. What's to cover up?"

"I don't know. You tell me if there isn't something strange about those murders up north."

"Yes. There's something strange."

"And then tell me there isn't something strange about the FBI not wanting to help."

He nodded, but said, "We don't do murder investigations, unless its peripheral to a federal crime. There is no federal jurisdiction indicated here."

"That you know about."

"That I know about, yes."

"Maybe someone in Washington doesn't want you to discover a federal concern," she said.

"Ah . . ."

"And then remember last Monday, when you moped around the apartment, didn't eat, and drank too much beer. Somehow, I figured that Carlos was your friend. I know I'm grieving over a friendship that wasn't allowed to develop for me."

That was the real hell of it. "Yes. I think he was my friend."

"You're the expert," she said. "The cop with all this experience. Can you make a difference for Carlos and Myra and the kids? At least in his memory?"

"Yes." There was no doubt in his mind.

"Then do it."

He snorted through his nose. "There's the matter of my job."

"Fuck your job. You've taken moral stands before. What's wrong with now?"

"I'm accustomed to income."

"I'll support you," she said, a wry twist to her smile. "I make twice what you do, anyway."

"Now, damn it—"

"You want to flex a bicep for me?"

"Cece . . ."

The Ramada's lounge was dark and nearly deserted when Janet arrived at eleven, and she picked out her own booth and slid in behind the flickering red candle. She ordered a vodka Collins from a waitress dressed in a long, embroidered skirt and white peasant blouse, then studied her fingers while she waited.

There were carbon ribbon smudges on her hand that she had not noticed. She still preferred working on her old portable Smith Corona to hunting-and-pecking on the new word processors. She slipped her hand under the table and rubbed it against the fabric of her jeans.

"Hello, Janet."

She looked up to see Blessing. "Have a seat, Mr. Candidate."

He sat on the other side of the booth. "Thanks for meeting on such short notice."

She shrugged, dug in her purse, and lit a cigarette while her drink was placed in front of her. Blessing declined to order.

"It's part of my job."

"This has to be off the record."

Shit. She almost got up and stalked off, but decided that he might say something that would lead to a bigger story later. "All right. What have you got?"

"It's hard to know where to start."

He looked almost pitiful, sitting there in a four-hundred-dollar suit, head down, studying his clasped hands. "Try the beginning."

"Very well. You know that after the, uh, Razor Murders, I often criticized Sheriff Rivera about the speed of the investigation?"

"Yes. And then you performed an amazing about-face."

"I was asked to do that."

Janet sat up, pushing her drink aside. "By whom?"

"I can't say, except that the request came from the highest levels of government. The thing is, Janet, the case has implications of national security, and of course, I support my country."

And she did not? She knew where this was heading. "So. National security, huh? Then the FBI is conducting the investigation?"

"I don't know."

"We're off the record, Del. Who told you to lay off? The FBI? Wayne?"

"I really can't say."

Maybe he did not know. "The President personally told you to stay away from it?"

"Of course not."

She sipped her Collins. "Why tell me this?"

"I'm hoping that you'll also see that it would be in your best interests, in the community's best interests, to kind of, well, soft-pedal the story for a while. Until we're ready to divulge the whole thing."

With the "we," he was aligning himself with the offstage powers that be. "Two people were hideously tortured and murdered. What's the national security angle?"

"I'm not supposed to say."

"But you know?"

He remained silent.

"Well, maybe that's your job, Mr. Blessing, keeping the public in the dark. It isn't mine. Tell me why, if the national security is involved, the case hasn't been officially transferred to another jurisdiction?"

"The intent is to downplay it, not to focus national attention on it."

"Not my intent," she countered. "My intent is to give the public what they're entitled to have. That's information."

It was difficult to tell in the dim light of the candle, but she thought his lips quivered. "Janet, if you persist, it could be somewhat . . . dangerous."

She took a long drag on her Marlboro. "You're threatening me?"

"Of course not. I wouldn't do that."

Maybe Blessing had been threatened? "But someone else would? Oh, Jesus Christ! Is that what happened to Carlos Rivera? He wouldn't quit, so your supersecret agency took care of him?"

Blessing was quick to deny. "Not my agency, Janet. All I'm saying is, you need to also look out for yourself. I'm trying to look out for your welfare."

"You *are* threatening. Well, just screw off. I live in this country, too, and I certainly live under its Constitution. You've got a law degree of some kind. Remember the First Amendment, Mr. Candidate?"

Delwin Blessing shook his head rather passively and stood up.

"What you need, Mr. Blessing, is some opposition in this election."

The would-be sheriff remained silent and walked away, skirting empty tables.

He did not even offer to pay for her drink.

Willow sank back into the cushions after realizing her spine had straightened on her during her bout with indignation. She had never considered herself an investigative reporter. What she had was the police beat, plus an assignment or two in city or county government when times were slow.

But it was her job to dig when she did not like the answers she was getting or if she thought that the respondents were fudging on the answers.

She was not afraid to ask the questions, and she had lots of them. What she did not have was answers.

Now, Blessing throws this crap at her, and she thought that it was crap.

Unless it could be confirmed.

She stubbed out her cigarette, already thinking about where she had to go for confirmations.

EIGHT

THE FIRST CONTRACT came within eight months of Pilo's discharge in 1970—he was the last to be released from active duty. The job came in through Lew, who knew somebody who had helped to arrange their last 'Nam jumps—probably the CIA guy, but nobody bothered to ask. After a year of successful high-stress missions in-country, the guys had come to trust Lew implicitly, like the Boy Scout leader they'd never had.

Andy's old man died after the ranch was foreclosed, and he hadn't made it home for the funeral. Never went back to Montana. Sweet never knew his father, and though he had a sister he thought was doing tricks on Sunset Boulevard, he never bothered to look her up. Brooklyn's parents had split before he was nine; his mother had a new name, and his father was doing twenty-five to forty at Attica for second-degree murder. C.B. went back to Tulsa every now and then and thumped a Bible with his folks, though he didn't think much of their total faith in their Southern Baptist church. Country had spent some time back on the farm, raising corn and sweet-talking some girl he fancied, while his arm healed, but he had seen the world, and the world wasn't in Gilt Edge, Tennessee. Pilo only lasted four days in Des Moines after he was discharged, then borrowed two hundred bucks from his father, an elementary school principal, and thumbed his way back to California.

After 'Nam, it was difficult to identify with much. Sweet wore his uniform in downtown LA once and got pelted with an egg. Some hippie crawled away from that encounter with two broken kneecaps. None of them found much solace or much empathy outside of STRAC.

It was Lew who came up with a name for the team.

The Strategic Ready Army Command had been composed of units supposedly on a 24-hour alert status, ready to go anywhere in the world on short notice. After awhile, STRAC had come to suggest tip-top condition, lean and mean.

The seven of them were STRAC.

Only three of them went out on the first contract, but everybody shared the revenue, using the same formula Lew had set up in Vietnam. It was kind of like being a shareholder in a corporation.

Lew, Brooklyn, and C.B. went because they could unobtrusively fit the trip into their schedules. Sweet was pissed at being left behind, but Lew had always been able to sweet-talk him when he needed it.

They flew first class into Windhoek, Namibia, and rented a Piper Aztec light twin. Lew, who had picked up his flying license, along with instrument and instructor ratings after his release from active duty, flew.

He took them at tree- and jungle-top levels into Huambo, Angola, dodging any radar coverage—which wasn't extensive, anyway, and put the plane down on a nearly deserted dirt strip half a mile outside the town.

The Aztec had been fully outfitted for them. Behind the cargo hatch were a dozen grenades, three Kalashnikov assault rifles, and K-bar combat knives. Brooklyn felt a little ridiculous, combat-geared in blue jeans and a black T-shirt. Felt it wasn't all that STRAC.

A suspicious but smiling Cuban walked up to the plane, and Lew opened the door and shot him. The Cuban flew backward into the dirt, raising a cloud of dust, and bleeding profusely. The blood dried almost immediately in the heat.

They had to shoot two more Cubans before they had control of the minuscule operations hut. Brooklyn stayed behind to protect the airplane, and Lew and C.B. took the single jeep sitting next to the operations building and drove into town. It took them all of five minutes to locate the hotel. Maybe it was a hotel. A play hotel. Four rooms.

The Soviet advisor was living in one of the rooms and using another for his office. Lew slammed the door near the handle with his cowboy-booted foot, and the door flew open, swung wide, and banged into the wall.

The Russian was behind the desk. He was a blond guy with a day's growth of beard, sweating heavily in a tan safari shirt. He looked up, startled, his eyes wide, and yelled something emphatic in Russian.

C.B. shot him in the throat. Went over to where he was sprawled over the arm of his chair and pumped one more round into his left eye.

They went outside and got back in the jeep, waved at the people congregating in the dusty street, and drove back to the airstrip.

"We're not going to get a medal for this one, C.B., but fifty grand isn't bad."

"Hey, Lew, it's only a Russian. Bastards ought to stay in Russia with the rest of the atheists."

Wayne tossed and turned for the better part of the night, awakened around three, made a compromise decision for himself, and then finally slept. At breakfast, Cece appeared at the table fully dressed. The beginning of the end?

Cece left for work first, chugging away in her Mercedes, leaving a blue haze behind her. Saving gas and polluting the atmosphere. Soon again, he was going to bring up the topic of trading her car off. Sensitive subject to her since she did not want to trade it. She loved it, or something. She did not like getting rid of the things she loved.

And then again, maybe he would not mention the car. The question of their future had a five-day decision deadline coming up.

He made the bed, hung up some of his clothes, and picked up yesterday's paper. He walked around the apartment. It was not a spectacular place, but then, as with all of his postings, he had only looked for respectable shelter. Knowing he would be moving on, just as soon as Special Agent Smith or Task Force Leader Jones or Deputy Director Ellington became disenchanted with him.

Locking the door, he ignored the elevator, took the back stairs down to the lobby, and went out the back door to the parking lot.

Disenchanted. Land of Enchantment.

Wayne's apartment building was located in a complex of seven buildings off one of the main cross streets in northeast Albuquerque, Candelaria Road. A mile to the west was the Rio Grande River, floating history from Colorado, past Old Town Albuquerque, clear to Mexico. To the east was Sandia Peak. South, he had flown over the Manzano Mountains a dozen times, enroute to Alamogordo. Occasionally, he had flown into Navajo territory to assist in some federal foul-up or another. He wondered how many hours he had accumulated, sitting in the back seat or the co-pilot's seat of small chartered airplanes flying the back country of New Mexico, Arizona, Mississippi, Missouri, Louisiana, Georgia.

Without realizing it, Wayne had assimilated the geography of New Mexico. It was becoming second nature. He liked it.

Crossing the parking lot, he was aware of the heat rising from the asphalt. At 8:15 in the morning, it was already eighty degrees, and by noon, it would be in the nineties. Hot, very dry. Attacking anyone stepping out of an air-conditioned federal building. Sometimes, he bitched about it like everyone else from out of state, but inside, he enjoyed it.

Carlos had said that Albuquerque was getting too big, and he was right. The city proper had a population of around 350,000 people, and like Los Angeles, it was spread out and spreading, rather than rising. It was a crossroads of intersecting interstate highways, and it seemed to be collecting a wide variety of people from all points of the compass. They got off the highway for gas or a burger or a taco, and did not get back on.

And yet, it was not particularly hectic. The sun and the land and the people moved with unhurried purpose, kind of a *mañana* mind-set. Maybe that was why they stayed. There was always tomorrow.

Five more tomorrows.

Maybe they'd promote Tom Edgerton to SAC in Sacramento and send him up to Santa Fe as Edgerton's replacement if he asked?

Wishful thinking.

Wayne left the Pontiac locked up and drove his government sedan the six miles to the federal car pool and turned it in. He walked the narrow 6th Street to Gold Avenue where his office was located. The downtown area was not as full of adobe as Santa Fe was, but the influence was there. The Civic Plaza, the Police Building, and others paid homage to the rounded corners, flat roofs, and lodge poles of adobe construction. He was going to miss it, going off to the glass-and-steel boxes.

Up in the Bureau's offices, he greeted Carmen.

She looked sad, saying, "I read the telexes."

Wayne was touched by her sadness. "One of those expected things, Carmen. Not much to do about it."

"Phil Norman got a telex, too."

"I'll congratulate him."

"It's not going to be the same."

"Chin up, dear. It'll always be the same."

In his office, he plopped behind his desk—the FBI's desk, opened the top left drawer, and found the government directory. He called Washington, DC.

"Personnel."

"Wilson DeForge, please."

Click.

"DeForge."

"Will, this is Steve Wayne."

"Hey, Steve. Long time."

"You want to call up my file on your trusty machine?"

"Ta-da-da-da, da-da . . . got it. Jeez, impressive as hell."

"Loaded with censure letters, no doubt."

"Well, yeah. But it's halfway balanced out with the commendations. Still, I wouldn't plan on becoming director any time soon."

"Fortunately, Will, that has never been a career objective."

"You're going to Sacramento. Congratulations."

"Yeah, thanks. Look, how much leave time have I got coming?"

"Hmmm, looks like thirty-two days as of today. You'd better use some of it before you lose it."

"That's why I'm calling. Drop a request for twenty-five days for me, will you?"

"Hmmm. You're supposed to report to California, Steve. Five days travel time involved there."

"I have a number of personal items I need to take care of, Will."

"Well . . ."

"You're the deputy director, aren't you? You can sign off without going higher."

"Okay, Steve, take it. I'll cover the bases and wire you a revised reporting schedule."

"I appreciate it."

It was not the first time he had gotten around the rules by knowing someone. In his experience, he had found that staff people often had more power and could facilitate more processes than the directors, legislators, or generals to whom they reported. Wayne had made it a point to meet lots of staff people who also felt that some rules had been written by cowboys riding backward on their asses.

Part of the penalty for getting caught circumventing the regulations, of course, was not revealing the names of those who had helped him, and he had taken the heat alone several times. Going around a stubborn Justice Department attorney got him a reprimand. One time, with the help of a master sergeant, he gained access to evidence that had been classified Top Secret by a lieutenant colonel who did not want anyone getting to the evidence. Why anyone would claim that $85,000 in hundred dollar bills was classified information, he still had not figured out. In the end, though, the rules supported the light colonel, and Wayne's folder gained another letter.

He called Cece at the McComb-Davis Agency. "Reprieve. I've got a month's leave."

"To do what? Delay a decision?"

"Think about that decision. And maybe do a little private snooping."

"I love you," she said.

He called Norman and Carmen into his office. Phillip Norman was elated by his status as the new acting Special-Agent-in-Charge and at the potential for promotion to the permanent position. Carmen had trouble smiling, and Wayne appreciated that. He asked her to box up his personal items, which were not many, and send them over to the apartment and promised he would not leave town without coming back to say good-bye. He gathered the printouts that Rivera had mailed to him and took them along, rationalizing the action by telling himself they had never been logged in since the office had never officially been part of the investigation.

Taking a taxi back to the apartment, he retrieved his Firebird, stopped on Candelaria Road for gas, then took the northbound on-ramp of Interstate 25. Fifty minutes later, he parked in the visitor's slot in front of the county building in Santa Fe, nodding at a couple of deputies who smiled at him. He was beginning to be recognized. He would not have hurried, had he known the kind of meeting Luisa Rodriguez was holding in her office.

He peeked through the open doorway, then said, "Pardon me, I don't want to interrupt."

Janet Willow seemed to assume she was in charge of the sheriff's office. "Come in, Mr. FBI man."

District Attorney Boyles and Dr. Hayman were also lounging in chairs around the acting sheriff's desk. Hayman said, "You're not interrupting, Steve. Come on in."

Rodriguez stood up and offered a hand. He shook it. Not soft, but not calloused, either. Her speech carried less of a Spanish overlay than had Rivera's.

"We've not really had a formal introduction, Agent Wayne."

She was a small woman, five-five, maybe. Pretty, even in the skirted uniform and tooled leather gun belt. Solid, steady gaze from soft brown eyes under arched brows. Young, unlined face, exuding more of a sense of competence and ability than of self-confidence. He guessed her for thirty-three, thirty-four. Her hair was a lustrous black. It was cut at the level of her jaw, which was square enough to make her face appear more oval than it really was. At the edge of her left nostril was a small white scar. In something besides the cotton drill uniform shirt, she would be buxom.

"It's Steve," he told her.

"And Luisa. Or Lu. Please sit down. Coffee?"

"I'm fine, thanks. This a weekly group?"

Keith Boyles had his handkerchief out, mopping at the perspiration on his neck. "Political activist committee, Steve. Three of us are, anyway. Tomorrow's paper will announce the write-in candidacy of Luisa Rodriguez for county sheriff. The editorial is going to support her."

"Congratulations," Wayne said. He was congratulating everyone but himself today.

"That's a bit premature," Rodriguez told him. "This

isn't my idea at all, and I have not agreed to it. I am not a political animal."

Hayman looked at his watch. "It's only ten o'clock. If we hang around until five, you'll be so political you can't stand yourself."

"What do you think?" Janet Willow asked him.

"I couldn't competently comment on the politics of Santa Fe County, Miss Willow. I'm definitely in favor of elections that have two or more people running for office." Wayne hoped that observation would not be twisted by her.

"Oh, come off it!" she said. "Don't you ever take a stand on anything? Or is waffling a bureau trait?"

Wayne had to smile. "You and my girlfriend have something in common. What's the opponent's experience?"

"Two years as a city councilman," Boyles said.

"I'd vote for you, Luisa, if I could vote," he said.

Willow turned to Rodriguez. "See?"

"Can I have until noon to make a decision? There's the matter of a husband and family who ought to be consulted."

"Jim will back you up all the way, probably be your campaign manager," Boyles said. He turned to Wayne to offer the explanation, "Lu's husband is a general contractor."

Willow stood up. "Call me at noon. Or I'll call you." She started for the door, then stopped. "What's the FBI doing here?"

"They're not here. I'm on official vacation."

"Sure you are."

"Call my office and ask."

"I'll do that." She whipped through the doorway, her heels hitting hard on the linoleum, raising echoes in the outer office.

"She will, too," Hayman said, flicking the remnants of a powdered sugar donut from his lapel. "You *are* vacationing?"

"Yes. Pending my transfer to an office in California next month."

"Must be nice," Keith Boyles said, "getting to see the country."

"I didn't ask for it."

Hayman displayed the acumen for which Carlos Rivera had once recommended him. "Your name's been in the paper too often."

"How do you come to that, Jerry?"

"The Bureau has been awfully reluctant when it comes to Santa Fe. We tried talking to Tom Edgerton a couple times, but it sounds like he has his marching orders."

Wayne felt as if he should defend his agency, but just shrugged.

The doctor eyed the group, then said, "You kept your mouth shut before when I asked you to. Can you do it again?"

"Sure."

"It seems our sole candidate for sheriff had a little set-to with Janet last night. Told her to lay off the Razor Murders, and explained he was doing just that at the request of an unnamed federal agency. It's a matter of national security. Yet, your federal agency doesn't want any part of it. Can you explain that to us?"

"No."

"Have you been told anything about a national security angle?"

"No."

"Do you have any reason to believe that those two people we found hanging in that barn were a threat to our hallowed shores?"

"You're beginning to sound as if you're working with Janet," Wayne said.

"Sorry. Satisfying my personal needs. Did the victims have a federal link?"

"No, not as far as I know," Wayne said, "though the first time I was here, you tried to convince me that they did. Where are you going with this, Doctor?"

"I wish I had goals and objectives all lined up, but I don't, Steve. At the moment, I'm just pissed at Blessing and his self-righteous, pompous behavior. I'm just as mad at him as Janet is."

"Making three of us," Boyles said.

"Janet," Hayman went on, "being Janet, got knocked out of shape at Blessing's suggestion, and hit up Keith and me this morning. The three of us decided a little healthy competition was justified, and so we came over to convince Luisa to participate in the election."

Boyles picked up the tale. "Except that, as it turns out, Luisa had also received a tactful hint from an unnamed federal agency."

Rodriguez leaned back in her chair. "After the commissioners named me acting sheriff, I got a call at home. Man's voice, moderately deep. Well modulated, but not particularly cultured. He said he was based in Washington and to keep any developments quiet."

"And you said?"

"I didn't say anything. I hung up on him."

"What have you done since then?"

"Well, maybe I've played it both ways, Steve. I haven't made any press releases, but I have continued the investigation. I also put a recorder on my home phone."

"That's the reason I drove up here, to see where you now stood. On a personal level, you understand?"

"Where you going to spend your vacation, Steve?" Boyles asked.

"I'm open to suggestions."

The DA looked hard at him. "You going to get yourself in trouble?"

"I've been there before."

Rodriguez looked to Boyles and Hayman and received nods from them.

She said, "This afternoon, the ME will release the results of the autopsies on the Rivera family. They were all murdered. One nine-millimeter slug each. The house was burned intentionally. There is no direct connection that I've been able to detect between those murders and the ones in the barn. I do, of course, believe that there is a relationship.''

''How about the ring? Anything come of that, yet?''

''You knew that we identified the manufacturer?''

''Creighton Associates, wasn't it?''

''That's right. We've got a list of their outlets, and have sent out letters asking about sales to 'Andy and Andrea.' No positive response yet.''

''How about the printouts?''

''What printouts?'' Boyles asked.

''Hang on.'' Wayne went out to his car and got the stack of paper. When he returned and dumped it on the table, he explained Rivera's feelings about a paratrooper involvement. ''Apparently, he kept it to himself, maybe until he had something more than intuition to go on.''

The acting sheriff added to that. ''He had asked forensics to check out the thread used in the harness, Steve. They determined that it *could* be the same kind of thread used in parachute rigging, but there was nothing solid.''

Rodriguez and Boyles leafed through one of the stacks while Hayman and Wayne went through the other. The sheriff said, ''Damn, there's a lot of names here. It would overwhelm my available manpower to check it all out. You think I should ask the bureau, Steve?''

''Somehow, at the moment, I don't think that's a good idea. I don't know what's going on just yet, but you'd better let me make some discreet inquiries first.''

''And in the meantime?'' Hayman asked.

''Carlos's copies may have burned in the fire, or they may have been the reason there was a fire. I'd suggest you immediately make a copy of each of these printouts and put them in a safe place. You have a vault or safe, Keith?''

''Yes. We'll do that.''

''Then, except for active duty personnel, I'd think that the Screamin' Eagle Association's mailing list is more up-to-date. I'd go through both lists and collate the names into one list. Then it's a matter of making phone calls and finding out which 'Andy' doesn't answer.''

Rodriguez looked at him. ''Do you know what my telephone budget is?''

''You're beginning to sound like a sheriff, Luisa,'' Wayne said.

''I'll put my staff to work on part of the calling,'' Boyles told her.

Hayman asked, ''You think this will get us anywhere?''

''Well, it's based on a hunch Carlos had. But if he was right, and we can get a name, it's a big leap. You yourself said the tortures were conducted to get information. I'd agree with that, and it seems reasonable to me that the victims, at least one of them, knew the perpetrators. If we get the name of the victim, we'll have a trail to follow.''

''There's something else to consider,'' Hayman said. ''Don't you think so, Steve?''

''Yes. I'd say you ought to address the matter of security for yourself, the DA, and the sheriff.''

''And the courageous reporter,'' Hayman added.

''And the reporter, if she's not taking any of these threats seriously.''

''Mother of God!'' Rodriguez said. ''Do you actually think there's a threat that reaches that far?''

''Carlos and his family are dead,'' Wayne said. ''Whether or not that's an overzealous reaction to something he had discovered, I don't know. The perpetrators of this thing don't seem to draw a line when it comes to family members. Personally, I don't think any one of you should be risking yourself or your family.''

''Judging by the reaction you've had from Washington, would there be somebody in the FBI behind this?'' Boyles asked him.

Wayne slumped back in his chair and sighed audibly. ''I'm naturally reluctant to say as much, and I wouldn't have thought so. The Bureau does not get involved in simple murder, Keith. You know that. There'd have to be some indication of a violation of federal law, and I suppose that's what the deputy director is basing his position on. If there is a federal angle that we're unaware of, and if no one in the Bureau is intentionally dragging his feet, there is somebody who has enough clout to apply pressure on me through my bosses.''

Boyles was leaning back in his chair, and he came forward, slamming the legs on the floor. ''What the hell is it all about? I still haven't come up with a motive.''

''There's a thread to follow somewhere,'' Wayne said. ''We just have to decide what color it is. Right now, it's blending in with the fabric, and we can't see it.''

Rebel called Boxer this time. ''This whole thing is getting out of hand.''

''How so?''

''There are too many players becoming involved, too many to effectively control. And your subcontractor has no tact at all. How in hell did he think he was containing the situation by blowing away the sheriff? And his whole damned family, for Christ's sake?''

''An error in judgment, I agree. But the man's a good commander, and he has a long history of success. You know that. Still, I agree with your assessment. I will contact the contractor, even guarantee that it will not happen again.''

''Do it fast,'' Rebel said.

''You took care of your situation?''

''I thought I had, but that's another place where we lost control. A deputy director in personnel approved his request for a leave. There's nothing I can do to change that.''

''So he has taken some vacation,'' Boxer said. ''Not much he can do on vacation, is there?''

''I hope not,'' Rebel prayed. ''Have you given thought to an abortion? To cutting the losses?''

"A thought only, my friend. Consideration of the need, however, is enough to overcome a faint heart. Like Cottonmouth says, it is, after all, our world that is at stake."

The desk was placed at one end of the dining area, against the glass wall overlooking the balcony and the ocean. It was a blue and serene day, not a cloud in the sky, and the horizon was an imperceptible merging of two shades of aqua.

On the desk were the two telephones, a blotter, a fake marble pen holder, and a small teak rack from which three chrome-plated metal balls were suspended. Lew was exceptionally neat; he hated having anything out of place.

He was giving some thought to driving up to Tuth's place and maybe the two of them going out on Tuth's boat, the *Contessa*. Lew had never tired of playing den mother, even at his age of forty-six, but Tuth needed a lot of supervision; he tended to be an unruly scout.

The scrambled phone buzzed, and he picked it up, simultaneously pressing the button under the lip of the desk. It activated a tape recorder located in the bottom drawer.

"STRAC."

"Boxer. Look, we're going to have to lie low for a while, until the dust you stirred up settles down. Suspend the timetable until I tell you to restart it."

"It's too late for that, my man." Lew stroked the bridge of his nose, pinching lightly where it had been broken; it had become a habit.

"What do you mean, too late?"

Lew looked at his watch. "At nine-thirty, your time, Target C gets his."

He hung up and reached out to swing one of the chrome balls. It followed the arc of its tether, striking the center ball and passing the energy on to the third ball, which swung up, then back, reversing the process. *Click-click ... click-click ... click-click ...*

Lew liked to watch that action, entirely aware of his ability to set in motion a sequence which had expected consequences.

And which was unstoppable.

NINE

THEY DISEMBARKED THE yacht at 3 A.M., drove the rubber Zodiak ashore twenty minutes later, waded through the surf, then slogged through the sand and into the tiny Nicaraguan village.

The dilapidated house was right where it was supposed to be, according to the map Lew had been given. Chunks of plaster were chipped out of the walls of the house and out of the low wall-like fence that surrounded it. Red bougainvillea were all but black in the night. Vines clung to the walls, trapping spiders. Country and Pilo took out the three guards with K-bars, silencing them by cutting their throats. Dark red blood spewed everywhere, staining the stucco.

They went over the wall, crossed a patio of red tiles and sand, and pushed open the unlocked back door. *Cocina*. Rushed through it and spread out in the living room.

Pilo swung his M–16 in a wide arc, taking out lamps and pottery with the muzzle.

The ceramics crashing to the tiled floor brought the mayor from his bedroom in a rush, his dark face pure white with fright. As soon as he came running through the doorway, Pilo tripped him, and the man landed on his hands and knees in the middle of the small living room.

"Sandinista shithead," Sweet said.

"Señor, señor, por favor—"

Lew killed the *alcalde* with one shot from his silenced Walther.

The mayor no longer had a wife, and that was fortunate for her.

Good old Sweet, with that hellacious wanger he was so proud of, raped the mayor's thirteen-year-old daughter before slicing her up a little with his surgical scalpel.

Wilbur Thomas Kincaid was thirty-nine years old, handsome in an overpolished way, twice divorced, and held a law degree from Georgetown University. He held some pointed views about his life and his society, and he did his utmost to communicate them to others, sometimes in less than subtle fashion, and frequently whether they wanted to hear his pointed views or not. He also enjoyed life as much as he possibly could.

At his age, he was often afraid he might have missed something worth experiencing, and he devoted the salary dollars beyond one alimony payment and one child support payment to an extensive and expensive casual wardrobe and to the financial institution which owned four-fifths of his red Ferrari 350GT. He devoted his free hours to a constant round of select parties.

Unfortunately, Keck and Battey missed him when he emerged from his favorite restaurant on Massachusetts, up from Mount Vernon Place, and had to follow the red sports car to a town house in Georgetown. Keck parked the stolen Plymouth half a block from the house in the shadows of wide-limbed trees, and they waited, slumped down in the front seat. They were accustomed to waiting.

A distant lamppost cast enough light to put a sheen on Carl Battey's hairless pate and to reflect off his highly polished, rimless glasses.

Danny Keck noticed and said, "You're going to have to start blacking out the top of your head, C.B."

"Fuck you," Battey responded.

It was kind of funny, because Battey had such a deep

tan, his arms and face almost black from burning in the sun, but he wore an LA Dodgers baseball cap when he was working, and it kept his head pale.

They waited, and Keck cleaned his nails and clipped them. He was meticulous about his appearance. He was five-ten with a slight frame that disguised hard muscles; he could bench press 275 pounds. His hair was dark and styled—hadn't grayed or disappeared on him like it had with the other guys, and his face was handsome, attractive to women. They liked his liquid brown eyes and soft smile. He had learned a lot about life in the two decades following, with a harried judge's help, his volunteering for the Army, rather than for a stint at Riker's Island.

"You been reading about Andy?" Keck asked.

"I been reading."

"So what do you think?" Keck thought maybe the message had been directed at himself. It bothered him.

And he had really liked Andy. Liked Andrea, too, and had even made a pass at her one time—at a barbecue or something, but she had been firmly attached to her man.

"I think he fucked up. Maybe he was gonna screw it up for all of us. I think we ought to shut up."

Battey was not the deepest thinker Keck had ever known. The guy could rattle on for hours about his religious philosophy, and though Keck did not know for sure, he thought the philosophy was a little disjointed. Keck, with a mostly solid Italian ancestry, had been a Catholic all his life, though he did not really have a solid grasp on it. As soon as his mother had remarried, he had bailed out of church and house.

"I don't like all the heat that's coming out of it," Keck said.

"Lew'll take care of it. He always has."

They had always relied on Lew, and that always seemed to be the answer. He got them through 'Nam, and he had helped them find Easy Street.

A little after two in the morning, Kincaid emerged from the town house, and they followed him back to his

apartment building on 10th Street. When
gotiated the Ferrari down the ramp into his pa
rage, using a card to open the automatic door,
whipped in behind him and drove inside while the door
was still up. He parked in the first open stall.

They were waiting for him as he walked toward the
elevator, eyes bright, and a self-satisfied smirk on his
ultraviolet-lamp-tanned face.

"He's flying," Battey whispered. "Fuckin' doper."

"He hasn't even started flying, C.B."

Kincaid stopped in front of them, checked to see that
the elevator was on its way down, and said, "Mornin',
fellows." He did not appear nervous. Too spaced out to
appear anything.

"Mornin'," Keck said.

The elevator doors parted and the three of them stepped
in. Battey reached forward, grabbed the man by the neck,
and applied thumb pressure to the carotid artery. There
was a flutter of weak reaction from Kincaid before he
passed out and Battey caught him.

Keck pressed the button for the sixth floor.

They used Kincaid's keys to let them into his apartment, and sprawled the man into a low white chair in
the living room. Keck took a small leather case from his
pocket, unzipped it, and extracted two hypodermic
syringes.

Battey rolled up the sleeves. "He's full of holes,
Brooklyn."

"Yeah, he's a big player. Free-baser, too." One of
Kincaid's activities of which Keck and Battey were already aware from their research.

"We punch him?"

"Yeah, it's all right. No one's going to notice a couple
more holes."

With thumb and forefinger, Keck searched for a vein,
then slid the needle into it, and slowly depressed the
plunger. That particular mixture was potassium chloride,
elements already in the body, and therefore undetectable.

... upset the body's electrolytes,
... attack.

... contained freebase cocaine, and
... Kincaid's other arm.

... sleeves down and reinserted the cuff-
... ned out the sleeves of the suit coat,
... wrinkles, then stood up. ''You want to
cat... ...rooklyn?''

''Why ...

It was cool inside the thick adobe walls of the church, and the bright sun outside brought life to the stained glass windows, making the colors brilliant. It had been so long since Wayne had been in a church that he had trouble identifying the figures represented in the stained glass. Jesus. Mary. Peter. Paul.

He finally gave up.

The flame points of the candles on the altar were steady throughout the mass, and the floral aroma from the wreathes and baskets stacked five deep on the other side of the altar rail blended with the sweet incense.

Luisa Rodriguez delivered the eulogy, standing at a podium behind the four matching burnished aluminum caskets. She was dressed in black, the first time he had seen her in a dress, and the tears slid unashamedly down her cheeks.

Closed caskets. Cece's eyes had filled with tears the moment she saw how small two of them were.

Holding her hand throughout the service, Steve Wayne felt the changing pressure of her fingers, the shift of her emotions, which intensified as twenty-four pallbearers made their procession up the aisle, out to four waiting hearses. The alto voice in the choir sang, ''Amazing Grace,'' and that tightened his throat muscles.

Afterwards, it was hot and bright and dusty outside on the steps where over two hundred people milled around and offered condolences to the surviving parents of Myra and Carlos Rivera. No one should ever have to attend a child's funeral, much less that of a grandchild.

Wayne saw Janet Willow—actually wearing a demure, dark brown dress—dashing down the street toward the Plaza and pointed her out to Cece, who did not care. He introduced Cece to Boyles and Hayman, almost not recognizing the doctor in a clean dark suit and tie. The two men introduced their wives, Wanda and Anne.

Boyles pointed to a diminutive figure in a light blue, pin-striped suit crossing the street, holding his hand up to stall a yellow Camaro. "That's Luisa's opposition, Steve. Delwin Blessing."

Rodriguez was one of the last to emerge from the church, accompanying the priest. She almost matched the priest, with the white lace of her cuffs and collar at wrists and throat. The two of them spoke for a moment, and then Rodriguez joined them.

"Hello, Steve. I'm glad you could come."

"Hello, Luisa. My friend, Carol Curtis. Cece, this is Luisa Rodriguez. She's the acting sheriff."

"I'm pleased to meet you, Miss Curtis."

"Just Cece, Sheriff."

"I'm glad you made the right decision," Wayne said.

While he and Cece had had breakfast and waited for the service to begin, he had read the previous day's newspaper in which Rodriguez had announced her write-in candidacy and had been supported by the editorial. She had proclaimed the safety of Santa Fe County residents as her first priority and the solution of the murders of the unknown transients and of the Rivera family as the second. Candidate Blessing had had no comment.

Rodriguez did not look exceptionally happy about her candidacy. "I hope it's the right decision."

"It is."

Luisa glanced at Cece, Hayman, and Boyles. "If you've got a moment, Steve?"

"Sure."

They excused themselves and stepped away from the crowd.

"George Henry Andropoulous."

Wayne stared for a moment. "You're certain?"

"I'm ninety percent certain. We didn't get it by calling through the list—that's less than a quarter done. No, a jewelry store in San Luis Obispo called on our query. They sold the ring. And there's a George Henry Andropoulous on both printouts. 101st Airborne Division, service in Vietnam."

"You call the police in California?"

Rodriguez grimaced. "Not yet, and I'll tell you why. The Screamin' Eagles printout had what I assume is a current address. I got the phone number and called San Luis Obispo. It's an active phone, but there was no answer. Then, I thought about having the police out there check on the address, but I got to thinking that maybe that might alert some people we don't necessarily want alerted. I haven't been too comfortable the last couple of days, considering I might have become a prime target. I tend to think about my husband and my girls a lot lately, Steve. Maybe I'm paranoid?"

"And maybe not. You want me to take a little trip?"

"I'd pick up your expenses. And I'd feel better if we knew more before this hits the papers."

Wayne checked his watch. "I think I can still catch a flight today."

Rodriguez handed him a folded memo slip. "Thanks. Here's the information we have on him. Meanwhile, I've got a couple people making a new list of anyone who served in Andropoulous's specific company during the period he was in Vietnam. And I've called the U.S. Army Records Center in St. Louis for a copy of his service record."

"That's good thinking, Luisa. You'll be a hell of a sheriff."

"Yes. Perhaps." She smiled at him, but grimly.

Wayne walked back to where Cece was talking with Anne Hayman, waited for a break in the dialogue, and said, "We'd better go, Cece."

In the Trans Am, headed for the interstate, she said, "I'm not going to any more funerals."

"I think so," he mumbled, but he was thinking ahead, not paying attention.

She scooted around to lean against the door. "Are we preoccupied?"

"Huh? Sorry." He told her what he had learned from Rodriguez.

"So you're rushing off to California?"

He grinned. "Couple days is all. Do you want to go along?"

"Yes. However, I'm not on vacation."

Which brought them back to his impending permanent departure. "You know what? I just thought about the way I introduce you to people. 'My friend' doesn't seem adequate."

"Adequate in what way? Is this an obtuse form of proposal?"

"I suppose it is, yes."

"Then I don't want to talk about it." She turned around and stared out the window for the rest of the trip south.

Wayne arrived in San Luis Obispo a few minutes before six in the evening, after a transfer from United to Southern at LA International, then a short hop to the airport at Santa Maria. He rented a Ford Escort there for the drive up to San Luis Obispo and used the map in its glove compartment to locate the address.

Driving along the coast, the ocean was serene and very blue, an appropriate accent for the sleepy city which was a few miles inland. He drove through the downtown area and found a through street that took him to a residential area on the west side of town.

It was a nice house—not ostentatious—on a nice street. Groomed lawns all around, two-car garages. In fact, George Henry Andropoulous's lawn was also freshly mowed and watered. It was too well cared for

for a man who had resided in the Santa Fe morgue for two weeks.

When he parked at the curb, Wayne saw the For Sale sign plugged into the sod. He got out of the car, wrote the name and phone number of the realtor in his notebook, and stood looking at the house. A pair of apple trees were planted on either side of the front walk. The neighbor to the west was trimming his hedge and keeping a covert eye on a potential neighbor.

He walked up to the front door, stepped into the shrubbery at the side of the door, and peered in the window. Not one piece of furniture to be seen. Walking across the driveway and skirting the east corner, he stopped to look in a garage window. It, too, was empty, and he went back to the front, crossing the lawn toward the inquisitive neighbor. Wayne considered using his credentials, then thought better of it. Sure as hell, it would get back to somebody who would take offense.

The man, in his fifties and grayed, looked up, feigning surprise. "Hi, there."

"Hello," Wayne said.

"Thinkin' about buying it?"

"Actually, no. This is the address I was given for a couple named Andropoulous."

"That would have been right. Andy and Andrea. Nice couple, but they moved a few weeks ago."

"That surprises me. Did you see them leave?"

"My wife did. She saw the moving truck that came, anyway."

"Did either of them say where they were going?"

"Naw. Angie would have told me if they had."

Wayne tried to look exasperated. "Well, darn! Andy had some antique jewelry he wanted me to look at."

"You try his businesses?"

"I didn't know about them."

"He's got a couple bicycle shops, he told me about. One downtown, and one in Lompoc, I think. And there's the Knights of the Sky in Santa Maria, of course."

"Of course." Wayne thanked the man and drove to a telephone booth to check the yellow pages.

Knights of the Sky was located at the Santa Maria Public Airport thirty-three miles to the south, but it was closed for the afternoon according to the yellow pages ad. The Cycle Store was open until nine. Returning to his rental, Wayne drove back downtown. He found a parking place directly in front of a glass-fronted store, but the painted letters on the window now read, BIKES PLUS. He went inside and asked for the manager.

The man was in his twenties, with a scraggly beard, and his shoulders straightened. "I'm the manager."

"Oh. I was looking for Andy."

"Don't want a bike?"

"I'm afraid not."

"Well, Andy ain't around."

"Do you know where I could reach him?"

"No."

"Will he be in tomorrow?"

"Not anymore." Wayne was rewarded with a row of broken teeth in a broad, proud smile. "I bought the shops."

"I guess I didn't realize he had them up for sale. When did this happen?"

"Last week. The fifteenth."

"You saw him at the closing then?"

"Just his agent was there."

"Where did you close?"

The questions were starting to create suspicion. "The bank. Wells Fargo."

"And you wouldn't know how I could locate either Andy or the agent?"

Shrug of the shoulders. "No. Maybe out at his house? I don't remember the other guy's name."

"I'll try there. Thanks."

"Anytime."

Wayne sat in the Escort for a while, thinking about it. Somebody helpful was closing up Andy's life for him.

Taking care of the loose ends. And probably not leaving much of a trail himself.

He started the car and drove the thirty miles back to Santa Maria.

Picking a Best Western near the airport, Wayne checked in, tossed his carryon into the standard room, then went to the restaurant for a chicken-fried steak dinner. He munched his way through it slowly and considered the possibilities.

This had to be the right Andy and Andrea. The neighbor's use of their names—especially the nickname, Andy—was all the confirmation Wayne needed. And yet, it was difficult to reconcile the couple who lived in a neat house in a neat little town and ran a bicycle shop with the couple depicted in the police photographs.

And just as certainly, someone was doing a very careful cleanup. There were any number of ways to accomplish it, but he guessed that the ''agent'' of George Henry Andropoulous, with forged power of attorney, was making the rounds, selling off the house, car, and businesses. Not too bright an agent, of course; he had forgotten to cancel the telephone service. Most of the bases were covered, though, and Steve was likely to find the same thing at Knights of the Air. It would be easy to sell everything quickly, if prices were set way below market.

The agent would very likely be somebody not connected with Andropoulous or the two who had murdered him. Still, when Rodriguez decided to release the ID, they should attempt to locate and put a tail on the agent.

Wayne could go to the local cops in San Luis Obispo, and perhaps here, too, press for an investigation of the financial transactions and perhaps get an identification of the bogus agent.

No. He was unofficial. That would have to be Luisa's decision. And as soon as the identification of Andy and Andrea was revealed, the locals would, or should, investigate the businesses, anyway.

Then, there was the important aspect. Why bother cleaning up behind Andy, at all?

Because.

Because why? Andy and Andrea simply disappear. Neighbors and friends begin to wonder why, but nothing would come of it. A boating accident at sea, maybe, or one of the many freaks on a street somewhere in some unknown city.

Life goes on. Why clean up?

Because there should be no unanswered questions at all. The perpetrators took teeth and fingers; they expect no linkup to be made with San Luis Obispo. Yet they go ahead and pick up the loose ends anyway, so that the local authorities do not look too closely at the connections Andy might have had, if he turns up missing.

The perpetrators were gaining in lead time. Over two weeks had passed since the bodies had been discovered, almost three weeks from the date Jerry Hayman had estimated as the night of the murders.

Abruptly, Wayne decided against waiting until morning, paid his dinner check, and went out to his Escort. He drove out to the general aviation section of the airport and cruised along the buildings fronting the runways. There was no Knights of the Sky.

Instead, in the middle of a long low hangar that backed on the parking lot and fronted on the tarmac was a brand-new sign that read TED'S JUMP SCHOOL.

Lights were on in the private aviation office at one end of the hangar, and Wayne could see several people moving about inside as he parked in the sparsely populated lot. There was a goose-necked light over the door to Ted's, and he avoided the pool of light, walking across the narrow strip of grass to peer in the big picture window. A single light had been left on, showing him a couple of baggy couches, a long glass counter with a cash register, and display cases neatly laid out with a variety of parachutes, helmets, jumpsuits, and other

sports paraphernalia. Behind the counter, in the middle
of the back wall, was a closed door.

He turned back to survey the parking lot and weighed
the consequences. No matter how he flipped his mental
quarter, it kept coming up tails; it had never done that
before. Tails was illegal. Checking the lot once again,
then finding no suggestion of an alarm system around
the window, he stepped into the pool of light and peered
at the door lock. Cheap. But well oiled; the bolt slid
easily under the pressure of his Visa card. Wayne knew
how to do it; he had just never done it before.

Slipping inside, he closed the door, ignored the outer
office, went around the glass counter, and opened the
gray metal door to the back. There was a short hallway,
barely defined by a light in the back room, rest rooms
on one side, and an office on the other side. He wanted
the office, but went to the back first to find long tables
for packing parachutes, a wall of lockers, a rack of stored
parachutes, and a big oak table with chairs all around it.
It was littered with Styrofoam cups, beer cans, and
overflowing ashtrays. Posters with a parachuting motif
covered the walls. There was a heavy-duty sewing machine on a big table in one corner.

There would not be anything for him here. Certainly,
Andy had not made up his own harness, so he did not
even try to locate a thread that might match that of the
harness. He wondered if Carlos Rivera had pictured a
room like this, and supposed that he had.

He went back to the office and turned on the overhead
fluorescent light.

The office held two file cabinets, a gray metal desk
with a typewriter perched on one pull-out shelf, and three
chairs. A picture of—he guessed—Ted and a short,
cheerfully smiling woman was secured in a black plastic
frame on the desk. He went through the file drawers,
finding neatly typed labels on each manila folder. The
one he wanted was labeled Company Papers.

Pulling the file, he found a copy of an application with

the Secretary of State for incorporation, a copy of a lease made out to Theodore and Samantha Orlon, and a set of the sale papers. The signature of Andy's agent was indecipherable, written in a back-slanted left-hand style. Ted had purchased his business on April 20 from Decon Company for $22,000.

Reasonable price, Wayne thought, though he had absolutely no idea of the going rates for skydiving businesses. He lamented the fact that the county clerk's office would probably be closed on Saturday morning, and that meant spending the weekend alone in Santa Maria.

When he got back to the motel, he telephoned Cece, but got no answer. He did reach Rodriguez at home and explained what he had found.

"You think someone's doing a good job, then?"

"I don't know how well the tracks are covered, Luisa. I suspect they never thought we'd backtrack Andy this far. What I'll do on Monday, though, is see what I can find out about Decon Company. There might be layers and layers of ownership transfers."

"I'll sit on what we have for the time being then, and not involve the San Luis Obispo or Santa Maria police."

"I guess I wouldn't just yet. And I'd stay a block away from Janet Willow. Otherwise she'll get the story out of you somehow."

"I don't know about that. I hold my own with her."

"Better than I seem to do, then." Wayne kicked off his shoes. "What have you done on security?"

"My girls aren't in school yet, so it was easy to send them off to Grandma's. My husband, Jim's, another matter. I ended up deputizing him and giving him a gun, which he can handle. Keith and Jerry sent their families out of town. And I put a couple of my more discreet deputies to following Keith, Jerry, and Janet around."

"Good. I'll call you Monday."

In his stocking feet, Wayne walked down the corridor to get ice, then made himself a drink from the bottle of J&B in his carryon case. He tried Cece again, and she picked up on the second ring. "Hello, hon."

"How's the California sun? You surrounded by beach bunnies?"

"I'm surrounded by emptiness. I thought maybe you'd gone out; I tried calling earlier."

"Do I detect a note of jealousy?"

"Yes."

"I was in the shower."

She refused to answer a phone while she was bathing. Wayne felt a surge of relief.

"Want to come to California for the weekend? I'll even pay for your ticket."

Howard Pyle stood slightly over six feet tall, and he had a pale aura. He was sun tanned, and his blond hair had turned nearly white under the sun. He weighed over two hundred pounds and often felt obvious and awkward, like an oversized neon sign with one letter burned out. In three activities he was graceful and accomplished: behind the controls of most small aircraft, parachuting from any aircraft, or focused on a dedicated mission.

This mission, for the past two weeks, had not been very dedicated.

He called the Culver City telephone number and listened to the familiar clicking as the relay was triggered. He had been bored to death with the assignment, but as always, was amazed at Lew's foresight. It had paid off.

"STRAC." Scrambler echoed.

"Pilo, Lew."

"Where are you at?"

"Santa Maria. I flew up this morning again, rented a car, and made the rounds to see if anything was happening." He had been coming up every other day.

"And?"

"Something's happening. I talked to the guy we sold the bicycle shops to—"

"Damn it! You didn't let him see you?"

"Aw, shit, no. I called, asking for Andy. He told me

someone else had also come by looking for Andy. I got a description of the guy and his car. Checked the house, but didn't see him. So I went out and sat on the jump-shop. About eight, he shows up and breaks into the place.''

"Breaks in?"

"Yeah. He's in there maybe ten minutes, then out again. I followed him to a motel, found the room, and got his name off the register. Bad news.''

"How bad?"

"The FBI guy out of Albuquerque. Name's Steven Wayne.''

"Shit!"

TEN

PILO'S SHOP WAS located at Orange County Airport, and he did a fair amount of business, though not enough to support his 500SL, his Piper Cherokee, his penchant for nubile young blondes, and other necessities.

He wanted to buy a condo in Newport Beach.

He called Malibu through Culver City. "Got us another contract, Lew."

"You what!"

"Yeah," proudly. "I was talking to a Marine major from over at El Toro Air Station. Seems he'd like his wife to disappear, and I told him 'no sweat.'"

"Fuck that. We're not doing it."

Pilo was disappointed. Ten grand was ten grand. "Why the hell not?"

"We go domestic, we'll get in trouble. We only do government contracts out of the country on targets hostile to American foreign policy. That's policy for STRAC and that's the way it's going to be."

Lew was firm on that.

But he was sympathetic to Pilo's needs and so decided to put him on the team for the Iranian hit.

Took five of them for that one. They went through Turkey on Pan Am to Istanbul and Shit-kickers Incorporated—an un-airworthy Twin Otter—to Karakose, near the eastern border. A very expensive and beaten-

118

up Land Rover took them across the border south of Urmia, Iran.

The target was a terrorist cell, part of the Shi'ite faction, composed of seventeen radical extremists and Adnan Boshogi. The Shah didn't like Boshogi, who was fond of raiding army posts and destroying American-built helicopters and tanks for which the Shah had paid with hard-earned petrodollars.

Boshogi was headquartered in his own village ten miles north of Mahabad, on Lake Urmia. It was rough mountain country, with roads that disappeared under rock slides, and with roads that weren't much more than goat tracks. Country drove and loved the challenge to his four-wheeling skills. There wasn't much that could take the Tennessee out of Country.

C.B., Pilo, and Andy bounced around in the back, and Brooklyn, who'd won the coin toss, hung onto the sides of the passenger seat. It was during that contract that Lew felt for the first time that he didn't need to come along.

They had aerial photographs to work from—taken from a spy satellite, no less—and that made it easier. By midnight, they'd parked the Land Rover, saddled up with the gear and struck out on foot to cross one ridge, then worked their way down into a low plain that flanked the lake. They got there at two in the morning.

It was cold, something Andy hadn't expected for Iran.

Using the tactics supplied by Lew, they spread out and surrounded the village. It didn't take much surrounding.

Five huts. Less than huts. Roofs caving in, doors missing, no windows. Garbage strewn around outside the doorways. Smelled like shit and piss, downwind. There were three rusty vehicles—a '54 Chevy and two mid-sixties Fords—parked in the hard dirt compound enclosed by the huts.

"Christ," Andy whispered to C.B., "how can people live like that?"

"Allah's taking care of them," C.B. said. "Allah's on an economy kick."

When Pilo got into position, he clicked the walkie-talkie three times.

Five huts, five men.

They all scooted forward, staying low, dodging bottles and cans. Andy stepped in a pile of human excrement, nearly gagged, then scraped his boot on a clump of weeds. He reached a doorway, and clicked once on the radio. After five clicks were heard, each stepped into a doorway and opened up with a Kalashnikov. Once around the room, emptying the magazine. Step to the side, and heave a fragmentation grenade inside.

If there were any screams left after the hosing with the assault rifles, they were stifled by the grenades.

They got twenty-nine. There were some women. And a few kids.

"But, hell," Pilo said, "they'd have grown up to be radical assholes, too."

Wayne picked Cece up at the airport in Santa Maria on Saturday morning, and they drove Highway 1 up toward Big Sur. Before they reached Atascadero, she leaned into the backseat and opened her suitcase, then stripped off her dress, panty hose, and bra.

"Make yourself at home," Wayne told her.

"You told me I'm on vacation," she said, struggling in the tight quarters of the Escort. Squirming, she fitted herself into white shorts, a blue halter top with a matching over blouse, and leather sandals.

"You do know how to make a guy feel overdressed for the party."

Wayne pulled his tie off, then leaned forward to shrug out of his suit coat. He unclipped his belt holster and shoved it into the glove compartment.

"You make your sale?" he asked her.

"You don't even remember who we were pitching."

"Sure I do. Desert Mix Floral on Friday morning."

"Sometimes, you surprise me," she said, patting him on the knee. "No sale, yet, but the presentation went well. And you? Why the free weekend?"

"The problem is that county governments do take the weekend off, and that interrupts the detecting. I didn't want to sit in some motel all by myself, so I though we could share this." He waved his hand to the left.

The ocean was an intense blue, the surf crashing on the rocks below was loud through the open windows, and the hills rising on the east were green with forest. A freighter plowed a watery furrow a mile offshore, and the sails of some kind of sailboat were bright triangles. There was little traffic on the curving highway, and Wayne drove easily, in no hurry. Cece found some easy listening on the radio, Chet Atkins playing "*Last Date*." The music Wayne's parents had hated was now easy listening.

"I think we're old fogies, now," Cece said when he mentioned it to her.

They stopped to tour Hearst's Castle at San Simeon, and they stopped at a convenience store to buy sun tan lotion, two towels, ham sandwiches, potato salad, and a six-pack of Bud.

South of Big Sur, Wayne found a shallow cove sheltered by gray rocks and parked the car in a graveled area off the highway. Feeling like a teenager, he led Cece down the steep slope, dodging boulders and scrub pine, and onto the narrow sand shelf of the cove. White spray crashed over the rocks, creating instant miniature rainbows, and the sand was hot under their bare feet.

"I've seen pictures that looked like this," Cece said. "I should have bought a camera."

Wayne spread the beach towels quickly and stepped off the sand. He took off his shirt, flopped on one towel, and opened two cans of beer.

Cece dropped her blouse on the beach, ran into the surf, squealed like a pig, and rushed back, slipping and falling to her hands in the surf.

"Oh, damn, damn, damn! It's cold!"

"In these here latitudes, ma'am, it don't get warm till later."

She came back, flicking water droplets from her fingers at him. "You could have told me."

"And miss your reaction? Not to mention your attire?" Her soaked shorts and halter top revealed almost as much as they concealed.

She stuck her tongue out at him.

Wayne grinned at her.

Sitting cross-legged on the other towel, she dug in the bag for plastic spoons, the salad, and the sandwiches. "Other than your ocean, it's kind of nice. I'm glad I came."

"I'm glad you did, too. I like all this natural, unspoiled beauty."

She looked up. "Me or the coast?"

"Both, but you most of all."

They ate their lunch and talked. Wayne told her what he had learned about Andy, and Cece told him she had clinched the Silver State account on Friday afternoon. Below the surface of the conversation, though, he thought they were both defending their own turf. Both of them building up credits for that final reckoning.

Wayne doused the freckles on her shoulders with Coppertone and rubbed it in, then spread some more on her forehead, nose, and cheeks. She kissed him.

After collecting the cardboard cups and waxed paper and dumping them back in the bag, they stretched out on the towels and held hands. The heat of earth coming through the fabric was reassuring. Cece was asleep in minutes, and Wayne listened to the slow rhythm of her breathing and watched the sky. Two gulls squawked and soared to the north.

Times like this, Wayne wished he had enough money set aside to sustain the status quo. He was not a big dreamer when it came to material goods, did not need cars with exotic names or ten thousand square feet of deep pile carpet or his name at the top of the page, like Hank Junior's. In that respect, he and Cece had something in common. She had not succumbed to the game that many in her field played—one-upmanship with Cads and Jags and addresses. She was happy with her diesel-swilling, blue-fog-belching, elderly Mercedes.

If you can get from here to there, that's the idea.

All Wayne wanted was to get from here to there with the windows down, sniffing the air along the way, hoping it was good air, the molecules undamaged by man's chemical progress. He did not want to run over dogs or people or candy wrappers or beer cans along the route, either. But the people and the beer cans and the bulldozers kept encroaching, making a cove like this one seem scarce, a last bastion of purity in a quickly deteriorating world.

He did not know for certain, but thought that he had around sixty-five thousand stashed in some CDs, money markets, and savings accounts. Not much for eighteen years. Most of it as a single man. There had always been the pension in the background, taking care of the future.

He also did not know what Cece's financial status was. He had not probed, and she had not offered. Her divorce was ten years behind her, with whatever settlement that had involved. Her widowed mother still ran the family ranch, but he had no idea of what that entailed. He suspected she made ninety or a hundred thousand a year, and she did not spend it, except on Uncle Sam. As far as he knew, her assets included only the smokey Mercedes and the furniture from her apartment, now in storage.

In that regard, she was right. If it came down to numbers, they were better off with Wayne abandoning his job. But what then? His law degree was so rusty, it creaked. He had never studied for the bar, nor attempted a bar exam. The Bureau had recruited him directly out of the University of Chicago's law program.

He could not lie on his back in a cove at Big Sur nor

loll around the kitchen table in an apartment in north
Albuquerque for the next thirty years. He needed puzzles.
Puzzles of people and motives and processes. That was
what the Bureau had given him, and he did not think he
could find them on his own.

Cece started to snore. Wayne rolled onto his side,
studied her face, then rolled back and pressed his shoulders into the towel. He wished he had a tape recorder to
collect the evidence of snoring. He was going to have
to tell her someday.

Before it all came apart.

Wayne had pulled off the highway so abruptly that
Howard Pyle had had to go on by, parking his rented
Olds a half mile further north. Taking the jack handle
from the trunk, he had hiked back, climbed the bluff on
the inland side of the highway, and sat in a copse of pine
trees to watch. Pyle wore Levi's, a jeans jacket, and dark
aviator glasses. It was hot in the sun, and he could feel
his nose starting to burn. He would be peeling skin by
nightfall if Wayne and the woman spent the whole day
staring at the ocean.

The woman was a surprise. When Lew laid down the
mission, he had assumed Wayne was alone, but Pyle
decided he could not wait until the fed got rid of her.
They looked like a weekend item.

Watching her in the wet halter top made him horny.
Watching the two of them eat made him hungry. Watching them sleep made him wish he had a different weapon.
Phut, phut! The two of them gone in two shots. But Lew
had said no. Nothing obvious.

After they had not moved for fifteen minutes, Pyle
slid down from his perch, crossed the road, and knelt in
the rocky dirt by the left front wheel. Tires swished by
on the highway behind him, raising a fine cloud of dust
and making him nervous, and he hurried. He popped the
hubcap and spun his lug wrench on the wheel bolts. He
left one nut in place, finger tight, dropped the rest in his

jacket pocket, and slapped the hubcap back in position.

Walking back to his car, he could already imagine how the single stud would snap under lateral pressure on one of the tight curves. It would be nice if they went off the cliff into the sea.

Hal Mayhew had gotten a tee-off time of 4:15 at Rock Creek, and he was the first one on the tea. He was a big man, with hefty shoulders and gray-black curly hair peeking from the sleeves and V neck of his Izod knit shirt. The hair of his head had gone gray a decade before and was long and sleek, slightly disturbed by the welcome breeze. There was nothing else out of place in his fifty-six-year-old body. He took two practice swings.

The deep green of the fairways and the heavy sprinkling of deciduous trees made it seem cooler than it was.

"Goddamn humidity never drops around here," Mayhew complained.

"Ten degrees cooler than yesterday, though," Doug Sanders told him.

Watching Mayhew made Sanders suck in his stomach. He figured Mayhew must spend two hours a day in the gymnasium at Langley. It was time Sanders did not have available. He had been known as Dauntless Doug in Vietnam, but across the river at the Pentagon, he was now respectfully referred to as Major General Sanders, and he put in sixty- and seventy-hour weeks. He was fifty-eight and aware of chunks of flab that golf would not erase. He appeared nearly bald as a result of keeping his blondish gray hair so closely cropped. In uniform, however, he still looked as solid as a concrete bunker.

"I don't know how these younger pups can take eighteen holes in mid afternoon," Sanders said.

"We talking golf or women?" Ellington asked, arriving from the clubhouse with a Styrofoam cooler full of iced beer. He placed it on the floor of the one electric cart they had rented; Sanders said he needed the walk.

"Either, now that I think about it, Mark," the general complained.

Ellington pulled a driver from his bag, rested it across the back of his neck, and stretched both arms outward. Like Mayhew's, his hair was gray under the billed Rock Creek cap, but much thinner. Everything was thin about him: nose, lips, neck, arms, legs, torso. He was conditioned from golf and tennis though, and agile. He called up to the tee. "You want to hit that son of a bitch, Harold?"

Sanders said, "Yeah, let's get on the fairway yet today, okay?"

Mayhew stepped up to his ball, addressed it with the driver, pulled back slowly, then drove in one fluid powerful swing. The ball zinged away, climbing, with a slight hook.

"Like a goddamned Trident missile," Sanders said.

"Looks like three hundred to me," Mayhew boasted. "That fairway enough for you?"

He went over to the cart, dropped his driver in the bag, and sat behind the wheel.

Sanders climbed onto the tee and bent to insert his tee in the sod.

Ellington said to Mayhew, "Don't drink all the beer while we're catching up, huh?"

"I ever drunk all the beer in the thirty years we've known each other?" Mayhew asked.

Sanders and Ellington answered as one, not laughing, "Hell, yes!"

Wayne woke at 2:20, his skin tingling from the sun. His New Mexican tan was dark enough that he did not think he would burn, but Cece's skin was much fairer. He gently shook her upper arm. "Hey, Cece. We've had enough."

Her eyes flickered, and she sat up. "What?"

"I think we've had enough sun."

She pressed her forefinger firmly against the soft skin

of her shoulder, then lifted it. There was a definite contrast between the white mark left by her finger and the pink skin around it. "How come I burn, and you don't?"

"Genes."

"My genes are good. In the good old days, when I was on horseback all the time, doing my chores, I looked like the Mexican hired hands."

"Not exactly like," he said.

"Almost. I bloomed late."

"Let's go."

They put their shoes on, Wayne gathered the towels while Cece carried the lunch leftovers, and they climbed back up the rocky slope to the car.

Approaching the Ford, digging in the pocket of his slacks for the keys, Wayne suddenly thought that something was different. He stopped, and Cece bumped into his arm.

"What's wrong?"

"I don't know. Wait here a minute."

He scanned the hills on the other side of the road, then the car. By habit, he was subconsciously aware of details, or rather the changes in them, and the car had changed. Or something. Something had changed.

How? He stood there on the grassy verge of the cliff and rotated his head. The hills? The highway?

A semi went by, its big tires whooshing on the asphalt. The car? He looked at the Escort again.

There was a light coating of dust on it, raised by passing traffic, undisturbed. After again checking the hills, Wayne stepped forward and walked around the car, staying ten feet away from it. The film of dust on the black rubber of the left front tire had streaks in it, like those from dragging fingers across a dusty table. It was noticeable because it did not match the left rear tire.

He stepped closer and looked at the ground beside the front wheel. In the soft sandy soil and gravel were the twin depressions made by knees and the gouges from toes. Several footprints were also clearly visible.

"What's wrong, Steve?" Cece's voice was an octave above normal.

He unlocked the driver's door. "Get in the car, hon. Quickly, please."

Cece's face changed from wonder to fright, but she ran forward and slid onto the seat. Wayne rotated, again checking the terrain. Nothing. A Cadillac with a family group of four went by on the highway. He reached across her to get his gun from the glove compartment.

"Steve? Are you going to tell me what's the matter?"

"I don't know, Cece, but I don't think anyone wants to steal a Ford hubcap. Let me check."

He clipped his holster on his belt, then unlocked the trunk and found the jack handle. He walked around the car again, looking at the footprints and checking underneath it. The hood had not been disturbed.

He bent down, lodged the spade end of the handle in place, and popped the front hubcap off. One lug nut.

"Son of a bitch!"

"Steve!"

He stood up and again looked around. The hair on the back of his neck bristled as if he were in someone's rifle scope, but nothing moved that he could see. For the first time, he considered the possibility that Janet Willow's articles mentioning the FBI had caught the attention of someone other than his superiors in Washington. He did not like it, and he regretted having brought Cece into it.

"Will you tell me what's going on, damn it?"

"We're missing some lug nuts, Cece. Hang on while I play mechanic."

Removing the rest of the hubcaps, he tossed them in the trunk, then borrowed one nut from each of the other wheels and tightened them onto the left front. Adequate, he thought, slamming the trunk and climbing behind the wheel.

Wayne started the car, backed out onto the highway, and headed south, pushing the Escort hard.

He did not like what he was feeling.

* * *

"Son of a bitch-bastard-goddamn-fucker!" Howard Pyle slid down the bluff, scraping his elbows on the rocks, and ran for his car.

Now what?

Everything was going wrong since they had started operating in-country.

After nine holes, Mayhew was four strokes under Ellington and six strokes under Sanders. Fifty bucks ahead. He felt good about it.

They sat in the shade of a big old elm tree on a wooden-slatted bench and drank from frigid cans of beer. Sanders tugged at the front of his perspiration-soaked golf shirt. "Jesus, it's hot!"

"Should have gotten another cart, Doug. You're going to kill yourself," Ellington said.

Sanders sucked at his can, crushed the empty, and got up to get three more cans from the cooler. He passed them around. "So tell us about your merry band of fuck-ups, Hal."

"My merry band! Shit, you're the one that found them in 'Nam."

"You used them there, too," Sanders defended.

Mayhew sighed. "Yeah. They've been good, you know? Over twenty years now, and very effective every time they go out. It's too damned bad the politicians didn't let us fight Vietnam with half a million troops like STRAC."

Sanders agreed with his friend. Being the only military man of the three, he had felt particularly betrayed by his own country. Washington had caved in to a bunch of damned hippies and anarchists.

Ellington pushed his sunglasses up, revealing his thin eyebrows. He said, "They haven't been very damned effective this time, Harold."

"Now wait a minute, Mark! The operation hasn't been compromised at all. That's still moving along just as planned, and there's no connection between it and the fiasco in Santa Fe. And Taylor tells me he's got that buttoned up now.''

Ellington was forced to agree. ''Well, maybe. It's been a week since the sheriff was taken out, and the major papers have pretty well dropped it. There's been nothing on the tube in four days.''

Sanders asked, ''Why in hell did Taylor have to make such a production out of executing one of his own? And the damned woman, too!''

''Dissension in the ranks, I suppose,'' Mayhew said. ''But he's the commander on the scene, and it's his decision.''

Until this operation, Ellington had not known any details about the STRAC Unit, and he preferred to keep it at arm's length.

Unless it threatened him. ''That's not good, Hal. If they're balled up internally, and it sure looks like they are, they're going to make mistakes.''

''A contingency plan is indicated,'' the general said, agreeing with Ellington.

''All right,'' Mayhew consented. ''We're a third of the way through the mission. After it's over, or if it looks like it's going to fall apart, we'll de-activate the STRAC Unit.''

''And if they don't de-activate congenially?'' Ellington asked.

''Then we'll do it the hard way.''

Sanders told him, ''Christ, Hal, they're professionals. Who are we going to get to do it?''

''I don't know yet, but we do have some private contractors available, you know. Let me think about how to handle it.''

The Olds was coming on hard, and Wayne studied it in the mirror and decided it was not just another speeder. The afternoon sun glinted off its windshield, and he could not see the driver.

The highway curved toward the ocean; he tapped the brakes lightly, swung with it, then goosed the accelerator. The Escort took its time getting back to sixty-five.

The sign read: SAN SIMEON—12 MILES.

Straight stretch of road.

The Olds pulled out to pass.

Its big V–8 brought it quickly alongside, and it edged ahead, then veered toward him.

"Get down, Cece!"

She went to the floor, and Wayne stomped the brake pedal. The Oldsmobile shot on by. The Ford slewed and slowed, and he twisted the wheel to left lock, slapped the accelerator pedal down, and skidded into a 180-degree turn.

Black smoke boiled under the Oldsmobile's tires as it braked hard and nosed toward the left side of the highway. It came to a full stop, jerked into reverse, backed, and again smoked the tires accelerating after him.

Wayne had always thought that high-speed chases were fraught with chances for error, and he did not intend to continue this one. He put the Ford in the ditch on the east side of the highway. Dirt and debris flew as the car slid to a stop.

Glancing down, he saw Cece huddled on the floor, holding her forearms against her cheeks, grabbing the back of her neck with her hands. Her eyes were huge.

The Olds came roaring back toward him, then faltered as the driver applied his brakes. Maybe he was confused by Wayne's stopping. Then he hit the gas again and edged to the side of the road, trying for a sideswipe.

Wayne pushed open his door, swung his legs out, and aimed the .38 through a cloud of dust, holding his right hand in the palm of his left. He was not as good as the guys on TV so he did not try for a tire. He squeezed off five shots directly into the windshield.

The windshield starred in five places as the Olds screamed by, drifting toward the cliff.

The car slowed, weaving. Slammed into the guard rail.

Rode it for a few feet. And broke through.

It did not burn when it hit the rocks fifty feet below, like it would have on television, but it made a hell of an impact.

ELEVEN

PILO PICKED UP Country in his Piper Cherokee at El Cajon, and they flew up to Santa Barbara and met Sweet. The three of them jumped in formation from 10,000 feet in the late afternoon and had a hell of a good time. Then they went out on Sweet's big Trojan cruiser in the evening and broiled one-pound T-bone steaks on a charcoal grill that clipped onto the stern rail.

Sweet's boat was forty-four-feet long and had a compartment fitted under the deck carpeting in the master's cabin that was large enough to accommodate the unit's arsenal. The autopilot took them south, four miles offshore as they drank beer, played poker, and cleaned the weapons they were taking to El Salvador.

Lew had already split the front money in the typical fashion—with nine grand coming to Pilo. With that and the Iranian money, Pilo had set the date of the closing on his condo in Newport. It seemed like a long time to wait, but Lew had coached them all on laundering the cash. Put some of it away in the hip pocket, to pay for odds and ends of expenses. Weekend trips and the like. Funnel some of it through the businesses, creating receipts for jumps and instruction that never took place, and pay taxes on it, then get it in the bank. Lew urged everyone to keep contributing to their Swiss and offshore bank accounts. Everyone was doing all right, though

Sweet seemed to do better. He had lots of toys like the Trojan. He had purchased a Ferrari the year before. But then, Santa Barbara was a big money town, with some people who liked a thrill now and then, jumping out of an airplane. A lot of what Sweet made was probably legitimate.

Country announced he was getting married. Sweet young thing from back home in Tennessee.

Sweet honed his scalpel.

Like on the Nicaraguan trip, they anchored far offshore and took the Zodiak into the beach. Unlike the Nicaraguan contract, the targets weren't in power, and it took them four days of tracking in a crunched '72 Ford sedan missing its trunk lid to run them down.

It was a compound of four houses in La Palma.

The inside of the houses, once they were in and got a look, were papered with posters and hand-painted slogans. Pilo could read a little Mexican, but didn't bother. If Lew said they were assholes, they were assholes.

It was disappointing. There were supposed to have been nineteen or twenty of them, all armed to the hilt with Russki weaponry supplied by Fidel.

There were only four, all sleeping in one house. Young soldiers, proud and defiant. They were sleeping in a neat row in an upstairs room, and Pilo, Country, and Sweet crept into the room without waking anyone.

Country gathered up four AK–47 Kalashnikovs stacked in one corner. Sweet got his dick out and peed on the first guy. Then, it was chaotic for a minute, lots of yells and blanket tossing, then lots of simpering, hot looks, as the four of them were forced back up against the wall, sitting on their hands.

"*!Puta!*"

"Wrong sex, asshole. You don't know nothin'," Sweet said as he unsheathed his scalpel.

The four of them must have thought the intruders were after information. The firm lips and disdainful eyes said there wasn't a man among them who was going to talk.

Sweet bent over and, without warning, sliced the first guy's throat. Blood squirted everywhere, but mostly down his bare chest. The first one wanted to talk then, but nothing would come out of his mouth.

Without ceremony, Sweet sidestepped once, and cut the next throat. The last two began to babble in Spanish, but they were the only two who understood what they were saying.

STRAC hadn't come after information, anyway.

Sweet did the last two, then they headed back for the Ford and the long drive back to the sea.

By four o'clock in the city room of *The New Mexican*, Janet Willow was visibly upset. The annual loss of the air-conditioning on a hot dry day aggravated her bad temper. Her hair was mussed from running her fingers through it, and she had a rash on her chest that she kept scratching. The suffusion was apparent on her skin at the vee in the mannish blue work shirt she wore. Her temper was short; she was snapping at everyone on the staff, and they left her alone.

Her word processor was on, but the screen was blank. On the pull-out shelf of her desk, the old Smith Corona portable had a sheet of paper in it, but the sheet was only partially filled.

She was beginning to think that she had erred in filing the Contrarez brothers story on Wednesday. AP had picked it up, but as far as she knew, no major daily outside of Albuquerque had run it. And now, with Sunday's deadline imminent, she did not have a damned thing. Not even follow-up on the brothers, except for some public comment from a couple of state legislators, because Pam Ostrander had alerted the principal at the school, and *that* son of a bitch had threatened to call the police as soon as she got out of her car.

And Luisa Rodriguez would not give her a thing when she called. "No developments that I can comment on, Janet. I'm sorry."

"It's been almost three weeks. Give me a step-by-step breakdown of your progress in the investigation."

"Generally speaking, Janet, in homicides of this nature, trails grow cold after seventy-two hours. Then it becomes a matter of rehashing old leads."

"What old leads are you rehashing?"

"Nothing substantial as yet. You don't want to publish conjecture."

"I'm supporting you in this election, Luisa." Willow was instantly sorry she had said it. She did not need to resort to threats.

"Sorry," Rodriguez said, her voice turning to ice.

"Lu, are you going to solve this before the election? That's five days away."

"Oh, I doubt that, Janet. There are a couple things that look promising, but it will be some time before we know for certain."

"How much time?"

"You'll be the first to know, if I can control it."

"That means there are other agencies involved," Willow said, continuing to probe. She was not one to give up easily.

"There are always other agencies involved. Laboratories, forensic specialists, the police departments in other states when we're trying to locate a missing person."

"FBI?"

"No, Janet. We have no evidence that a federal crime has been committed. Not yet, anyway."

When she hung up, Willow felt as frustrated as she had ever felt. Part of it, she knew, was a result of not remaining as detached from the Razor Murders as she should be. She had seen the confusion and fear in Roberto Contrarez's eyes. She had spent some time thinking about the female victim, what had been done to her, what she might have been feeling. And damn it, she had liked and respected Carlos Rivera. It was beginning to seem as if, rather than objectively reporting the case, she was too immersed in it, wanting to be part of the solution, pressing too hard.

And not asking the right questions. Luisa would not lie to her. But Luisa had to be approached with the right question. God, if only she knew more about the evidence held by the sheriff's department.

And then, Luisa had mentioned missing persons. . . . Willow hit the redial button on her phone.

When Rodriguez came back on, she sounded resigned. "Yes, Janet?"

"Do you know the identity of the victims?"

Pause, then: "Yes, we think so. But Janet, there has to be some confirmation, and we have to trace next of kin before I can release any information."

"Are they locals?"

"No."

"What state?"

"California."

"What city?"

"Ah . . . let me hold on to that, until we're certain."

"Do you think it's a drug-related crime?"

"No. I do not."

"No motive, then?"

"Not at the moment, Janet, no."

"Thanks, Lu. That's enough for now." She had written front page stuff based on less.

Steve Wayne and Carol Curtis had been waiting in the San Luis Obispo County Sheriff's Office for two hours. The two promising developments were that Cece had stopped trembling and that they were allowed to wait in an undersheriff's office rather than an interrogation room.

Cece still wore her halter top, over blouse, and shorts and looked cold in the air-conditioning, but Wayne did not have his jacket to offer her. Her brief immersion in the Pacific Ocean was revealed by the whitish lines of salt dried on her shorts and halter.

"Cece, I'm sorry I got you into this."

"Would you stop saying that? I'm not blaming you. It's just that I've never been so frightened in my life. It was so utterly unexpected."

For her, yes. For him, no. He was disgusted. He should have had his eyes on his back track from the moment his name appeared in the paper, or at least from the night Carlos was murdered. The nature of the murders—all of them—should have told him that these guys played for very high stakes. Anyone asking questions was a target.

The frosted glass door opened and Undersheriff Dale Whiteny entered. He was a big amiable man in brown suit slacks, a white shirt, and a green tie. He carried Wayne's Smith and Wesson. Reversing it, he passed it butt first to Wayne. "Ballistics're done, Agent Wayne."

The fact that his revolver was returned to him was promising. Wayne checked the cylinder, found it unloaded, and returned it to his holster. "And?"

"You got 'im. Once, in 'is cheek. Dead before 'e hit the rocks."

Cece flinched. He felt the jerk of her arm against his own. He raised his arm and put it around her shoulders, and he could feel the rigidity in her muscles. Very tense.

That was three people he had killed in eighteen years of service. The fact that Wayne was still walking around and the perps were not did not make it easier.

"Anything else?"

"The DA went over your affidavit. We checked you out with the Feds, who say they want your report forthwith. We checked the skid marks against your story. We found your lug nuts in 'is pocket. We checked with the Santa Fe Sheriff. Everythin' holds up, an' the DA's reportin' it as justifiable homicide. You can go."

Undersheriff Whiteny's eyes kept drifting toward Cece's bodice.

"You release it to the press?"

"No choice in that matter, Agent. They been crawlin' all over the buildin'."

"What about the victim? Who was he?"

"Howard Jason Pyle. Spelled Y-L-E. Newport Beach. On 'is driver's license an' 'is pilot's license. We're lookin' for next of kin an' havin' Newport check out 'is house."

Wayne thanked him, and he and Cece went out to the car, followed by the undersheriff's eyes, using a back door to avoid the press piled up in the lobby. The right front fender was scratched from the slide into the ditch, and the rental agency would probably charge him for that. They got in and drove back to the motel in Santa Maria.

The first thing Cece did was to pour two large, strong Scotches, hand one to him, and take a long gulp from the other. Then she headed for the shower. She was not being very talkative, but Wayne did not want to press her. He sipped his drink and sat on the bed next to the phone. Flipping through his notebook, he found the number he wanted, and he caught Rodriguez at home. Wayne brought her up to date quickly, though the acting sheriff had already heard most of it from the San Luis Obispo undersheriff.

Luisa sounded concerned. "You sure you're all right?"

"Cece is a little strung out. I think she'll come out of it."

"What was the name again? I've got the printouts here."

"Pyle. Howard Jason."

He heard pages fluttering. "Right here. Same damned outfit as Andropoulous in Vietnam, May '69 to May '70. Steve, Carlos had the right instincts about this thing."

"Yeah, he did." Could they have moved any faster? Before this Pyle guy shot up the Rivera house, if he was the one who'd done it.

"I've asked the St. Louis Records Center for a copy of the 201 File on Andropoulous, and I'll do the same for Pyle," Rodriguez told him.

"Good. Pyle was a pilot, too, according to the un-dersheriff. It's probably a private license, and it might be worth checking the airport to see if he might have parked a private plane there around the time of Andy's or Carlos's murders."

"That's good, Steve. I'll do that."

"This thing is going to break all over the papers and the local TV here, Luisa. You're going to lose some control now, with San Luis Obispo and Newport involved."

"Yes, I know. And Janet's going to be all over me. She thought her Razor Murders was a personal exclusive."

Tough for Janet, Wayne thought, then softened the thought a bit. She was irritating, like a pugnacious and stubborn bulldog, but he kind of liked her.

"You'd better call Janet and tell her what's happened out here. We're better off with her on our side than we are with her ticked off at us." Wayne was thinking, too, of Luisa's write-in campaign. The politics wormed their way into everything.

"All right, but I'm probably too late for her next edition."

"Shows you tried, Luisa. Give her the 101st Airborne connection between Andropoulous and Pyle."

"You sure?"

"Yes. It'll be something she alone has, and when it gets out, it may spook someone else. Now, with Pyle dead, we've got one more to go."

"You think just two?"

"The odds lean that way. Your people found two sets of tracks in the barn. And that reminds me. Maybe you should send photos of those shoe prints to San Luis Obispo and Newport?"

"Looking for a match with the shoes on the body or those in his closet?"

"You got it."

"And I'll do it."

"You get a list of people in Andropoulous's company in Vietnam?"

"Yes, but it's still a long damned list. People transferred in and out irregularly or were wounded or killed, you know? During Andy's tour, there were two hundred and thirty-five men in his company at one time or another."

"Well, we've two hundred and thirty-three to go."

"We'll keep plugging. Steve?"

"Yeah?"

"Something really bothers me."

"What's that?"

"We've got Pyle living in Newport Beach and Andy living up the coast, right?"

"Right."

"Why bring Andy all the way to Santa Fe to dust him?"

"Damn. Luisa, it's stuff like that that's going to keep me awake all night. And make you a good sheriff. Goodbye."

Wayne hung up as Cece emerged from the bathroom in a thin robe.

"I don't like California anymore."

"Understandable, hon. You want to talk about it?"

"Not now. Maybe later. Now, I just want to go home."

"Right now? Right away?"

"As soon as I can get a flight."

Unfortunately, they found connections for her at 9:30.

Janet Willow had her story polished and ready to submit when the telephone on her desk rang. Still reading her third draft, she picked up.

"Willow."

"This is Luisa, Janet."

"You're working late, are you?"

"Janet, I think I've got some real news for you. Tell your editor to save you a few columns."

"I'll be over in ten minutes."

* * *

Wayne went to the county clerk's office in San Luis Obisbo on Monday morning. It took him less than an hour of leafing through the records to learn that Sidney Gregg, agent for George Henry Andropoulous, had sold the bicycle stores to their present owner. Gregg's Los Angeles address, listed on the power of attorney, turned out to be fictitious.

Then, since Santa Maria was in Santa Barbara County, he had to drive eighty miles down to the clerk's office in Santa Barbara to dig up the records on the Knights of the Sky parachute center. He learned that Decon Company was Andrea and George H. Andropoulous, and figured that that was going to be a dead end. All of the businesses most recently sold had been purchased with certified checks, delivered at closing, and he suspected that tracing the checks, looking for endorsements, would not reveal much. Andy certainly had not received them.

Somebody was a little richer.

Sidney Gregg's phone number, also listed on the power of attorney, turned out to be an answering service for a group of doctors in LA, and the service had never heard of Gregg. He knew Gregg would have disappeared by now, would never have existed. Especially after yesterday's news coverage.

Wayne checked his notebook and drove back to San Luis Obispo to find Clarkson Realty. The middle-aged lady who greeted him wore glasses and a hairdo two sizes too large for her. Her smile was also oversized. "Yes, sir? How can we help you?"

"I have some questions about the house on Mars Way."

The smile evaporated. "The police have already been here. Are you a reporter?"

The San Luis Obispo newspaper had splashed the names of the Andropoulouses, Pyle, and Wayne and Carol all over the Sunday edition. Through the sheriff's office, the California reporters had connected the Santa Fe murders, but had not yet discovered the relationship between Andy and Pyle. If the wires picked up Willow's story, though, they would soon know.

Wayne reluctantly produced his credentials.

"Oh. FBI."

"I'd just like to look at the listing."

"Not the house?"

"No."

He followed her bouffant back to her desk, and she produced a file for him. The house had been listed for sale by Sidney Gregg.

"This Gregg have a power of attorney?"

"Certainly. The police took it, along with copies of the file. The sale is under suspension, of course."

"Of course. What did Gregg look like?"

"I already told them."

"Please."

"Brown hair, very short. Blue eyes. Five-ten or eleven. He was in his mid-forties, perhaps. It's difficult to tell about his age because he looked like he was in pretty good shape. He has a very good tan and a little white scar on his forehead. His nose was a bit crooked, I think."

Wayne wrote the description in his notebook, thanked the lady, and went back to his rental. It looked funny without the hubcaps.

For his next stop, he drove back to the neighbor's house on Mars Way. Wayne had forgotten to mention his conversation with the man in his affidavit for Undersheriff Whiteny. Subliminal withholding of evidence?

The neighbor was not at home, but his wife, Angie, was. She was matronly and plump. Wayne asked her about the moving van.

"United Moving and Transfer. That was it."

"You're sure."

"I'm positive."

She wanted to talk to the FBI some more about her

infamous neighbors, but Wayne fabricated an excuse to leave, located United Moving and Transfer in the phone book, and drove to their warehouse.

A dumpy, bald man checked his credentials with utmost care, nodded vigorously, and said, "Thought you might get around to us."

"You know what I'm here for?"

"Sure. The Andropoulous murders. I been expecting you, so I got the file right here."

He shoved a manila folder across the desk, and Wayne sat down to leaf through it.

"You'll find everything in apple-pie order there, Agent. Every piece was tagged. Weight couldn't be off more than a couple pounds."

"I'm certain it's correct," Wayne acknowledged, reading the inventory sheets.

Sidney Gregg had arranged it, naturally.

"Where did you deliver the consignment?"

"The furniture went to Zack's Used Furniture. Wardrobes and kitchen stuff we dropped at Goodwill. They got a good deal."

"I'll bet they did," Wayne agreed.

He stood up. "The local police will be around to talk to you and get copies of this. Thanks for your help."

"Anytime. Always glad to help the cops."

Wayne stopped at a café for two tacos and a beer, then went to the pay phone on the back wall and called Undersheriff Whiteny.

"Woman called from Clarkson Realty, checkin' on your authenticity. You gettin' yourself involved in our case?" Whitney was not as congenial as he had been on Saturday.

"I just remembered something I forgot to tell you. Maybe you don't want it?"

A long pause. "What'ya got?"

Wayne told him about the conversation with the neighbor. "It's United Moving and Transfer."

"Well, uh, thanks."

"Anytime."

Wayne gassed the Escort and found his way onto the southbound Highway 101, headed for Newport Beach. Since putting Cece on the plane Saturday night, he was feeling more lonely than he had in years. The next few hours were not going to help, and he wished he were back in Albuquerque. Fishing his notebook from his pocket, he held it against the steering wheel and went through the information he had collected. It did not look like much, but that was police work. Sometimes it all came together.

He drove through Santa Barbara for the second time that day. The traffic on Highway 101 thickened and picked up speed. Wayne held sixty-five and watched the Volkswagens and Nissans and Buicks go by him at eighty.

Itching away at the back of his mind was that "forthwith" report he was supposed to file with Ellington. Washington always wanted to know immediately when one of its agents was involved in a shooting. He would call it in first thing in the morning, he promised himself.

Unless he ran into Howard Jason Pyle's buddy first.

TWELVE

LEW WAS NOT only a competent leader, strategist, and tactician; he was also a good teacher.

He taught the others how to launder their contract money through their businesses, how to invest for the future, and how to avoid attention by lavish spending. He had the most trouble with Sweet, of course, who liked lots of expensive toys and couldn't seem to wait to buy them. Pilo was almost as bad.

By 1979, when Andy was married, Lew's records showed that the STRAC Unit had made over 1.7 million dollars on thirteen contracts. In the next ten years and by the mid eighties they upped the take by over four million. The targets had changed drastically, and Lew could demand a higher premium for their services. Some of the guys didn't like the change in mission objectives, though they put up with it for three reasons: they respected Lew's judgment, they were professionals, and they had become accustomed to the bucks.

In fact, they liked the bucks well enough to have struck out on their own, if Lew didn't watch them. He had to keep an especially tight rein on Pilo and Country. He knew, also, that C.B. had once tried to trace the Washington contact, maybe looking for some solo side action. But Lew was the only one who knew Boxer. Lew controlled the contracts and the flow of dollars, and that was the best authority he could have.

They still got together frequently, even though a few of them were now married. The tone changed. Backyard barbecues, a few less cases of beer. More hunting trips.

Hunting trips were good cover for absences of several days, and Lew made sure everyone took up hunting, whether they hunted or not.

Lew bought himself a used Cessna Model 337 Skymaster, a unique twin-engine airplane. It sported twin booms from the high wing to the twin rudders and a 210 horsepower Continental engine in the nose, with a second, aft-facing engine in the rear of the fuselage pod. It had space for six seats, but only the pilot's and co-pilot's were normally in place. The rear compartment was used to haul jumpers with all of their equipment.

It was a good hunting plane.

Loaded up with Remingtons and Winchesters and Brownings and maybe an AR–10 Armalite for fun, Lew and one or two of the unit would fly up to Nevada, over to Arizona, or down to Mexico, land in the desert, and shoot prairie dogs and rabbits.

It was like the old training days.

Janet Willow had pinned Luisa Rodriguez down in the sheriff's office on Monday morning, the day after her Sunday exclusive had been lost among all the other exclusives coming out of the LA area.

"Steve Wayne's working with you?"

"Wayne's on leave, I understand."

"Who's this Carol Curtis?"

"I think I met her once. However, I don't know anything about her."

"Come on, Luisa. You gave me some good stuff Saturday night, but it was just enough to keep me in line. You're using me, damn it!"

"Now, now, Janet. I was trying to help you."

"And then, come Sunday, I find out the whole West

Coast has the same story. You wouldn't have told me a damned thing if it hadn't broken out there first.''

"I gave you the bit about Andy and Pyle being in Vietnam together," the sheriff told her. "The others didn't have that information."

"Placebo," she said. "I know you know more than you're telling me."

"If we ever find the other guy, we've got to have something to check his story against. You can understand that, can't you?''

She let her lips pout.

"Come on, Janet. I'm being as straightforward with you as I can be. You could at least write something about the sheriff's office actually making some progress on the case.''

"How did you identify Andrea and George Andropoulous?''

"A wedding band," she said.

"What about it?''

"It was sold in San Luis Obispo.''

"So Wayne's doing your legwork?''

"The papers said he was taking a long weekend when he was attacked. I suppose that's right, but you never know about the papers.'' Rodriguez's face was a model of Mexican stoicism.

"Sure. And it just happens that Andropoulous was from San Luis Obispo?''

The acting sheriff shrugged. "The papers said Wayne had gone to Big Sur. Maybe they're wrong?''

"Who's Howard Pyle?''

"I'd never heard of him until this weekend, Janet. Had you?''

Willow smiled. "You're tough enough to be sheriff, Lu. How'd you get the scar on your cheek?''

"Dog bite.''

"Damn, I thought it'd be something more exciting.''

They were disturbed by the opening of the door, and Jerry Hayman came in, hitching up his baggy pants. He looked directly at her, grinned, and said, "I guess I'm not interrupting anything important."

Janet shoved her notebook into her big purse and stood up. "Nothing informative for sure."

As she went through the doorway, Hayman called after her, "Been scooped yet today, Janet?"

"Go to hell!" she called back. Bastards.

Taylor finally reached Tuth on Monday afternoon at his shop in Santa Barbara. "Where in the hell have you been, Sweet?"

"I been out on *Contessa* for a few days. Just come back in."

Taylor pinched the bridge of his nose. "You've got to buy a damned answering machine and leave messages so I can find you. Look, we've got to talk. Give me time to reach the phone, then call me from a booth."

He hung up, told his office manager he was leaving for the rest of the afternoon, and went out to find his Eldorado in the parking lot.

Leaving the general aviation section of the Van Nuys Airport, he took the San Diego Freeway south, got off on Sunset, and followed it over to the Pacific Coast Highway. The day was hot and oppressive, the brown cloud hanging low in the valley. Traffic was heavy enough that it took him fifty minutes to reach his house in Malibu. It was not a big house, less than two thousand square feet, but it was on the beach, and Taylor was glad he had bought when he did, right after returning from Vietnam. He had paid an ungodly hundred and thirty thousand then, but today it was worth over a million and a half.

The red telephone on the desk was already ringing when he let himself in.

Scrambling for it, he knocked the teak rack with the three chrome balls off the desk. It shattered on the floor.

"Goddamnit!" he shouted into the phone.

"What'sa matter, Lew?"

"Nothing. Look, you read the papers?"

Stupid question. Tuth didn't read anything, much less watch the news.

"I told you. I been gone."

"Pilo's dead, Sweet."

"What the fuck? That's really something. How?"

"The FBI guy took him out."

"What the hell's goin' on, Lew? How come I didn't know Wayne was gettin' that close? You don't tell me shit."

"You were gone, remember? Read the papers and you'll know as much as I do."

"Gimme a fuckin' hint, Lew. You're controllin' the intelligence input."

Taylor told him about Pyle's phone call from Santa Maria and his instructions to Pyle. "He screwed it up, and so he's dead, and Wayne's blowing his big mouth to the papers."

"Damn. I liked Pilo. The two of us, we jumped good together."

"Listen, goddamnit! They've got Andy's name and Pilo's. I don't know how much more they have, but that new fucking sheriff in Santa Fe won't listen, and it looks like this Wayne's moving around on his own."

Taylor realized that the way he was yelling was going to make Tuth even more nervous. That was no good. He had to get hold of himself.

"What about the Blessing jerk?" Tuth whined. He did that when he was agitated. Like some little kid.

Taylor steadied his voice and his tone. "He's no good to us until he's elected. I've been checking the Santa Fe paper at the library, and the coverage had been dying off until now. Hell, the Willow broad made the one-oh-one connection between Andy and Pilo. That's more than the California papers had."

"Yeah but, Lew, so what? Maybe they got Andy and Pilo, but it don't mean shit. Ain't no direct connections to us."

"Maybe, maybe not. Ten to one, they have another listing of jumpers, like the one we took from Rivera. Somebody will be calling us."

"You told me Washington had it blocked. Boxer said Wayne was off it, gettin' transferred or something."

"I just now told you Wayne's on his own, Sweet. He's on leave."

"We can't trust Boxer."

"I trust Boxer," Taylor said, trying to reassure. He didn't trust him fully, but he understood the man. He knew why Boxer did what he did, and he agreed with the philosophy.

"We shouldn't of done Andy."

"Had to be taken care of. And you enjoyed it." Taylor knew that.

Tuth ignored him, the whine increasing in his voice. "Sure as hell, Lew, if they've got a listin', they're gonna see five more fuckin' names that mean somethin'. We'd better slide on out, man."

Taylor was ready to agree, but his panic subsided, and he reconsidered. One of the reasons he liked talking to Tuth was that it made him feel smarter, more in control.

"Let's not go overboard just yet, Sweet. Think about it. It's no big deal if we all know each other. Hell, all that happened, we started the same kinds of businesses when we got out, right? The rest of us can't help it if Andy and Pilo drifted away, got hung up in something we don't know about, right? We can stonewall it."

"I guess that's right." Tuth did not sound convinced.

"You covered for this weekend? You have somebody with you on the boat?"

"Yeah, but she's not gonna want to talk about it."

"If the cops force her, she'll talk, and that'll protect you."

"Yeah, sure." Tuth sounded more worried about that than he was about Pyle.

"What we need to do is get the unit together and check out alibis for each other anytime a couple of us were gone. Yeah, that'll do it. We'd better meet tonight, my house.''

"Country and C.B. are on the east coast, Lew."

"I know. It's okay. We'll fill them in when they get back.''

Thinking about alibis, Taylor had a brilliant thought. "One more thing, Sweet. Pilo's Cherokee is parked up at Santa Maria. Get that scalpel of yours and run up there and stick it under the seat before the cops find the plane."

"Now, Lew, goddamn it—"

"Hustle. When they find the plane, we want them to find the scalpel."

Wayne left the San Diego Freeway for Newport Boulevard, found a Holiday Inn, and checked in. FBI agents did not splurge on hotels, especially they did not splurge when they were paying the bill themselves.

He had an early dinner of spaghetti and spicy Italian sausage, then confiscated the phone book from his room, looked up Pyle's address, and drove out to find it clustered with a long series of condominiums and palm trees a couple blocks from the bay. The light was beginning to fade fast in the west, but from his car, he could see the police seal on the door and the young lady arguing with the guard stationed in a lawn chair on the porch.

When she turned to come back down the walk, he got out and started across the street. They met at the curb, and he saw the tears streaming down her cheeks. She had blond hair that went halfway down the back of her tight coral blouse. Her thick mascara was streaked and her large breasts heaved with her sobs; she was trying to be twenty years old, but he added ten or twelve years to that.

Wayne stopped. "Something wrong, miss?"

She hesitated, suspicious.

"I was just stopping to see Howard Pyle." He pointed at the guard. "Nothing the matter, is there?"

She sobbed audibly, "He . . . he's dead."

"Dead? My God! What happened?"

More sobs. "I don't know! The pig wouldn' tell me anything."

"You knew Howard?"

"We were going to be married." She looked like she meant it.

He wondered if she could read, or she had ignored the headlines. Maybe she did not watch television.

"Oh, damn! I'm sorry to hear that. Look, maybe it'd help to have a drink?"

"I don' know you."

"I'm safe." Wayne flipped open his credential folder.

"FBI? Really?"

"Really."

"Howie worked for the governmen' too, you know?" He did? "I know."

"All right. Jus' one drink."

She crawled into a beat-up MGB and led him to a neoned pizza joint a couple miles down the coast, on the beach side of the street. It was definitely not part of Newport Beach. He got out of the Escort and waited while she repaired her makeup in the cracked rearview mirror of the MGB. The sidewalk was covered with sand. Between the buildings, he could see the white flash of surf washing on the beach. Several couples wandered shoeless in the night.

When she was finished with her touch-up, they went inside, took a booth, and ordered two draught beers.

"You wan' a pizza?" she asked.

"No, I've eaten, but you go right ahead."

She hesitated.

"I'm buying."

"Gian' sausage and pepperoni with mushrooms, black olive, green peppers, onion, and anchovy."

Grief had not affected her appetite. The waitress shook her head and walked back to the counter.

"I didn't know Howie was getting married."

"We've been talking about it for a year. Had been. Oh, God!''

"He was a nice guy," Wayne admitted. "How much did he tell you about his work?"

"You governmen' people're worried about that, huh?'' She sniffled. "Well, he didn' say much, excep' that he did special jobs every once in a while. He couldn' talk about them. He was a hero in the war, you know?''

"I know."

"He showed me the medals a couple times. You know wha' a Bronze Star is?''

"Yes."

"He had two of them. Little Vs on the ribbons. He was very brave.''

"That's what I understood," Wayne said.

"And they came and asked him to do special things for them, every now and then.''

"Maybe he was doing one of those special jobs and got hurt?'' Wayne suggested.

"Oh, Jesus! You think so? He said they were dangerous, but I didn' believe him. Sometimes, he liked to brag, you know?''

"I know. Hey, I'm sorry, I didn't even ask your name.''

"Dazi Noyes. It used to be D-A-I-S-Y, but I changed it to D-A-Z-I.''

She dug in her voluminous bag, came up with a mirror and a department store sampler of eye makeup, and started again on her eyes. "I mus' look awful.''

"Not at all. Quite pretty.'' Her too-tight blouse squashed her breasts into flat melons.

She smiled lamely. "I feel awful for Howie.''

"Did Howie tell you which government agency he worked with?''

"Oh, no! It was secret, he said.''

"That's right, it is. He mention the others he worked with?''

"The others?''

"I guess not. He wouldn't have. But he did all right with his regular work?"

"For sure! He has that neat car, and the jet boat, and the condo, and the airplane, and simply jillions of dollars, you know?"

Wayne was getting tired of responding to "you know." He waited.

Dazi's eyes went dreamy. "His favorite song was the Green Berets' thing, you know? By the sergean'? Only he mixed up the words when he sang it, like 'a hunerd men will testify, only fools jump out of the sky.' Something like that."

"But he jumped?" Wayne prodded.

"Almost every day. I bet we jumped together fifty, sixty times."

Steve arched his eyebrows. "That's a surprise. I wouldn't have picked you as an enthusiast."

"Oh, yes! It's neat." She squinted her eyes at him. "I'll tell you a secret, you don' tell anyone. Twice, I jumped topless. Howie liked that."

"I can imagine." And he could.

"Usually, it was cold. I got all prickly, you know?"

"It must have been nice for him, being able to jump any time he wanted to."

"Yeah. He never charged me, either." She put her makeup away as the pizza arrived. Wayne ordered two more beers.

Dazi worked a wedge out of the pie, chomped on it, and asked, "You been . . . out . . . there? To . . . Silk?"

"Silk?"

"Silk . . . Dreams?"

"No. Where is it?"

She swallowed. "Orange County."

Wayne checked his watch. "Hey, Dazi. I've got to run to another appointment. It was nice meeting you."

"You just ordered more beer."

"You can have them. Really, got to run."

Her mouth turned down. "Come back some time."

"I'll try. I'm sorry about Howie."

"So'm I." She levered another wedge into her mouth as he got up. He stopped the waitress, paid her, and took his car back to the motel.

He used the multiple Yellow Page books in the lobby. Silk Dreams—Skydiving Instruction and Support was located at the Orange County Airport.

Damn, Carlos, my friend. You knew what you were talking about.

For the second night in a row, Delwin Blessing drank more than his normal evening two cocktails; his wife was keeping the tally. When he poured his fifth Jack Daniels, Delores got up and left the living room. She believed in silent punishment.

He carried his drink into his den.

The story in *The New Mexican* on Sunday had scared him mightily. Apparent to him was the fact that Rodriguez and Wayne knew a hell of a lot more than they were letting on. The story left him with a series of hopes, however.

He hoped that Wayne had killed the man responsible for the murders and the phone calls to him, and that the man had acted alone, as far as the calls to Blessing. It could be all over. Yes, with a little luck, it would all be over. He hoped that no one found the tape of the telephone call. The duplicate that he had received in the mail had gone into his trash masher. At one point, he had even hoped that the groundswell building for Luisa Rodriguez's write-in campaign would be successful.

Now, maybe things were going to straighten themselves out. With this Razor Murders case out of the way, he could show people the kind of job that could be done. It was not his fault that the jerk had taped his conversation. Completely illegal.

The phone rang.

He did not want to answer it, but he did.

"Del, ol' boy, just checking in. You did a nice job

on the Willow broad there for a while, and believe me, we appreciate it. But I think you need to have another long talk with her. Real soon, hear?''

The dial tone buzzed amid Delwin Blessing's shattered hopes and dreams.

Rebel had not been able to reach Boxer in two days, so he finally called Cottonmouth at his home. ''Boxer show you a contingency plan yet?''

''Not yet.''

''It's damned well time to put one in place. Those crazy sons of bitches are going after my people now.'' Rebel was angry.

''You mean Wayne?''

''Yes, I mean Wayne. Boxer's STRAC Unit isn't supposed to be killing off my people. They're deviating a long damned way from the plan, and they've got to be stopped.''

''It's been going pretty well, Rebel. Think about what it means for the country, for all of us.''

''I am thinking about what it means for us. You'd better do the same.''

After a long pause, Cottonmouth said, ''I'll see if I can locate him.''

Willard Travis and Carl Battey stole a Chevy Caprice with air-conditioning in Brooklyn.

''Too bad Brooklyn ain't with us,'' Travis said.

''Yeah. He could show us the old homestead. He's always talking about it, as if it were one step short of heaven.''

''Too bad Pilo's no longer with us.''

''I don't know how he screwed it up so bad,'' Battey said. He had called Lew as soon as he read a day-old paper, but Lew had not given him much. Told him to finish the Koenig job and get back. But that was Lew. Always on the ball, always keeping his eye on the objective.

Travis was driving, lanky and nonchalant and slumped behind the wheel; in New York City or anywhere, he drove like he was on a deserted gravel road, hauling a trunkload of glass jugs topped off with moonshine. His eyelids were half lowered over blue eyes, and his short cornsilk blond hair was tucked under a rolled-brim straw cowboy hat tilted low on his forehead. He looked as if he should be toting either a Colt .45 or a flattop guitar.

He took Flatbush to the Manhattan Bridge, crossed, and turned onto Franklin D. Roosevelt Drive. Battey polished his rimless glasses and studied the pictures he had of Walter Koenig, close-ups of his face and snapshots of the whole man. He was in his sixties, balding, broadly set, and wore thick horn-rimmed glasses. He was a respected economist in some international circles.

Travis got off on 42nd, just before the United Nations enclave where their man was making big deals in some kind of economic conference. They would never find him there, they knew, and Travis drove on up to Sixth Avenue, turned north, and found a parking place a block south of the Taft Hotel at 50th.

Battey got out and wandered up the street to the hotel. He wore a navy blue leisure suit with white stitching he had bought in 1971. He wasn't big on ties.

Travis sat behind the wheel and watched the girls and smiled at some of them. They all smiled back at the cowboy. Two of them bent over next to the car, showed him some tit, and suggested private parties. He begged off politely. He was a happily married man, and Doreen had just as much, and more, to offer.

At 8:20, Travis saw the Cad limousine approaching in the side mirror, and he crossed the ignition wires to start his engine. As soon as the limo passed, he pulled out behind it and followed it to the front of the hotel.

Koenig got out, his door opened with a flourish by the uniformed doorman.

The limo eased away. Travis drove ahead and stopped in its place.

Battey pushed away from the brick wall he had been leaning against, skirted the doorman, met Koenig head-on, and threw an arm around him, turning him back toward the Caprice.

"Damn, Walt, it's good to see you!"

The man spluttered.

"Hell, we've just *got* to have us a drink or two, ol' buddy."

Travis leaned back over the seat and shoved the rear door open.

Battey heaved Koenig into the backseat and crawled in with him.

Travis pulled the Chevy out into traffic, dodged a taxi, and flipped the cab driver a finger.

Koenig continued to splutter. "Vat's this? Vat's this? Who are you? Vat are you doing vith me?"

SOB couldn't even speak American.

"Somebody's bound to call it a mugging," Battey said. "Lots of muggings in this burg, I heard. Don't you think so, Country?"

"Sure do."

Battey broke Walt's neck.

The crack of snapping vertebrae was crisp over the hum of the air-conditioning.

"Go with God," C.B. said.

THIRTEEN

BROOKLYN, C.B., AND Lew took out a Saudi Arabian deputy minister for oil export. The man was objecting to a large contract with US oil companies because he thought they were trying to break his country's monopoly, though STRAC never worried unduly about the reasons. The unit was apolitical, or at least, learning to be. If anything, they were simply patriotic. As in 'Nam, they always assumed their contracts were in support of American objectives, and that was the only rationale necessary.

Maybe they never grew up.

The target had a lavish apartment in Riyadh and the STRAC Unit arrived in Riyadh by way of commercial flights through Paris and Cairo. They checked into the Hilton under false passports, and decided right away to make it a quick trip.

No liquor. Not even a lousy beer.

Lew called the airport and finalized their return tickets for 9:40 the following morning.

"It's got to be today, guys," he said.

"Fine with me. Sooner the goddamned better," C.B. said. He was still sullen about the customs agent confiscating a full quart of Jack Daniels.

Lew opened his hanging bag. It had come through as regular baggage, and even though the customs agents had gone through it, they gave up their search as soon as they found his bottle of J&B Scotch.

In the bottom of the bag was his aluminum-sided camera case. He took it out, opened it, and extracted the big video camera from its nest of soft rubber. The customs agent had done that too, holding it up on his shoulder, and faking a pan of the customs area. He had grinned hugely at his own good humor, and Lew had grinned back at him.

Now, he popped the camera's film cassette cover and pulled the cassette out. Prying the lid of the cassette open with his penknife, he poured the barrel and frame of the Walther onto the bedspread. There hadn't been room in the cassette for the grips.

Two of the five spare cassettes also gave up automatic pistols. The three silencers were in his Dopp kit, wrapped in plastic and submerged in aftershave, shaving cream, and toothpaste containers.

The three of them disassembled and cleaned the pistols, double-checked the feed of the magazines, and reloaded them. Then they left the room and went down to find a taxi.

The cab driver only had command of ten or twelve words of English, and Lew just pointed in the direction he wanted to go, tapping him on the shoulder whenever he wanted a turn made. They passed the address and C.B. almost mentioned it, but Lew rapped him on the knee to keep him silent.

A block later, he ordered a right turn, then a stop, and they got out. After the cab was gone, they started back up the street.

It was hot and dry. The sunlight glared harshly, reflecting off white concrete sidewalks and buildings, and making Lew squint. He put on his sunglasses.

Brooklyn said, "This is a first. Daytime and all."

"First daylight shot since 'Nam, anyway," C.B. said.

"Maybe it's not so good, Lew," Brooklyn said. "Hell, we stand out as foreigners."

They were dressed in lightweight summer suits, complete with white shirts and striped ties. Except for C.B.'s, their shoes shone with spit shines.

"There are foreigners all over the place," Lew told him. "All of them after oil."

"They sure as hell ain't after a drink," C.B. said.

The apartment building was eight stories high, set back from the street, with a large, two-story parking garage at the back. Probably full of Mercedes and Cadillac limousines. Modern building, all cement with a coating of stucco, including the balcony walls.

One security guard in a small guardhouse at the single gate, handling both pedestrian and auto traffic.

Brooklyn walked up to the guardhouse, tapped on the window, and when the guy looked up at him, shot him in the heart. Glass cracked and tinkled. The guard dropped like a steer banged between the eyes with a mallet. Country had told Brooklyn about meat-packing plants one time, and Brooklyn didn't eat meat for a month.

Brooklyn used the silencer mounted on his gun to break out the glass around the bullet hole, reached through, and toggled the gate motors. The gate slid to the side, and they all walked through. C.B. stepped into the guardhouse, straddled the body on the floor, and put the dead man's peaked cap on his own head. He closed the gate, then leaned back against the wall and shut his eyes.

Lew and Brooklyn walked up the wide sidewalk, entered a marble foyer, and rang for the elevator. It was on the first floor and the door opened immediately. They got in and Lew used the knuckle of his forefinger to press the button for the third floor.

The oil minister wasn't supposed to have bodyguards, so Brooklyn knelt on the carpeted floor in front of his door and worked the lock with picks. Lew watched the hallway.

The lock gave after three minutes, Brooklyn pushed

the door open, and they went inside. Magnificent place. Acre of deep pile, plush white carpet. Black sofas spotted around. Glass-topped tables on brass legs. Wall of glass overlooking a broad, concrete balcony with yellow wrought iron furniture. Lew thought the prints and paintings hanging on the walls were all good, very expensive, and wished he had space to take a few back with him. Brooklyn had never seen a stereo entertainment center that cost $30,000 before. That's what the background brief had said. He didn't think it looked much better than the one he had paid a grand for.

Nobody there.

Then they heard giggles coming from the back.

They went down a long hallway and walked through the open doorway into a bedroom with a round bed that must have been twenty feet in diameter.

Lavender and pink upholstery. Same for the drapes. Big bed. Large enough for four, with room to spare for more.

Right now, it held a frozen-faced, balding oil minister with a goatee and a lapsing erection. Also, three naked, first-class broads, one each of blonde, brunette, and red-head. They were spread all around the minister, ministering to him in various ways.

"Sweet's gonna shit, I tell him about this," Brooklyn said. "Ten to one, he'd have had the endurance for all three."

"No bet," Lew said, appreciating all of the flesh. Made him wonder if Sweet didn't have the right idea, just once in a while.

The oil minister said in English, "What do you want?"

"Nothing you've got," Lew said.

A slight relaxation of his face.

Then Lew shot him. *Phhht!* One right in the left temple. Not much blood. Just a tiny hole.

Girls screaming, yelping, rolling.

Brooklyn surveyed all those lovely breasts jouncing as the girls tried to scramble out of the bed.

He shot two of them, and Lew took care of the third. The STRAC Unit never left a witness behind.

Steve Wayne called the Bureau in Washington at nine o'clock, their time, on Tuesday morning. Outside his window, he could see faraway clouds on the Pacific horizon.

"Director Ellington's Office."

He recognized the voice. "Mrs. Wagner, this is Steve Wayne. I wonder if you could tape a report for me?"

"Oh, Mr. Wayne! The Director's been—"

"I don't have any equipment with me, and I'd sure appreciate a transcription, Mrs. Wagner."

"Well, uh, just a moment, Mr. Wayne."

Dull echo of hold.

Ellington came on the line. "Wayne! Where in the hell are you?"

"Good morning, Mr. Director."

"You going to answer my question?"

"In Los Angeles. I—"

"I want you here, in my office, as soon as you can get a flight. This afternoon."

"Mr. Ellington—"

"No excuses. And you'd better have a good rationale for this rampage you've been on."

"Mr. Ellington—"

No hold this time. Just the steady dial tone.

Dead-ended against the bureaucracy one more time. He might not even make it to Sacramento. How about Nome?

Wayne sat on the edge of his bed for five minutes, his mind broiling, then called room service and ordered coffee, orange juice, pancakes, a manila envelope, and ten dollars' worth of postage stamps.

He dressed and packed while waiting for breakfast, and when it arrived, sat down at the small table by the window. He could stare at the Pacific while eating and composing. Using Holiday Inn stationery and his copy of his affidavit for the San Luis Obispo Sheriff as a guide, he wrote a concise report for Ellington. He added the visit to Andy's neighbor that he had forgotten in the affidavit, but he did not provide many details of the earlier investigation in Santa Fe. Simply as a favor, he had checked on the purchaser of a wedding ring.

And when he thought about it, that's about all he had done. Favors. For a friend. It was done all the time. Why in hell should he feel guilty, as if he were deceiving his superiors?

Why in hell should Ellington be incensed at all? When he was done, he signed and dated the report. Then he took a single sheet of paper, addressed it to Ellington, and wrote two words: "I resign."

No explanations. No excuses. No bucking the system. He signed and dated that one also.

From his credential folder, he extracted the credential, tossed the worn leather folder in the wastebasket, added the credential to the report and resignation, and slipped it all into the envelope. Standing, he unclipped his holster from his belt and packed the .38 into his suitcase. It would no longer be legal for him to carry it.

The lack of weight on his hip was noticeable. It had been there for eighteen years. The lack of authority in his pocket was a new blank space in his life. Wayne was not certain how he felt. Numb. Somewhat emasculated.

Ironically, somehow freer. Less bureaucratic weight to carry around.

He thought about Gary Poole, wondered if he was still chasing spooks and mounting undercover operations in Latin America for the CIA. Wondered why they had ever been friends.

He went down and checked out, arranging at the same time to have the envelope posted in the overnight mail.

Finis.

That's all, folks.

Carrying his case out to the Escort, he got in and drove north unhurriedly on the Pacific Coast Highway. There was no urgency requiring a freeway. The highway transformed itself into Sepulveda Boulevard on the other side of Torrance, and Wayne followed that north, crossed through the tunnels under LA International's runways, and weaved his way into the airport complex. He turned the car into Hertz, confessed the scratched fender, showed them where to find their hubcaps, and paid the bill.

United found him a seat, but he had a wait that lasted him through five cups of coffee and every page of the *Los Angeles Times*.

Wayne's Boeing 727 landed at Albuquerque International at 11:15 on Tuesday morning. It was hot and dry and bright. On the other side of the airport, out of Kirtland Air Force Base, several flights of F-15 Eagles took off to practice the delivery of destruction. As they passed over, the sleek fighters appeared incongrous against the dark tan, adobe-style buildings of the airport terminal. A nice study in contrasts, the fat, solid past placed against the slim and speeding shape of progress.

Wayne retrieved his Firebird Trans Am from the lot, followed the access road out to University Boulevard, and joined Interstate 25 after a traverse over Cemetery Boulevard. Cemetery seemed particularly appropriate. Prelunch traffic was light, and he reached his Candelaria turnoff in ten minutes.

Wayne did not expect to find Cece home at that time of day, but he also did not expect to find the apartment so empty. Inside the door was a cardboard box of his personal items from the office. Leaning against the wall were the four paintings of the old Navajo men. Displaced once again.

He tossed his bag in the bedroom and wandered through the rooms, and the more he did not see, the more disheartened he became. The little things—accessories, pictures, her plaque from the New Mexico Advertising Association—were still there, but quite a few of Cece's clothes were gone. It also explained why she had not been picking up the phone since Sunday.

The agency told him she was out when he called. No, they thought she would not be back today. Her phone number? They gave him his own. He almost phoned Rodriguez, but then decided to leave the woman alone. The acting sheriff would be busy enough with the election.

On Wednesday morning, Del Blessing wore his best summer, western-cut suit and ate breakfast at the Village Inn with Aaron Clark and Humphrey Moore while they waited for the results of the recount. Blessing had scrambled eggs while Clark and Moore each dug into spicy Mexican omelets.

Blessing was not hungry and pushed his eggs away, nibbling on one piece of bacon. He poured coffee from the insulated pot while Clark, as county GOP chairman, got up to make yet another call.

"I hate the waiting," Blessing said. "Last night was hell."

"You should have been a reporter instead of a lawyer," Moore, the old newspaper man said. "You learn patience. Some do, anyway."

Clark appeared in the doorway from the vestibule, his face grim, and they both watched him thread his way through the tables. Clark's dismal face gave Blessing hope.

"Well?" Blessing asked.

Clark sat down and poured himself fresh coffee, being deliberately slow. "It's ironic."

"What's ironic, damn it?"

"You lost your council seat by seventeen votes."

Blessing's spirit soared.

"You won this one by seventeen votes. Congratulations!"

Delwin Blessing felt faint.

* * *

"I took the rest of the day off," Rodriguez said. "It'll be the last time I can order myself on leave. Hell, next Monday, when Blessing takes office, I might not even have a job."

"He's got to give you something like patrol or investigation captain," Hayman said.

Keith Boyles said, "I'd like to have him try to fire you, Luisa. Jesus, I'd have a field day with the SOB. Female and Hispanic, not to mention election loser. 'Discriminatory, arbitrary, and capricious' is a phrase I can use well in front of a judge."

The four of them sat around a big old oak table in Hayman's dining room, and Wayne could see Anne Hayman through the kitchen door, talking to someone on the phone. Big platters of sandwiches and chips and dips, along with four cans of Coors, adorned the table. It was a comfortable room in a big old house on the east side of town. Navajo rug hanging on one wall. A prized Georgia O'Keeffe was centered above the sideboard.

Luisa Rodriguez wore an off-white full skirt and a pale blue blouse. Her dark, shining hair was blow-dried and seemed to have more body in it than it did under a deputy's Stetson. Except for the sour downcast of her lips, she did not look like someone who had lost an election.

She did not look hard enough to be a cop.

Then again, he was not a cop, anymore, either. He was not anything. And yet, he did not feel out of place in the group. These were people who halfway liked him, he thought.

Wayne had just arrived after Hayman's telephone invitation at ten o'clock.

"I'm disappointed as hell," Wayne told her. Then he said to Boyles, "Congratulations, Keith."

Boyles tipped a can at him in thanks.

Hayman took a long drink from his tall can, his Adam's apple bobbing. "You're only disappointed? I'm mad as hell. I've lost all faith in the discernment of the general public.''

"It's a big town, Jerry," Boyles said. "But it's still an old-fashioned town in a lot of ways. I think Lu ran into some resistance from people who couldn't see a woman as sheriff. Plain and simple, like that. Many of the voters didn't show any real feeling for either the competency or the politics. One thing, though, Blessing sure didn't get a mandate.''

"But he'll take it as one," Hayman said.

Boyles had shed his suit coat and large perspiration stains circled his armpits. He still wore his vest and was the only one with a tie in place. Wayne was in jeans and a sport shirt. The non-requirement to wear a tie was almost as confusing to him as was the absence of a weapon on his belt.

"You can't go anywhere without getting your name in the paper, can you, Steve?" Boyles asked. "I'm damned glad to see you, by the way. Alive, and all that.''

"Thanks.''

Boyles reached for another sandwich. "What's the story behind the story?''

Wayne related the details of his snooping around San Luis Obispo, Santa Maria, and Newport Beach. He skimmed over the confrontation with Pyle.

"Cece's okay?" Hayman asked him.

"She was a bit shaken, but I think she'll come out of it all right." Wayne based the statement on faith. He had not been able to find her anywhere.

"Both Andy and this Howard Pyle owned skydiving centers?" Rodriguez asked.

"That's right.''

"Franchises?''

"No. They were independently owned.''

"I have a bit of a downer for you, Steve," the exacting sheriff said.

"Just what I need.''

"None of the shoes owned by Howard Pyle matched

the shoe prints we got from the barn. The size doesn't match, either. Pyle wore size twelve, and the ones in the barn are both size ten.''

''Damn it. That means we've got at least three perps. Pyle and the two in the barn.''

''Yeah, and something more confusing,'' Rodriguez added. ''The sheriff's department investigators from San Luis Obispo found a Piper Cherokee registered to Howard Pyle at the Santa Maria Airport.''

''That's confusing?''

''The Piper has never been in Santa Fe, as far as the records here show. And the plane's log supports that.''

''Okay. It was a long shot,'' Wayne said.

''We also checked out Pyle's name, Steve, in case he rented an airplane. No one named Pyle parked an aircraft overnight at Santa Fe. I got a list, though, of every transient aircraft on the ground for April third to the tenth and for April seventeenth to the twenty-first. There are a lot of them.''

''Good. However, you must have a 'but.' ''

''But,'' she said, nodding, ''they found a scalpel in the plane in Santa Maria.''

''They're shipping it to me, to see if I can find any matches with the wounds on the victims,'' Hayman said.

It took only a couple seconds for Wayne to hash it over in his mind. ''Pyle has the scalpel, but Pyle was apparently not on the scene.''

The DA grinned at him. ''How's that for a puzzler?''

''Sounds to me,'' Wayne said, ''as if someone was taking advantage of an opportunity. Since Pyle was done for, anyway, drop the evidence on him. Maybe the dumb New Mexico cops will close the case.''

''That's the way I've been thinking, *amigo*,'' Rodriguez said. ''And I don't like having anyone think I'm stupid.''

''You have the computer printout with you, Luisa?'' Wayne asked.

''I've got one of them. Hold on.'' Rodriguez went out

to her car and came back with six sheets of paper stapled together. "It's a bit thinner now. This is the 235-name roster I told you about."

Wayne scanned the names. Andropoulous and Pyle had stars next to their names. The rest of them did not mean much. It was just a roster of people who had served in the same company in Vietnam during the same period as the two dead men, a period which now spanned fourteen months with the overlap in Andy's and Pyle's tours of duty. Some of them were probably dead, a result of the war or of civilian tragedy in postwar years. Each name had a rank and an address derived from the Pentagon or Screamin' Eagles list. A few had telephone numbers which might or might not be accurate. Among the A, B, C, and D names, many phone numbers had been written in longhand by someone from the sheriff's office or the DA's office attempting to call them. There were a lot of gaps. Modern technology could not keep up with transient people.

"What did you learn about Andropoulous and Pyle?" Wayne asked.

"Their two-oh-one files indicate exemplary military service. Andy was a buck sergeant and Pyle a spec four. Eight or nine decorations apiece. Bronze Star and Silver Star for Andy. Two Bronzes for Pyle."

Pyle had told Dazi the truth, there.

"Any detail for the citations?"

"Not much as I recall. Something like outstanding and selfless action at Chu Lai on such and such a date."

"Have you looked for a commanding officer?"

"No."

Wayne ran his fingernail down the column of ranks. There was one captain.

"Peter G. Conrad. He's the only captain, and he must have been the company CO."

"What's his present status?" Boyles asked.

"Civilian, I guess. Lists an address and phone number

in Pocatello, Idaho. I assume the data is from the Screamin' Eagles.''

"We can try to run him to ground," Rodriguez said. "By all rights, he should have been at the top of the list.''

"I don't know Blessing," Wayne said, "but I get the feeling from all of you that he's not going to jump right into this.''

"He won't want to get his hands dirty," Hayman said. "Unless Janet gets right on his ass, I don't think he'll push too hard. If he's smart, which I won't vouch for, he'll make Luisa chief of the investigative division and leave the case to her.''

"We're not going to know anything about that until Monday, if then," Rodriguez said.

Boyles chewed his lip. "There's still a couple of perplexing problems.''

"Like motive?" Wayne asked.

"A good start.''

"Like why bring Andy and Andrea here to knock them off?''

"Even better.''

Hayman said, "What if there was just a problem within the group? Even if it's just a group of three. Say between Pyle and Andropoulous, and they had it out?''

Wayne told him, "Jerry, you said the perpetrator was after information. Indicating something more than a feud.''

"True," Hayman admitted. "Keep in mind, however, that, once or twice in my life, I've been wrong.''

Wayne mused for a moment. "Let's come back to the geographical problem. Andy, Andrea, and two more people, males, were in the Santa Fe area for some purpose. On or about the eighth of April. Is there some way we can check out what else was going on at that time?''

"I'll have my office do a search," Boyles offered. "We're looking for any activities in that period that are out of the norm, right?''

"Yes. Something that might have made the newspaper, for instance."

"Okay. I'll start my people on it in the morning."

"Jerry, would you mind a long-distance call on your phone?" Wayne asked Hayman.

"I'll send the bill to the DA."

Wayne went into the kitchen. Anne had gone outside onto the patio and was chatting with a woman Wayne did not know. He flipped though the computer listing to the Cs and called the phone number in Pocatello. A monotone recording told him the number had been changed, but also gave him the new number. He dialed that one, and when a woman answered, asked for Peter Conrad.

"He's at the office."

"Could I have the phone number, please?"

He had to go through a receptionist advertising Conrad Insurance Agency before he reached Peter Conrad.

"Mr. Conrad, my name is Steven Wayne."

"The name rings a bell."

"I'm afraid it was in the news last weekend."

"Ah, yes! You're with the FBI."

Wayne did not deny it.

"There was something out in California involving Pilo."

"Pilo?"

"That was Pyle's nickname. Claimed he was a pilot before he was drafted, I think, and they shortened it from there. Those people did funny things with names."

"You remember him, then?"

"Sure, after I saw the name in the paper, though I didn't think he'd end up like he did. He was a hell of a soldier. I decorated him twice, I think."

"I wonder if you'd remember the names of any men he was closely associated with?"

"We're talking twenty years ago, Mr. Wayne. There were one hundred and eighty people in the company at any one time, and they kept shifting on me. They died, they got shot up, they rotated home, and they were replaced."

"I understand."

"And during that period, I think it was difficult for most of them to get too close to each other. You never knew when a buddy was going to be wasted. Getting too close was too hard emotionally. And beyond the formality that came with being their commander, it was the same with me. I knew a lot of my people by name, but I didn't get buddy-buddy with them. Especially at the platoon level."

"How about Pyle's platoon leader? Remember him?"

"Well, hold on . . . Be . . . Ba . . . Barker? No, he was the Fourth Platoon. Must have been Taylor. I think that's right. Frank or Fred . . . Frederick Taylor. Oh, hell, yes. First Platoon." There was a change in Conrad's tone.

"Do you recall something significant about Frederick Taylor?" Wayne found Taylor's name on the listing. Malibu, California.

"Yeah. Taylor got himself in some deep trouble one time."

"What kind of trouble?"

"The kind we weren't supposed to talk about, but well, hell, the war's lost anyway, isn't it? We weren't supposed to be making combat jumps, but Taylor and a few of his people scrounged up some equipment and made a few jumps on their own. They got caught at it, of course, but it was buried. Then they made a few more—let's say unsanctioned—jumps at the request of some people in the US Embassy. You've heard of the Special Operations Group?"

"I have."

"All I know is that whatever missions they were, they were highly successful."

"Kind of a commando team?"

"That's right."

"You and others in higher authority were aware of what was going on, though?"

"Blindly aware, Mr. Wayne. Mainly because those missions were not announced to our allies. Avoided all kinds of leaks that way."

"Do you recall who else was part of that unit?"

"Ah, hell. I probably knew at the time, but you know how it is? I try not to remember most of it. It seems as if they were all in the First Platoon, Taylor's. Just because their names have come up in the papers, it seems to me that Andropoulous and Pyle may have been part of it. I think I gave Andropoulous a decoration of some kind, too."

Wayne took a quick look at the computer listing. The platoon assignment was not part of it. If it came down to it, Luisa could mail Conrad a list and see if he could identify people by platoon.

"And *your* commander at the time was . . . ?"

"Dauntless Doug Sanders. He was a full bird then, but I think he's made general since."

"Mr. Conrad, I appreciate your time."

"No problem. Sometimes, I miss it. We were a gung ho outfit. And then I think about how dumb we all were, and I don't miss it anymore."

Wayne went back to the dining room, and his three colleagues looked up at him expectantly.

"Directly from the horse's mouth, lady and gentlemen. First Lieutenant Fred Taylor and probably Andropoulous and Pyle were part of a covert hit team in Vietnam."

Boyles sighed. "That's just great. Can we prove it?"

"Probably not. It was a Special Operations Group exercise, and they'll have buried it deep. There won't be any paperwork now, if there was any at the time."

"But the FBI . . ."

"Forgot to tell you," Wayne said. "I resigned."

"No shit?" Boyles's face showed surprise.

"No shit."

"Not because of us?" Rodriguez asked, concern in her voice. "Did you get in trouble for helping us out?"

"It's a combination of lots of things, Lu. Don't worry about it."

"Do you want to be a deputy?" Rodriguez asked. "At least until Monday?"

Boxer called Taylor on the scrambled telephone line.

Taylor was at his desk, halfway expecting the call because he had not answered the phone when it rang for the past few days. He was not eager to talk to Boxer. He also missed his chrome inertia balls and reminded himself again to replace them.

As soon as he heard Boxer's voice, he pushed the button to start the recorder.

"You see on TV where they pulled Koenig out of the river?" Taylor asked. "Four down and eight to go."

"I saw. You see on TV where they pulled Pyle out of the sea?"

"Yeah, well, he made a mistake." Taylor pinched the bridge of his nose, rubbing at the disjointed cartilage.

"A big one. What are you doing about it?" Boxer's voice was harsh.

"It's covered."

"How?"

"You work strategy, Boxer, and I'll work tactics. How's that?"

"Like hell! You've been fucking up regularly."

"It's covered, I told you. Don't sweat it."

"I *am* sweating it. And a few others are also sweating it. In fact, Lieutenant, it has been suggested that the ties be cut. Permanently."

Taylor sat up in his chair, alarmed for the first time. "Permanently?"

"That's right."

He tried bravado. "Can't be done."

The snap of Boxer's fingers echoed hollowly in the receiver. "Just like that. You think you're professionals? I've got a full-time team here that puts you to shame.

You call me immediately if the cops or the press get any closer to you.''

"Then what?"

"Then we evaluate it."

"And if it looks bad?"

"We shut it down. One way or another, we'll shut this thing down."

On his way out of Santa Fe, Wayne had an inspiration. He pulled the Trans Am off Cerrillos Road into a gas station and parked in front a public telephone.

The phone book was half of its original self. Pages had been ripped out haphazardly. He dropped a coin, dialed information, and got the number he wanted.

Then he called the Lazy-C Ranch.

A female voice with half a load of gravel in it answered with a drawn-out "Hello."

"Mrs. Curtis? My name is Steve Wayne. I wonder if—"

"Let me get her, Steve."

After a minute, he heard her say, "I didn't think you'd remember the name of the place."

"Desperation does strange things, Cece."

She sighed.

"I love you," he said.

She sighed again.

"I resigned from the Bureau."

"Where are you?"

"In Santa Fe."

"Get a room at the La Quinta. I'll be there in a couple hours."

FOURTEEN

SWEET WANTED TO do the Moran job alone, but Lew sent Andy and Country with him.

Maureen Moran was an Irish national and a highly successful fund-raiser for the IRA, working the American-Irish ghettos like an Avon saleswoman. The money rolled in, bought AK–47s and plastic explosive, blew the shit out of Brit soldiers, little boys, and little girls.

Somebody in Washington didn't like it.

It was snowing in Montreal, and it was cold as hell. December was the time to be home in So Cal, not slogging through the slush covering someplace where they thought it was France.

It was twilight, but they hadn't seen the sun all day. Just went from light gray to dark gray. The hotel was brightly lit, though, and when Andy stood in the lobby near the windows, standing sentinel on the corridor containing the elevators, he could see the jetliners taking off and landing over at Montreal International.

Every time one of the elevators chimed, he turned to see who was getting off. Just people.

Finally, the doors rolled back and Country stood there, Maureen baby by his side. Big green eyes, wide and rolling side to side, showing lots of white. Dark, dark red hair, shoulder length, flying all over when she jerked her head around. Andy couldn't see her mouth; there was a chunk of duct tape over it. Couldn't check out the body, either. It was hidden under a wool coat, green like the eyes. Country had her arms taped behind her and she struggled, but not too much. She was tall, tall as Country, who was five-eleven.

Andy swept the lobby once for watching eyes, nodded at Country, then turned and went down the elevator corridor, headed for the side door.

Country shoved her ahead of him and followed Andy. Andy opened the side door and waved. Sweet came rolling up in the rented Chevy Citation, and Andy opened the car doors.

Country tossed her into the backseat and followed her in, while Andy crawled in front with Sweet. She was moaning under that tape, and she kicked out at Country.

"Where to, gents?" Sweet asked. His pitted face beamed, showed the sheen of sweat on his forehead.

The woman thrashed around, grunting.

"Just get it rolling, Sweet," Andy said. "And turn on the headlights, so we don't get picked up."

He took the Boulevard Ste. Anne east, then turned south on the Honore Mercier Bridge to cross the St. Lawrence River. Deep in the Caughnawaga Indian Reserve, Sweet found a graveled side road into the forest. Damned near got the car stuck several times. Smell of pine, snow falling in lazy flakes. Just like Christmas.

Andy and Country stayed in the car.

Sweet left the engine running and the headlights on, got out, and jerked her out of the car. Pulled her around in front of the car.

She's trying to scream.

Lights reflecting off snowflakes.

Unsheathed the scalpel.

Bigger eyes.

Used the blade to cut her clothes off her. Pieces of sleeves, lapels, fabric littering the snow-covered road. Blade between her breasts, snick, the bra fell away. Small nick of the skin that trickled red down her belly.

Good-looking girl, standing there in nothing but panty hose and high-heeled shoes sinking into the snow. Sweet peeled the panty hose down around her ankles. Standing proud, not thrashing now. Staring Sweet down, daring him, thinking it was only a rape job, maybe.

He reached out with both hands, keeping the blade up and away from her flesh, grabbed her shoulders, and brought her down to her knees. He unzipped his pants and made her blow him first. You could tell she was cold. The shivers were running visibly over her fair skin.

Then Sweet whipped her around, throwing her onto her hands and knees. He sodomized her, fondling her breasts, then he sliced her throat.

Dark red snow under the headlight beams. Andy watched and thought that things might be getting out of hand. Squinting at Country in the backseat, he sensed the same thoughts behind the Tennessean's eyes.

It was the first one they'd done on the North American continent. It seemed a little close to home.

On Friday, the saleslady showed them a broad range of offerings. Broad being two hundred to four hundred thousand dollars. She managed to skip a couple in the seven-hundred-thousand range.

Wayne studied the saleslady's eyes in the saleslady's rearview mirror, but all he could see was, commission, commission.

He sat in the backseat, next to Cece, and looked at her, trying not to show his frustration.

Cece told the driver, "Mrs. Angst, let's go back north, on Sunset."

"Very well."

Studying the photos, statistics, and numbers in the Multiple Listing book, Cece reached over and took his hand. Wayne took the gesture as reassurance.

They had spent Wednesday night and most of Thursday and Friday in their room at the La Quinta and walked a lot of streets in the evenings and talked.

"You call Bart and tell him that McComb-Davis needs a branch in Santa Fe," Wayne suggested. "Tell him that you'll manage it."

"Tell him or ask him?"

"Tell him."

"You want to commute all the way to Albuquerque for these refresher law courses?" she asked.

"It's only for the fall semester. Then I'll attack the bar exam."

Cece called Bart McComb on Thursday afternoon and said, "Bart, I'm going to manage a new shop for us in Santa Fe. McComb-Davis is going to put up the capital to get it under way."

Silence while she listened.

"Me. I say it's the right time."

More silence.

"Great! And, Bart, I think now might be a good time for me to buy shares in the firm."

Brief pause, and then she laughed.

"Well, maybe not tomorrow. How about Monday?"

By two o'clock on Friday, they had looked at a dozen houses. Wayne could not believe the prices, but Mrs. Angst had explained about the influx of California people. Some of them were actually treating Santa Fe as a bedroom community to Los Angeles. They worked in LA and commuted in private jet aircraft. They did not care what they paid for a house, as long as it was a little bigger than the one next door.

"Turn left here," Cece said.

Mrs. Angst turned off Sunset Street onto a narrow, newly paved road. They were several miles north of Santa Fe, in low rolling hills cut with arroyos and eroded ditches. The manzanita and scrub oak were thick, hiding flat-roofed houses set on small acreages. As Angst's Cadillac followed the dips and curves of the road, Wayne tried to spot the houses hidden amidst the foliage. It was difficult, and he was impressed with the privacy, despite the number of houses.

"Left here, again."

Mrs. Angst pulled into a long graveled drive and followed it for a hundred yards to where it ended in a small car park. There was a detached two-car garage situated at an angle to a house that was not much bigger than the garage. From where they sat, neighboring houses could not be seen.

They got out, Mrs. Angst worked the combination on the realtor's lockbox, found the key, and opened the house. The tour was over in ten minutes.

It was about forty years old, or maybe more. There were two bedrooms of adequate size on either side of a large bathroom, a long and narrow living room with a curving adobe fireplace on one end, a small dining room, a kitchen, and a utility area. A large deck of cedar planks extended off the back, southern side of the house, over the descending slant of the hill behind. The lights of Santa Fe would be visible at night, Wayne thought.

He had a vision of Cece walking through the house naked, and the vision almost made the house theirs.

The neglect was evident. The varnish coats were peeling from the oak plank floors, and there were chips in the plaster walls. A water stain on a bedroom wall suggested a leak in the flat roof. The kitchen appliances were antiquated. Outside, large pieces of the adobe-style finish were scattered in the weeds crowding the walls.

"Square-foot wise," Carol said, "it's about twice what we have in the apartment."

Mrs. Angst waited stoically while Wayne and Cece went outside and tried the deck. The manzanita closed right up to the cedar-railed deck.

"Three quarters of an acre," Carol said.

"It doesn't matter," he said. "You'd never get through the foliage to find the border."

"No neighbors close enough to keep tabs on you."

He bounced up and down the planks. "Seems solid. It won't fall down right away."

"Cedar box planters. Black wrought iron furniture."

She was dreaming ahead.

"Could even sink a spa into the deck, over in that corner," Wayne said, helping her.

She smiled at him.

"How much does the book say?" Wayne asked.

"They're asking eighty thousand."

"Jesus, Cece! I've often wondered why I never bought a house. Now I know."

"I love it," she said.

He scanned her face for sarcasm, but found none.

"This is what they call a fixer-upper?"

"I already see the final result," she told him, tapping her head with her forefinger.

"I haven't lifted a hammer in twenty-five years. I don't even own a screwdriver."

"But you're willing to try, aren't you?"

"Ah, hell. As long as I'm out of work anyway."

Wayne leaned forward and kissed her on the lips, then turned to find Mrs. Angst waiting in the doorway.

"We're going to offer seventy," he said.

She frowned, but took them back to the realty where they each wrote out a five-hundred-dollar check for the earnest money.

Mrs. Angst got on the phone to the listing realtor, and twenty minutes later, they had settled at $74,000. They signed the papers and went looking for a home loan.

Willard Travis drove his big-tired Bronco up from El Cajon to Malibu early on Saturday morning and spent some time with Taylor.

"Hey, Country! Come on in."

"How you doing, Lew? I hope you've got the coffee on."

They sat at the table in the kitchen and drank the hot and extra strong coffee that Taylor liked. Travis slumped in the kitchen chair and stared across the living room, out the wall of windows toward the Pacific.

"What happened with Pilo?" Travis asked.

Travis suspected the story was slanted strongly toward Lew's point of view.

"But I see in the *Times* that they found out Andy and Pilo were in 'Nam together."

"So?"

"So I think they're going to be making a bunch of phone calls. I get up in the morning, I expect to see some cop standing on my doorstep."

"Big fucking deal, Country. We got the alibis set. No way anyone's going to put anything together."

"You hope."

"I know. Damn it, almost every operation we did was outside CONUS. The New Mexico and California cops don't even know about those."

"But they might know about the in-country stuff. Like Koenig."

"I doubt it all to hell, Country. Most of it's on the other coast. There's just no way for them to put it together."

"But there's Andy."

Lew shrugged his big shoulders.

"Why Andy, Lew?" Travis pressed. "I mean, hell, we all got the message, but that was shitty, turning him and Andrea over to Sweet."

"He backed out right in the middle of a mission. Right in the goddamned middle. He lost the guts for it, and that hurts us all. We're a team, Country."

"You were expecting it, though."

"What do you mean?" the ex-lieutenant asked.

"That reporter in Santa Fe wrote something about the harnesses you used to hang them in the barn. You had them with you when you went."

"Sweet put them together," Taylor admitted. "Just in case."

"You should have let him go."

"He was going to go right to the cops."

"Shit! Not Andy."

"That's what he said."

"No goddamned way, Lew. Andy was as straight as they come. You should have just let him out of it. We all got to retire someday."

"You looking to retire?"

"I'm thinking about it, Lew. We got off the road, somewhere, and hell, all of us have a chunk put away. We don't need it anymore."

Travis studied Taylor's face. It had not changed much over the years. The little white scar on his forehead captured the eye, made it difficult to look him in the eyes. It was a bayonet scar. Tight night, that. Living here on the beach gave him a good tan. He looked like some easygoing movie star, played the rugged, lovable, but ruthless hero. War stories. The nose was bent to the left from a gun butt.

Travis waited.

"Yeah, well, I've been talking to Boxer about that," Lew said.

"About disbanding?"

"Yeah. Maybe, after we finish the current contract, we'll cut it off."

Travis felt better right away. "Good deal. It's time."

"You think the others feel the same way?"

"I haven't talked to them about it, but yeah, I think they'd go for it. Except Sweet."

Taylor pursed his lips. "Yeah, well, I'll handle Sweet."

"You always have, Lew."

"Even if we decide to shut it down, Country, we still have a security problem."

Travis sipped at his coffee, then said, "Boxer."

"Him and a couple others in Washington."

"You know who his contacts are?"

"Oh, hell yes. I've been tapping their phones for years. Got a lot of it on tape."

Travis wondered if Taylor had been recording the telephone calls to El Cajon. Probably. "It's okay, Lew. We don't need a contract to eliminate security problems."

* * *

On Monday, Delwin Blessing was sworn into office by a county judge at eight in the morning. He had elected not to wear the ugly khaki uniform of his predecessors, but he had purchased a white Stetson that went well with a light blue, western-cut suit. He wore high-heeled cowboy boots covered in a bluish-gray rattlesnake skin; they diminished the height problem. He was fidgety, trying to remember what he had been told on the phone at 6 A.M.

There were not many dignitaries at the ceremony. The paper did not even send a photographer over. The small auditorium was packed with deputies, feeling duty bound, no doubt.

As soon as the short ceremony was over, he went down the hall to his new office with Rodriguez, the patrol captain, the acting captain of the investigative division, and the lieutenant who ran operations.

The office was barren of decoration and had been that way since Sheriff Dawes had died. Rivera and Rodriguez had not had the time to make it their own. Blessing waved his subordinates to seats and pressed the intercom button.

''Yes, Sheriff?''

''What's your name?''

''Marilyn Baker.''

''Well, Marilyn, would you send someone over to my law office to pick up four cardboard boxes?'' Blessing was damned well going to put his imprint on this office.

''Yes, sir.''

He released the button and said to the operations lieutenant, ''Ron, I'd like to have you prepare a condensed report for me on budget, current status of expenditures, vehicle condition, and the like. We'll meet at one o'clock.''

The lieutenant nodded and left.

''Patrol, Jim. I'd like to see a map of routine patrol routes and a report on manpower, shift strength, and the like. Let's do that around two." Blessing thought he was sounding very professional.

The patrol captain left.

"Investigation. Main thing, I guess, is the Razor Murders and the Rivera murders. One of my campaign promises, of course, and I want to get it out of the way, first thing."

Luisa's eyebrows went up. She was in her uniform, Stetson and cotton drill skirt. The skirt and the polished gunbelt with all of the accessories on it were not very becoming, Blessing thought. Not for a woman.

The acting investigation head said, "Luisa's been handling that one, Sheriff."

Rodriguez said, "I'll go get the paperwork."

They both left, and Blessing sat in his high-backed desk chair. He was becoming calmer, and the chair felt good. The whole thing felt good. He had never commanded his own troops before.

Rodriguez came back with an armload of paper and sat in the straight chair across the desk from him. Elected Sheriff Delwin Blessing liked having that symbol of authority—the desk—between them.

"Where we at?"

Rodriguez passed over a report form. "Let's start here. Angela Schwartz positively identified the bodies of Andrea and George Andropoulous. Andrea was her daughter."

"All right."

"Here's the pictures from the murder scene."

Blessing took the stack of photos from her and started through them. He dropped them after the fourth picture, nearly gagging. His good feeling evaporated, and he thought he might throw up. That was what the voice on the phone could do to him. His sphincter muscle tightened and he was suddenly very conscious of his genitals.

"Next," he mumbled.

"This is my report on the ring. That's what made the connection with San Luis Obispo."

Blessing read it quickly. "Right."

"Here's a report of what Steve Wayne learned in California."

Blessing read through it. Not much more than what was in the papers. Then, he read it again, feeling better. Hell, they were not getting anywhere.

"Okay, good. What else?"

"Here, this one's from Hayman. The scalpel found in Pyle's aircraft can be matched in three characteristics—depth, width, and cross-section—to the wounds on the bodies."

Cough, cough. "Uh, sorry, Luisa. Been fighting a little cold."

Rodriguez did not care. She smiled grimly and went on. "This is the inventory of what the Orange County Sheriff found in Pyle's house and automobile."

Blessing went over it carefully. There it was, just as the voice had promised him this morning.

Another sheet of paper. A list of . . . fifty-six names. "What's this?"

"That's the roster of the men assigned to Andropoulous's and Pyle's platoon in Vietnam over a fourteen-month period. We think that at least two of them may be involved in the murders at the barn. And of Carlos and his family."

"Jesus. You've got it pinned down that close?"

"We think so," Rodriguez said, nodding.

"And the next step?"

"We've got to get hold of the first name, the guy named Taylor who was the platoon leader."

"What for?"

"We want the names of the men in that platoon who were assigned to an assassination squad in Vietnam. It was controlled by the CIA."

Blessing's stomach rumbled. He felt positively ill, but managed to say, "That it?"

"That's it."

"Okay. This is good."

Rodriguez sat quietly, waiting.

"Now, Luisa, we have a problem."

"What's that, Sheriff?"

"It's going to be difficult for the two of us, you having sat in this chair for a while. And honestly, I just don't see demoting somebody to put you in a captain's slot. Be best for both of us, I believe, if I could have your resignation. Say, by noon."

Janet Willow hated sharing press conferences with others. She preferred being on her own, chasing the slim leads of a story, and she ignored the other reporters and camera people milling around. Christ, this one had even brought out the TV and radio people from Albuquerque.

On top of which, Blessing had scheduled the damned thing for four o'clock. The broadcast media would have it for their evening news slots, but her story, if she decided to write anything at all, would not hit the stands until morning. Blessing had a lot to learn about taking care of the newspaper side of the media. He was the kind, though, who would play to the immediacy of TV and radio.

Blessing entered the small auditorium briskly. He was wearing a bright white shirt that would play hell with the cameras. Photographers began searching for filters. Spinning on his heel at the podium, he smiled widely and said, "Thank you for coming, ladies and gentlemen. I have a statement, and then I'm open for questions."

The press waited, silent and less than expectant. Blessing spread open a sheet of paper and laid it on the podium. "This afternoon, at three o'clock, I officially closed the Andropoulous and Rivera murder cases."

Cameras whirred and pencils scratched.

Shit. Willow started writing, furious. She had broken the damned case, damnit, and now, he had not even given her an exclusive on the finish.

Blessing smiled benignly. He had solved his first case, first day on the job.

"The weapon utilized in the Andropoulous murders was discovered in the airplane of Howard Jason Pyle, recently killed during a confrontation with an FBI agent in California. Subsequently, Orange County law enforcement officers searched a Mercedes automobile owned by Howard Pyle and recovered a nine-millimeter Walther automatic pistol and silencer. Ballistics comparisons made by telex this morning confirm the weapon as the one used in the Rivera murders.

"This office is confident that Howard Jason Pyle was responsible for the deaths of six people. With no suspect to bring to trial, we have closed the cases."

He smiled again, a little uneasily this time, Willow thought, and asked, "Questions?"

Tower of Babel.

"Easy, easy. One at a time."

A hand shot up in the back of the room. "What weapon was used in the Andropoulous murders?"

Janet saw Delwin Blessing's right hand tremble. He saw it, too, and pulled it down behind the podium. "A surgeon's scalpel."

"Jesus!" The hand went down. No follow-up question desired.

She waited while a dozen other questions were ably fielded by Blessing. He was growing comfortable.

Then she raised her own hand.

"Yes, Janet?"

"What was the motive?"

He paled, but held the insipid smile. "Motive? What do you mean?"

"Why did Pyle kill them?"

"The Riveras? To protect himself from discovery."

"Oh. Then you're saying that Carlos Rivera had pretty well solved the case?"

"Uh. Well, I don't know. I didn't talk to Rivera." The new sheriff licked his lips.

"Why did Pyle kill the Andropoulous couple?"

Blessing cleared his throat. "Uh, we're assuming a drug connection."

"With what?"

"With what?"

"Drug connection with what?"

"You know, a connection. Drug dealing."

"Drugs have been discovered, then?"

The smile finally died. "No."

"What about the other man?"

"The other man?"

"The one who helped Pyle slice up George and Andrea Andropoulous. The evidence at the scene indicated the presence of two persons."

Blessing's face was pale and tinged with green now, and Willow felt good about that. "Uh, we believe there was only one man."

"Who's 'we'?"

"We?"

"Does the medical examiner and your forensics unit agree with your assessment?"

"Well, we're still working on that part of it."

"So the case is not really closed?"

"Just part of it."

FIFTEEN

ONE TIME OR another the members of the unit had saved one another's asses, and that drew them together, made them look out for each other.

It could not go on forever though, Andy thought. Here he was, coming up on forty years old, and still walking point for C.B. and Lew and Sweet in a stinking African jungle while they hunted down some primitive who thought he was going to take over the world. Or providing cover for Country and Pilo while they stalked some guy in a business suit. In an American city. It still didn't seem right.

Andrea was tired of his little hunting jaunts with the boys, kept pushing him for details, and he told her about prairie dogs and rabbits, mountain lions and bears, deer. Pheasant and duck, in season.

"You guys still think you're twenty years old," she said. "Get out the guns, chase up a mountain, drink beer. Keep playing soldier, any way you can. Andy, those days are long gone. Grow up."

He was still fit, and prided himself on his physique. The jumping and the bicycling helped keep him that way. But if he leaned in close to the mirror, he saw the crow's feet growing at the corners of his eyes. A couple of deepening lines across the forehead. The bright blue eyes seemed to have sunk a little deeper in his face. He got tired a little sooner. He'd rather come home to the house Andrea had put together so well than stop off for a couple quick ones with the clients.

For that matter, they were all in good shape, though Sweet and C.B. had put on some weight. Sweet's disposition hadn't changed that much. It had never been good, but he was so quick and capable and loyal, like a good spaniel, that everybody overlooked it. In a bind, you wanted Sweet with you. His blond hair was thinner and he wore it longer to compensate. Still thought it was the sixties. He wore dirty jeans and T-shirts—bulging over his beginning paunch—all the time, and Lew was forced to take him shopping sometimes, to outfit him for commercial travel to some place in the world. He'd lost a couple back teeth, and when he grinned, the gap showed. Didn't like dentists. Sweet's eyes were still dark and hard below a protruding brow, and he liked to stare people down. Usually scared them. He had liked to do that in 'Nam, too, only he wasn't very fierce back then, in the beginning, and he'd gotten himself beat up a few times by bigger guys in the company. Until he learned to fight dirty.

C.B. was bald, or almost. He'd had a real head full of thick hair in '70, but it'd slowly drifted away. His balding head was shiny, and the brownish-gray fringe around the sides was getting long, hanging over his ears. He had a small, round face, deepening crevices running from the corners of his mouth down his chin. He wore big round, rimless glasses, and every time Andy saw him, it seemed as if the lenses were thicker. They made his hazel eyes seem larger, almost fanatic. He *was* an introverted fanatic, though, still studying religions, and pretty well decided that he was going to have to found his own. There were faults in all the other religions the world had to offer or so he said. C.B. was the shortest in the bunch, barely topping five-five, but his shoulders and the arms were muscular, almost black from the sun, and the tattoos on his forearms had faded to blurred reds

and blues and greens that were almost indecipherable.
Mother. God and Country.

Brooklyn was a clotheshorse. Must have a closet thirty
feet long and thirty feet deep. He was always immaculate,
even in designer jeans and sport shirts. Big on Topsiders.
Five-ten, with the Italian ancestry showing through in
unblemished skin, brown eyes, and swept-back hair that
was so black it was blue. He was suave, and he had
some slick moves. Brooklyn was on his third wife and
probably looking for a newer, younger one. He'd been
a Californian for twenty years, but he still talked about
the streets back home. Brooklyn's reflexes were a hell
of a lot slower than they used to be, but he didn't admit
it to anyone, and probably not to himself.

Pilo was something of a braggart. Liked to talk up the
women, and his exploits in the big war were his favorite
subject. Lately, as the real war got farther away from
him, Pilo was filling his stories with the details of some
of their contracts. He was still big at six feet and 220
pounds, but the outer layers were softer, the good muscle
submerged in new fat. He was still a hotshot pilot, taking
some chances that weren't required, but he was damned
good, a better pilot than Lew. Wore the big aviator sunglasses day and night. When he took them off, there
were large, pale circles around his eyes. Like Sweet, Pilo
liked his toys—the cars and airplanes and stereos and
boats. His condo in Newport drew in the women. Though
he'd always professed a distaste for marriage, he'd been
talking about it the last couple of months. Even Pilo
wanted to settle down.

Country'd gotten married a few years before. Of them
all, Andy supposed that Country had changed the least.
He still had a nasal Tennessee twang, still the easy, slow
movements. Never in a hurry. Studied the situation carefully before making a move. His hair was thin and corn
colored. He was long and lean, six three, skinny as a
pole. Country'd never fit the commando image, but he
knew the drill, and he was the best marksman among

them. Brave and loyal. He and Doreen should move back to Tennessee and raise Boy Scouts.

Lew was a Boy Scout, once. He told them he'd made Eagle Scout, but he didn't have any memorabilia hanging around, like he did the Army medals. Lew was only five ten, but he stood ramrod straight, like they'd taught him at Benning, and he appeared taller. He commanded rooms. People listened to him. Gave him their money. Over the years, Lew had done all right, channeling his bucks into the right investments. He didn't blow it, for sure, not even on women. Andy had double-dated with him in the early years, but Lew would only spring for a Big Mac and a movie. Forget he lived in Malibu, or there were ten thousand night clubs around, it was always Big Mac and a movie. Cheap bastard. He was in good shape, though, wore silk shirts open to the navel to show off the hard pecs and the tan. Steady, washed blue eyes, and Ivy League haircuts. His nose had been broken by a pistol butt in a hand-to-hand tussle, and the slight asymmetry gave him a kind of mysterious air.

Lew had it made, could hop out anytime, but he liked command. Liked all of the arranging, logistics, strategy, and tactics. Liked the guys saying, "Yessir." He should have stayed in the Army.

Lew thrived on it, but someday, Andy thought, Lew was going to have to admit the war was over and the troops were exhausted. Not that he wouldn't back up Lew on anything. Andy wouldn't be where he was if it wasn't for Lew.

But damn, he was tired.

He thought that Brooklyn and Country might be as tired as he was, but he didn't know if he should approach them before he talked to Lew.

On Wednesday, Frederick Taylor drove his Eldorado over to the Los Angeles Library and read the account in the Tuesday edition of the Santa Fe *New Mexican*. Blessing must have really garbled his first press conference, the way the Willow bitch wrote it up. Still, the wires and major media had only reported the closing of the cases. It looked as if the national hoopla would die away, though he would have to keep an eye on Blessing.

That pleased Taylor for the most part; he was always gratified when his plans were executed exactly as he had envisioned them. He enjoyed strategic and tactical planning. He liked being a commander, with the authority and responsibility it entailed.

Fred Taylor had grown up in Lubbock, Texas, the son of a carpenter who was too easygoing and too nice a guy to get much respect from Fred. In high school and in college at El Paso, both of which were academic struggles, Taylor had not been able to make the football teams or even the baseball teams. He joined all kinds of clubs— debate, thespian, aviation—but the memberships would never elect him an officer. Only in ROTC was his natural leadership recognized.

At Fort Benning and at Fort Bragg, he had been orally reprimanded by commanders for fraternizing too closely with enlisted men, but damn, those guys would work for him. He had proven that in Vietnam, and he had been recognized for it. He had proven that to Boxer and his buddies over and over since 'Nam.

Taylor was grateful for Boxer, though he would never have told the man as much. Without Boxer, the STRAC Unit would not have a purpose, a reason for existence. And Taylor respected Boxer, as well as Rebel and Cottonmouth. They were men of conviction, not afraid to take action, determined that debacles like Vietnam would not happen again. Their vision made the STRAC Unit possible, and Taylor lived for the unit.

Yes, Taylor liked his command.

He had the power of command, and he had the power of fear. He was not afraid of using either.

He also thought he might give Blessing a call and pat him on the head. It was amazing the way compliments could instill the same kind of fear that threats did.

* * *

Ellington met Sanders and Mayhew at their familiar pub in Arlington, and they all ordered martinis. It was an out-of-the-way place, not on the schedule of watering holes for government or military people. There were self-contained booths with high walls, black Naugahyde bench seats, and small, forty-watt light fixtures suspended over the tables. Coming inside the lounge from bright daylight resulted in temporary blindness.

Under the watered-down light of the fixture, Harold Mayhew had a self-satisfied smirk on his broad face. Ellington had seen it any number of times before, when they were working the Saigon SOG together.

Mayhew had already been with the CIA at the time, working on rural pacification projects, and he had been as dedicated as Ellington, who was then with the State Department's intelligence division. They worked out of the Saigon Embassy, frequently on the same projects. Ellington remembered long late night conversations over drinks and dinner in the balmy breeze on the Caravelle's roof terrace, bitching about the corruption rampant in the revolving door Vietnamese governments—and using it where necessary, of course.

They had perfected the art of manipulation in Saigon. Washington made the decisions, and they were told to implement them, however they could. They dipped frequently into the bag of covert funds and used the money to buy history, to influence elections, to eliminate opposition to White House desires. What was good for America had to be good for Vietnam.

It had not changed much since.

Mayhew had been the first to meet Douglas Sanders, when the colonel stopped by the Embassy and offered the use of a squad of gung ho paratroopers. Sanders had been seeking brownie points toward promotion, of course, but when Ellington met him, he had liked the brusque battalion commander.

The three of them had a lot in common, then and now.

Twenty years had served only to cement their friendships, and Ellington appreciated that. Not many men could claim, and rely on, the loyalties exchanged between Harold Mayhew, Doug Sanders, and Mark Ellington. Sometimes, Alice Mayhew and Sandra Ellington showed a little jealousy over the relationship of the three men. Sanders was widowed and no longer had to explain himself to a spouse.

Mayhew's good humor had resulted in a new suit, Ellington thought. A nice lightweight summer wool in silver gray. He was also wearing a new pale gray shirt and dark maroon tie, both in silk. The Deputy Director for Operations at the Central Intelligence Agency could be downright natty sometimes, despite the heft of his physique.

"Well?" Mayhew asked them.

"I guess Taylor pulled it off, Hal," General Sanders said. He was wearing a suit and tie, too, but had a few hundred dollars less invested in it than Mayhew had in his. He always looked less comfortable in civilian attire than he did in a full dress uniform.

Ellington had been surprised by the recent news, too. "I don't know how he reached that new sheriff, but that man's in his pocket. The *New Mexican* may keep some pressure on him, but I think maybe this Blessing will be able to stonewall it."

Mayhew grinned, "Hell, Mark, I think it's a nice wrap-up. Now maybe we can get on with the rest of it?"

"Yeah, I suppose so," Ellington agreed.

"No contingency plan called for?" Mayhew pushed.

Ellington looked at Sanders. "Doug?"

"No. I guess not."

"I'll suspend my request then, too," Ellington said.

The waitress arrived with a new round of martinis, placed them precisely in front of each man, then waltzed away.

Sanders played with his olive. "Is anyone seeing any effect yet?"

Mayhew swallowed his own olive. "It may take a couple years before we see the total effect, Doug, but yes, I'm seeing a couple benefits. The requests for information are down, the voices sound a hell of a lot less strident. That helps my shop a lot."

"Well, we're still in a defensive posture," the general said.

Mayhew reached out to pat the general's shoulder with a beefy hand. "Yes, but that's a result of some global issues that we can't control. Keep the faith, babe. It'll come around again."

Luisa Rodriguez and Jerry Hayman said they had driven down to Albuquerque to get drunk and had decided to stop and get Wayne to help them.

Wayne thought they might be well on the way. "You sure you need help?"

"Ah, hell yes!" Luisa said.

"Well, don't stand in the hall. Come on in."

"Cece here?" Hayman asked.

"No."

"Booze here?" Rodriguez asked. Her hair was in slight disarray, and the small amount of lipstick she wore was smudged. Wayne decided he would not ask about her husband.

"Scotch and brandy and a few cans of beer."

"That's all righ'. We can mix 'em together." Rodriguez led the way into the living room, and the medical examiner followed, hitching up his pants.

Wayne got three cans of beer out of the refrigerator, popped them, and they all sat in the living room.

"I got fired awhile," Rodriguez announced.

"But now she's an investigatin' captain," Jerry enlightened. "That's what we're celebratin'."

"What happened?"

"Delwin, ol' asshole, can' me. Had to. Wouldn't resign. Nice 'n' neat like he wanted it." Rodriguez took a long swig from her can of Budweiser. "Wants ever-

'thin' nice 'n' neat 'n' all package' up. Screw' up his head plans, did.''

"You want to try, Jerry?"

"Keith went over and raised unholy hell. Discriminatin' 'gainst Mexican-Americans and women and that stuff. Comin' on top of that hellaciously bad press conference, Delwin went right to the wall. Ca-pit-u-la-ted. And Luisa's a cap-i-tan.''

Wayne decided the night was a loss and went across the hall to borrow two six-packs of beer from his neighbor. By the time Cece got home from her meeting, everyone was happy.

Cece took one look around the living room, then opened up the Hide-a-Bed in the spare bedroom for Luisa, tossed blankets and a pillow on the sofa for Hayman, and collected everyone's car keys.

Wayne awakened at 5:30 in the morning, slipped out of bed without waking Cece, and carried clothing into the bathroom. He showered and shaved, put on jeans and a plaid sport shirt, and went into the living room.

He peeked into the spare room. Luisa Rodriguez was twisted up in a comforter and pillow. Hayman was sprawled out on the couch in the living room in rumpled shirt and suit pants, but that was normal. His clothes always looked as if he had slept in them.

Passing through to the kitchen, Wayne started a pot of coffee, then checked the refrigerator for bacon and eggs. No bacon, but he found a dozen link sausages. He laid them on the counter and took a loaf of frozen bread from the freezer and tucked it into the microwave oven.

By the time he could pour himself a cup of coffee, Cece appeared. Fully dressed.

"I hate having company around," he told her.

She grinned and kissed him. "Oh, I don't know. You're making breakfast for a change."

"Practice. I may end up a short-order cook."

He kissed her again and wrapped his arms around her waist.

"Do I get to grade your efforts? At the stove?"

He could not reply before a hoarse voice spoke, "Oh, sorry."

They parted, and Cece smiled. "Come in, Jerry. You look awful."

Hayman straightened his shoulders and came to his full height, his trousers dangerously low on his hips. "Thanks. I feel like a daisy."

"Is that a medical euphemism for an aspirin?"

"It wasn't until just now. I'll love you as much as Anne will let me."

Hayman flopped in a kitchen chair, and Cece got him the bottle of aspirin and a glass of water while Wayne poured three mugs of coffee. He poured a fourth when the deputy appeared. Her skirt, blouse, and jacket were wrinkled.

Rodriguez had her head tilted back, and she looked through half-squinted eyes at the bottle of aspirin Hayman was tipping over his palm.

"That's a nice bottle you have." She took a chair at the table. "Pardon me for ignoring you, Cece. You're looking *muy esplendido*."

"*Gracias, señorita benevolo*."

"*No es benevolo. Yo es desconcerto*." Rodriguez pointed the fingers of both hands at herself. "See what Hayman's done to me?"

"I've never had a more willing follower." Hayman passed the aspirin to Rodriguez.

"Jim's going to kill me," she said. "Providing I don't die first."

"Jim?" Cece asked.

"My husband. He doesn't think I'm supposed to act like a cop out of a Joseph Wambaugh story."

Wayne retrieved the bread from the microwave and plugged in the electric skillet. Cece sat down with her back to Wayne and held her coffee mug in both hands. "I'm sorry you lost the election, Luisa."

"I wouldn't be, except that Blessing's such an as—a sniveling wimp. I got my job back, but I'm not going to like it much, working for him."

Wayne started the toast and broke eggs into a pan to scramble them.

Hayman sat up straight in his chair and leaned toward Cece. "You doing all right? After your experience in California?"

She had not talked very much about it to Wayne, and he was alarmed that Hayman brought it up.

"I'll survive," she said.

"Most of us do that," Hayman said, "but it's not much good if you're hiding some feelings. I've seen some bad things come out when cops have to kill."

Cece did not respond right away, but then said, "I can't say that it doesn't bother me, but Steve did what he was trained to do. I'm glad he did."

"Good," Hayman said. "I don't want you two to get all fouled up."

"Steve didn't tell you?"

"Tell me what? He's a closemouthed SOB."

"That we're buying a house in Santa Fe?"

"Oh, oh," Rodriguez said, holding her head. "This an excuse for another celebration?"

"Damned right," Cece said. "We close on the house in three weeks, and we've set June fourth for another closing."

They accepted congratulations on their coming wedding while Wayne served his breakfast. He got As from Rodriguez and Hayman, but only a B-minus from Cece, who said that people with hangovers had numb palates.

Cece left right after breakfast, on her way to Santa Fe to look for commercial space for the new McComb-Davis branch office. Wayne poured the last of the coffee and started another pot.

"What made you decide on Santa Fe?" Hayman asked. "To live in, I mean."

"Carlos once made a comment about the size of Albuquerque and the direction it was taking. He was right." Wayne still got a lump in his throat when he thought about Rivera.

"The more time that passes since the funerals," Hayman said, "the easier you'd think it would be to say, 'well, we got one of them,' and let it slide. I can't though."

"After I moved back here from LA, Carlos was my mentor, taught me almost everything I know," Rodriguez said.

"You lived in LA?"

"I spent a year with the Los Angeles sheriff's department, thinking I needed to be far from home. I was wrong. I needed the ties. And I needed Carlos, too."

Wayne could not forget the dead sheriff either. He vividly remembered his conversations with Carlos, Myra, and Jeff Rivera. He wished he had gotten to know Tracy.

His two guests looked better after breakfast and showers and calls to their spouses. Wayne opened all the drapes, and they sat in the living room with another round of coffee.

"Is Blessing going to get away with closing the case?" he asked.

"No," Hayman said, "Keith won't let him. But good ol' Del is playing PR and politics and budget. He seems convinced that he's got the primary perpetrator, and he's told Keith that his resources only go so far. He can't afford to devote dollars and manpower to it the way Carlos and Luisa did."

"I'm supposed to work on it in my spare time," Rodriguez said. "It's no longer a priority."

"So what have you done in your spare time?"

"I've got a friend named Hogan, one I met in the LA Sheriff's Office, who's now a sergeant with the LAPD.

He's on Robbery, but what the hell? I gave him a call, he verified that one Frederick Taylor lives out in Malibu, and he's going to run him down and interview him.''

"All right. Good."

"Maybe we'll learn something that gives us a new path to follow. Who knows?"

"In this whole damned thing," Wayne said, "I've been stymied by the lack of motive. Or the lack of knowing what the motive may have been."

"For Carlos, the motive was silencing him," Hayman said. "For Andy, information. Or, if I'm wrong, maybe just a message sent to person or persons unknown."

"Okay, sure," Wayne said. "I'm talking about a reason for Andy and Andrea to be in Santa Fe."

"Boyles didn't come up with anything," Rodriguez said. "There wasn't much out of the ordinary going on when Andy was in town."

"Give me an example, Luisa."

She squeezed her eyes shut. "I wish my head would quit throbbing. Let's see. There was an art auction. There are lots of auctions during the year, but this was a big one, brought in some heavy spenders."

"Art, huh? The Andropoulous house was cleaned out when I got there. I don't know whether or not they collected Southwestern art. We might be able to check it out with the man who runs United Moving. What else?"

"On that weekend? Carload of teenagers ended up in the hospital. One of them died. A Greyhound bus broke down and stranded a college choir in town overnight. DeLamma died in a motel room."

"DeLamma? Senator DeLamma from Connecticut?" Wayne knew who the Appropriations chairman had been. He was always a topic of conversation when the Bureau's budget was up for review, and the man's committee usually cut any substantive increases from the budget request.

"Yeah. He and a couple of his aides were touring Los

Alamos. He had a heart attack sometime Sunday morning.''

That did not go anywhere.

"You two are the cops," Hayman said. "Where are we going from here?"

"One, we have to wait for Hogan's interview with Taylor in LA," Rodriguez said.

"I just thought of another angle," Wayne said. "After Jerry said he felt like a daisy this morning, I remembered Dazi.''

"Who's Daisy?" Hayman wanted to know.

"Spelled with a Z and an I. You'd love her. She told me she was supposed to have married Howard Pyle, but I think she'd be happy with anyone who could afford endless giant pizzas.''

"You're losing me," Hayman said.

Wayne grinned at him. "Pyle apparently told Dazi several times that he still performed special assignments for the government.''

"What agency?" Rodriguez asked.

"She didn't know. And it sounded to me like Pyle loved to tell stories, true or not. I didn't put much credence in it. But since Peter Conrad, the company commander, mentioned the secret missions of the Special Operations Group, I've started to wonder about it.''

"What would the CIA, or one of those three-letter gangs, want with Pyle and his friends?" Rodriguez asked.

"Sabotage? Espionage? Executions? Assassinations?" Hayman suggested.

"It happens," Wayne said. "Could be anything."

"And then something went wrong within the group," Rodriguez said. "Andy may have spilled the beans, or threatened to spill them.''

"Something happened, and the thing got out of hand."

Hayman sat back on the sofa, his face slightly puzzled. "I guess I can grasp that theory, even if it isn't much of one. What do we do with it?''

"It'd be nice to know from Taylor, or someone, just who all was in the group," the deputy said.

"Andy and Pyle probably were," Wayne said. "Again, I didn't think about it at the time, but Andy seemed to be doing pretty well. He had a nice house and three businesses. Nothing ostentatious, but more than I would expect him to earn out of a skydiving club. I'd like to know more about Andy's and Pyle's life-styles. Did they spend more than they appeared to make? From Dazi, I'd guess Pyle did. Fancy car and an airplane, big-buck condo in Newport, and as she said, 'jillions of dollars.' "

"Hogan might be able to check on some of that for me," Rodriguez said.

"Don't push your friendship too hard."

"I won't."

"Then, if this theory is to hold up," Hayman said, "there's got to be a connection to the federal government somewhere. That might be tough to find."

"Maybe not," Wayne told him. "I know Washington fairly well."

"We keep talking about what we're going to do," Rodriguez said. "I'm damned if I've figured out what it is, from what we've been discussing."

"That's because you're still engrossed with last night," Wayne said. "Luisa, you're going back to Santa Fe to keep up your contact with your friend in LA. Jerry can go back and help Keith keep the pot boiling. Get Janet involved if you can, Jerry. A little pressure on Blessing might spook someone."

"What are you going to do?" Hayman asked.

"I'm going to Washington. I've got a lead to chase."

SIXTEEN

BROOKLYN AND ANDY did the first in-country job.

It wasn't as if the guy was any kind of national hero, or even had a name anybody would remember, but still Andy felt a little . . . traitorous. He wasn't in this thing to sell out his country, and Brooklyn had to remind him that it was the other way around, the other guy was the traitor.

Brooklyn didn't really give a shit. The in-country stuff was bigger bucks, covered the risk and inflation. He'd finally caught on to what Lew was doing. The ex–first lieutenant was salting away some hefty dollars in Swiss and Cayman accounts, plus living the good life in Malibu. Sure, Lew was smart—had told them all to set up their own accounts, but Brooklyn thought maybe Lew was smarter than he should have been. He'd begun to suspect that Lew, who had the only contact with the contractor, had maybe skimmed more than a little off the top, more than the formula called for.

Brooklyn didn't know why Lew should have so much more than he himself did, even though Brooklyn's expenses were heavier than Lew's. He was laying off four grand a month in alimony for Linda and Aura Lee, for one thing, and that made it easier to fall behind. He wasn't going to confront Lew, he was going to emulate him. Pare back on the luxuries, dump everything he could into the offshore accounts. He had a couple hundred thousand set aside now, but he figured he could get it up to a million in three or four years. And as soon as he did, it was good-bye Linda, good-bye Aura Lee, good-bye Monica. He and Julianne were going to take the first flight they could to Brazil. Dump the house and the shop and everything in Riverside and live off the interest.

He had asked Lew for more assignments. And they got this quick one.

Andy drove the rental after they landed at Dulles, found his way into Georgetown, and parked down the street from the guy's apartment building. It was hot as hell, humidity up in the nineties, and Andy kept the Ford idling and the air-conditioning running.

"This is shit," Andy said, for maybe the tenth time.

"Hey, man. It's all right. Pigs come in different nationalities. This one just happens to have been born in the U.S. and A."

"I don't give a—"

"There he is, Andy. Punch it!"

A Chevy Caprice was trying to back into a tight parking space almost in front of the apartment building.

Andy pulled the shift lever into Drive and slapped the accelerator down.

The Ford's tires squeaked as the car shot into the street. He raced down the block and slammed on the brakes, sliding right in beside the Chevy.

It wasn't quite parked.

Brooklyn shoved the door open and stuck the .357 Colt Python in the guy's face.

Guy gagged. Throat working, face jerking.

Brooklyn got out, yanked the Chevy's door open, and pulled the guy out of the car. He was little, a puny bastard in a three-piece suit, and Brooklyn manhandled him with ease.

Still in gear, the vacated Chevy banged into a Toyota parked behind it.

"What the hell're you people doing!" the guy yelled as Brooklyn shoved him into the backseat.

Andy stepped on the gas.

Brooklyn had the syringe ready, sat on the guy's stomach, and pumped him full of stimulants.

In the rearview mirror, which he angled down, Andy saw the fear in the guy's face. His eyes were almost white, a pair of beacons in the darkness of the backseat.

Holding the speed steady now, avoiding attention. Left and right turns, working through the neighborhood. Turn right at the Old Stone House. West on Jefferson Place.

Swinging onto the Key Bridge.

"Coming up, Brooklyn."

"Gotcha. Hey, man! You alert? Yeah, just look at those eyes."

"What're you doin' to me! God, I've got money! You want money?"

"Nah. Lew wants you awake enough to think about it all the way down."

"Down. Think about what, damn it!"

"How you've fucked over your own country."

Water of the river black, way down there. Short gleam of the moon on its surface.

In the middle of the bridge, nearly deserted except for a car entering from the Virginia side, Andy jabbed the brakes.

The Ford slid to a stop.

Brooklyn popped out of the backseat, dragging the guy with him.

"No! God, no!"

Brooklyn took two steps, and heaved the guy over the railing.

He had maybe two seconds to think about it.

Then Brooklyn was back in the car, and Andy got it up to speed.

By one o'clock in the morning, they were on a 737 headed for Chicago.

Andy never could figure out how a little wimpy guy
like that, with a name like Moscowicz, could have so
much influence in Washington. It didn't seem right.

Tuth ought to cut his hair if he was never going to
wash it, Taylor thought. It hung uncombed to his jaw,
and it was all right when he was around his boat, skin
diving and the like, but on the red-eye flight early this
morning, Taylor had seen the stewardess actually wrinkle
her nose when she had to lean over him.

Tuth always took an aisle seat so the stewardesses had
to lean over him. And Taylor was always half afraid that
the man was going to reach up and grab the goodies
someday.

He was something of an embarrassment to travel with,
in an unpressed suit and no tie and running shoes, but
he was so efficient on the other end. He did not make
mistakes.

His face was hard with awkward angles, lightly pock-
marked, and downright ugly, and his eyes were like chips
of cold flint, way back under his brow. Except for a few
VC and a couple SOG cowboys, Taylor had never known
anyone whose sole motivation seemed to revolve around
killing. Tuth did not like the subtle variations of assassination; he derived more pleasure from open confrontation with the target, especially with his scalpel. He had
been totally pissed at having to give up the scalpel he
had carried since Vietnam, but he was getting used to
the new one, he said.

Unlike the VC and the cowboys, Taylor thought that
Tuth's killing emotions were more sensual, touching
nerves that tingled in the right lobes of his brain. He
liked the danger, the risk of getting caught, the chance
to slip away. When he was jumping, he was always the
last one to jerk the ripcord.

Taylor knew the others did not like to pull assignments
with Sweet though they had never said as much. Taylor
did not mind because he could remain objective about

it; it was just a job. Well, not just a job. He knew his
own motivation was as patriotic as it was monetary. The
jobs promoted American goals, as well as padding the
offshore accounts. In the nationalistic respect, Taylor and
the STRAC Unit were just like Boxer and his friends,
Rebel and Cottonmouth. The by-product, the untaxed
cash, was frosting to Taylor, maybe a little less so to the
others. Pyle had always been strapped for cash.

"There they are," Tuth said, "and here we go."

"He was supposed to be alone."

" 'S all right, Lew. We'll take 'em both." The sallow,
pocked face grinned.

Sweet backed away from the living room window,
letting the drape fall back into place. It was a small town
house condominium in Arlington Heights, cramped between similar structures, and though it was raining hard,
Taylor knew they could not allow much noise.

"Who's he with?" Taylor asked.

"Daughter, looks like. Gonna be a nice night."

In the light from the hallway, which had been left on,
Taylor could see the slim smile on Tuth's face, the sheen
of perspiration on his upper lip.

The key clicked and grated in the lock, and the two
of them entered the foyer. Taylor and Tuth stood to
either side of the wide living room entrance, Taylor
holding his new Beretta nine millimeter with the silencer
by his side. The girl came through first, flicking on the
light, and Taylor grabbed her from behind, clamping
a hand over her mouth. Martin Dubose, columnist, came
in next, wiping raindrops from his glasses with a
handkerchief.

Tuth slapped a meaty palm over his mouth and ran
the scalpel deep into his liver. The man struggled and
trembled for nearly a minute before his wild eyes glazed.
Tuth dropped him on the floor.

The girl was screaming silently against Taylor's hand,
struggling, hysterical, out of her mind. Tuth unzipped

his fly, pulled his dong out, and grinned. "Try it. You'll like it."

Taylor shoved his automatic into the girl's armpit and squeezed the trigger. In ten seconds, she was just a body losing heat, hanging heavy over his arm. He dropped it to the floor.

"Ah, goddamn, Lew!"

"We don't have time, Sweet."

"Ah, goddamn!"

Delwin Blessing sat in his soft leather chair, smiled across his desk at Boyles, and wondered how anyone that fat could look so good in the custom tailored suits. He wished he had run against Boyles for DA, and maybe he would, next election. Blessing had already begun to consider his future, after locking up this election so handily. He picked at some lint on his cuff.

Boyles checked out the wall of pictures behind the desk. Blessing had some good pictures, the one of himself and the governor centered behind him. His favorite, though, was the one that had been taken when he was shaking hands with Barry Goldwater.

"All I can say, Delwin, is that it would be in your best interest to put Captain Rodriquez on the Andropoulous and Rivera cases full-time."

Blessing was adamant. He had to be, after the reassuring call from the voice on the phone. "They're way down on the totem pole, Keith. It wouldn't serve any purpose to go on searching for a killer who we already know is dead."

"There were two in the barn."

"I'm less confident in Rivera's evidence than you are. Who's to say the one set of footprints wasn't made earlier, Keith?"

"The department's forensics team. And you know Pyle's shoes didn't match any of the prints."

"I was a smart killer, I'd dump the shoes, too."

"You're demonstrating a lot of avoidance behavior,

Del. If I didn't know you better, I'd think you were on someone's payroll."

"Hey! Goddamn it, Keith! You can't accuse me of anything like that." Blessing was getting angry.

"I'm talking appearances, not necessarily reality."

"Well, it's bullshit."

"You going to do what I ask?"

"You have an investigator in your office. Use him. Call Tom Edgerton over at the FBI."

"The FBI won't touch it. It's your job, damn it."

"I haven't got the money, and I'm damned sure not going to ask the commissioners for a budget increase. We'll handle it the way we're doing it now."

Boyles reached inside his jacket, pulled out an envelope, and tossed it on the desk.

"What's that?"

"Your invitation to the hearing I'm asking Judge Oliver to conduct. Bring lots of evidence to support your position."

Wayne arrived at National Airport just before 10 A.M. Washington time. It was raining torrents, which eased the heat problem, but the humidity was still high.

He rented a car and made a phone call, then drove into the district on the Mount Vernon Memorial Highway, taking the Arlington Bridge across the Potomac. The heavy rain slowed the traffic down and jammed it almost as badly as during the rush hours. Large bow waves rose off the cars in the lane next to him and sluiced over his windshield.

He went directly to the State Department on 23rd Street. Somebody had been courteous enough to leave a visitor's slot for him in the parking lot, but he had to make a long run in the rain to reach a door, and he was soaked by the time he reached it. His separation from the Bureau seemed to have also terminated his common sense; he had forgotten to bring a raincoat with him when he traveled.

Danny Endover, an assistant secretary on the Pacific Desk and a man he had known for ten years, helped get him access to the archives. Having to ask the favor made him realize how much he missed his credentials. It only took ten minutes to find the directories he wanted, and a clerk photocopied the rosters for the Saigon embassy staffs, 1969 to 1973, for him. Wayne paid for the copies and went back up to the main floor.

It was still raining, and he had an hour to kill before his appointment with Hunsecker, so he found a chair upholstered in gold tweed in the lobby and read through the directories. His suit smelled like a damp sheep, and he wanted a cup of coffee, but decided to skip it.

The directories were long and, he suspected, not entirely accurate. Like the military units in Vietnam, the embassy had people floating in and out, plus they had a lot of people whose names they would not have committed to a roster. He found some names he had not expected to find—people he knew in various agencies that had never mentioned Vietnam time, and a few names that he had been certain he would discover. A lot of people never mentioned Vietnam, for one reason or another.

Looking out through the rain-streaked window, he could see the Lincoln Memorial on the Mall. The weather had discouraged the tourists this morning, and the monument looked very solitary, very white against a gray day. The grass was deeply green, and the magnolia and cherry trees were densely leafed out. It used to be that this part of the capital had always reaffirmed Wayne's mission in life. Lincoln and Jefferson and Washington gave him a thumbs-up. But wander off the Mall at night, and the flip side of the founding fathers' ideals was too apparent. Murder for a buck or two or a couple rocks in a plastic bag. The city was breeding kids whose idols drove hundred-thousand-dollar cars and wore neon suits and pimp-style shirts. Not one of them cared whether or not they were ever memorialized in white marble and granite. It sickened him, and Wayne was surprised to discover himself somewhat relieved that he no longer had to fight those unwinnable battles.

He met Bert Hunsecker for a lunch of sauerbraten and good German ale at noon, in a fake *biergarten* way out on New Hampshire Avenue. Hunsecker was in his fifties, pale from office work, but still as slim and fair haired as he had been in their first assignment together twelve years before. Hunsecker was now an assistant director in the logistics branch of the Bureau.

He tapped the briefcase under the table with his toe. "It's my ass if you get caught with this stuff, Steve."

"I won't get caught, Bert. I'm going to be very low profile, and that's why I need it. It'll be on your back porch around midnight."

"Better be."

"Take a look at these would you?" Wayne handed him the photocopied rosters.

Hunsecker leafed through the sheets and frowned, then went back to the first one. "They're old lists. State Department people."

"Saigon, sixty-nine through seventy-three. You recognize any of those names as current Langley people?"

Laying the pages flat on the table, Hunsecker took a pen from his inside jacket pocket and began to check off names.

"Looks like it's going to be most of them, but that doesn't surprise me or you, huh?"

The three of them took a table in La Fonda's dining room and ordered salads for lunch, though Hayman also ordered a burrito, an enchilada, and a chili relleno. The man could put away ten pounds of food at a sitting and never fill out his hips enough to keep his pants from sliding down. It was too bad he could not transfer some of that stomach to his hips.

The *Dos Equis* arrived first, and Boyles poured Willow's into a glass for her. No matter what else she thought about the DA, he was always courteous.

At the moment, Janet Willow was nervous. Hayman and Boyles had never taken her to lunch before. They were always friendly enough, though in a remote way. Teased her a little, maybe, about her devotion to her job.

They had never ganged up on her before.

She would have to watch her step, especially with these two.

"There is no longer a free lunch in this country. What do you guys want?"

Hayman asked, "Did you ever think that you might suffer from a trifling bit of tunnel vision, Janet?"

"Me?" She did not answer the question, nor did she quite understand it.

Boyles said, "Contrary to what you might believe, the two of us think you're a pretty good reporter. Sometimes, however, it does appear that you're so focused on whatever is in front of you, that you don't look back."

"Hey . . ."

Boyles held up a hand. "Did you know that, until Monday, when Blessing took over, you had a shadow you didn't know about?"

"A what?"

"Did you know that Luisa was so concerned about your safety, what with the way you were pushing the murder cases, that she detailed an around-the-clock body-guard for you?"

Oh, shit. Her stomach churned, but she said, "I don't need a damned bodyguard."

"Even Carlos needed a bodyguard," Boyles said, "but he didn't have one."

Hayman dipped a tortilla chip in the hot sauce. He smiled. "Into every life a little debt must fall. Time to pay the banker, Janet."

She stood up, angry. "Listen, I'm a reporter. I only report. See you."

Boyles used his courtroom baritone, "Sit down."

Reflexively, she sat.

The attorney told her, "Face it, Janet. You're just like anyone else in this old world. I like attention, Jerry likes it, you like it. You hit the attention jackpot, nationally, and it's difficult to give that up."

She started to get up again. The bastard.

"Sit."

She sat.

Hayman took over. "We don't want you to give it up."

"Where in the hell are you guys going with this?"

"Your last articles on the Razor Murders fell to page ten," the ME said. "Nothing new in them."

"You want to write them, Jerry? With what Blessing's giving me? He's doing nothing."

"We can't disagree with that," Hayman said.

Boyles grinned at her. "Janet, we happen to think you're on the right track. You don't like Blessing's handling of the cases. That was apparent in Tuesday's paper. You don't even like Blessing. You just don't know where to go from here."

She did not know how to shake her head, from side to side or up and down.

"Since, deep down, we like you, we're going to help you out, Janet," Hayman said.

"We're going to give you everything we've got," Boyles added.

Willow squeaked, "On the record? Attribution?"

"On the record, and you can quote us, but with one qualification. You can start writing it, but you can't go to print until Jerry or I give you the word. We may want to suggest the order in which you publish the stuff we'll give you. In the next couple of days, we may even have more information for you."

"Nobody dictates what, or how, I write."

"Think of what Luisa did for you," Hayman said.

"But I guess I'm open to suggestions."

"Maybe we could start with the shoes," Boyles said.

"What shoes?"

"We can't find the shoes. That's a real problem. More of a problem for Del, though."

She dug in her purse for her notebook.

Hayman asked, "Where in hell is my burrito?"

It was a big wiring panel since there were 120 apartments in the building located in Arlington Heights. Conveniently, however, each wire pair was marked, and Wayne had no difficulty locating Apartment 1012's line and clipping in the leads to the recorder.

Entry to the building had been simple. He had buzzed nine apartments simultaneously, and someone had released the door. There would be a few calls to security, and some people would be screaming about the damned kids screwing around.

His VISA card got him into the locked basement.

Wayne had spent the afternoon trying to narrow the list of names Hunsecker had checked off. In the US Embassy in Saigon in those years, CIA people were behind most of the desks. Telephoned inquiries around town, trying to find out who had retired or quit, had narrowed the list, but he still had over seventy names to trace.

This particular ploy was a long shot, but it was founded on the one name he had of someone in power in Vietnam who had known of the activities of Frederick Taylor and his squad. Wayne was accustomed to playing the cop's game of patience, waiting and watching, but tonight he was going to be impatient. He was no longer a cop.

At eight o'clock, he retrieved the lineman's telephone from Hunsecker's briefcase, selected an apartment at random, and connected into the line. No one was using that phone at the time, and turning his handset over, he used the line to dial the number.

It rang twice. "Hello?"

"General Douglas Sanders?"

"Yes."

"My name is Steve Wayne, special agent with the FBI."

Instant hostility in the tone. "What do you want?"

"I have a couple questions, if you don't mind, sir?"

"Over the phone?"

"It saves my traveling to Washington."

"Well, what is it?"

"You were a colonel with the 101st Airborne in Vietnam?"

"I spent six tours in Vietnam."

"This would be in seventy, going into seventy-one?"

"Yes, I was a full colonel then."

"And you were aware of several clandestine parachute drops made by a commando team headed by a Lieutenant Fred Taylor?"

Hesitation, then, "That's classified material."

"I have a Top Secret rating."

"I don't give a shit what you've got. It's still classified, and I wouldn't talk about it on the telephone, anyway."

"Are you aware that Taylor's group still conducts clandestine activities for government agencies?"

"Look, Wayne. I don't know what the hell this is all about, but you'd better send your information to one of your bosses. I'll talk to them."

"Well, thank you, sir. I believe you've answered my questions." Wayne disconnected.

He started the recorder and put on the headphones. Sanders was already dialing.

"Hello?"

"Rebel, Cottonmouth."

"Not a good time."

"Wayne called me."

"What?"

"Said the FBI had questions for me."

"That's bullshit. Wayne resigned."

"Well, goddamn it, why didn't you tell us?"

"It didn't come up."

"He knows things."

"What things?"

"Not on the damned phone."

"Let me look into this, and I'll get back to you."

Dial tone.

Wayne was almost surprised, but not quite. He knew the voice.

Sanders dialed another number.

The phone on the other end rang seven times before it was answered. "Hello?"

"Boxer, Cottonmouth."

"Wrong phone, goddamnit!" Wayne did not know this voice.

"No choice. Go to Boardwalk." Sanders hung up.

Damn it! Wayne had hoped, if his suspicions about Sanders were correct—that he had some knowledge, the man would have spent some time on the phone. But they were using code names, and they had preplanned meeting points. That was just as ominous as it was encouraging. He was certain that he was on the right track.

Unplugging his equipment, he crammed it into the briefcase, slammed the telephone box shut, and headed for the stairs. He wanted to be in his car before Sanders made the elevator descent from the tenth floor.

He had to wait twenty minutes in his rented Dodge opposite the exit ramp from Sanders's sublevel parking garage before the man appeared. He had to assume he had the right man since he had never seen Sanders before. He was not in uniform, and he was driving a new silver Buick Regal. There was an urgency in the way he drove that settled the identification for Wayne. Waiting until the Buick was a block away, Wayne pulled away from the curb and followed.

It was not far. Out of Arlington Heights, Sanders took Highway 244 east to the Henry G. Shirley Memorial Highway, skirted the Pentagon, and crossed to DC on the Arland D. Williams Memorial Bridge. He then turned south on Ohio Drive, headed for the point of East Potomac Park. The rain had stopped, but there were few cars in the park at that time of night, and Wayne stayed well back. He switched off his headlights and followed the reflections of lampposts on the wet street.

Before reaching the point and turning onto West Basin Drive, Sanders parked in an alcove off the street, shut off his lights, and stepped out of the Buick. He disappeared into the trees. Wayne found a parking spot, killed the engine, and got out. He stayed away from the street, walking in the shadows of the leafy trees. Nearing the Buick, he heard the crackle of underbrush off to his right and followed the sound down toward the shore of the Potomac.

The lights from Washington National Airport across the river shone dimly on the trees, but Wayne could make out a shadow moving sixty yards ahead of him, working south along the bank of the river. He waited while it merged into a clump of shrubbery, then scurried ahead, staying within the dark protection of the trees. The ground was wet, and his loafers were soggy within minutes.

It was a good meeting place. Wayne could not get closer than forty yards because of some open terrain. He settled to his knees behind a juniper to wait it out and felt moisture from the soaked ground penetrate the knees of his slacks.

He listened for another car. The man Sanders was meeting should arrive soon.

Sanders was no longer his objective; rather, he wanted to pick up the trail of the man the general was meeting.

A few cars drove by on Ohio, their tires squishing against the damp asphalt, but none of them stopped. On the river, the running lights of two large ships passed, and one freighter close to shore left a babble of voices drifting over the water. Aircraft departed and arrived at National on a steady schedule. They followed the river route, keeping the noise of their passage away from the neighborhoods.

He waited.

Just before ten o'clock, the darkened hulk of a large powerboat, its engine idling, drifted down the river from the north, scraped into the bank, and was hidden by the shrubbery where Sanders waited. The engine died.

Damn. Wayne had not expected an approach from the water.

He continued to wait, shifting on his knees, trying to decide if he should attempt to get closer, but saw no way he could do it undetected.

Fifteen minutes.

He could not hear a thing. He should have gotten a nightsight and a boom microphone from Hunsecker.

Twenty minutes.

Something was not right.

No more waiting.

He rose to a crouch and half ran toward the cluster of shrubs, stopping every few yards to listen. He was thirty feet away before he thought that Sanders might have boarded the boat and drifted on downriver without power. He stopped again, but heard nothing.

Slowly then, he crept toward the bushes. They were tall—junipers and forsythia. The leaves were still dripping, though the rain had stopped an hour ago. He pushed his way into them, until he saw the gleam of lights on the surface of the water.

He did not see the silhouette of the boat.

When he had alerted no one, he withdrew the .38 short-barreled Police Chief's Special he was not supposed to be carrying, parted prickly boughs, and stepped into a small clearing.

At first, he thought there was no one there. He moved

closer to the water, stepping into mud, to get a look downriver. His toe bumped something soft, and he bent down.

Dauntless Doug Sanders.

The top of Sanders's head was gone, and he had the long cylinder of a silencer stuck in his mouth. His right hand was still locked around the grip of the Colt Python.

Wayne had not run into many suicides involving guns where the despondent person had wanted to be quiet about it.

SEVENTEEN

"SHIT, LEW. THAT'S inside the country again. I don't like it."

"We're too good to let it worry us, Country. The hell of it is, the country's being threatened by its own citizens. That's what this whole contract is about, protecting America from America. And it's *mucho* bucks, too."

So Country, C.B., and Pilo flew into Atlanta's William B. Hartsfield Airport, rented a car, and drove up to Savannah. They got there at three in the afternoon, carrying duffel bags and lots of fishing tackle, and rented a forty-foot power cruiser named *Champagne Flight*.

Pilo, who was a boater like Sweet, took the helm. C.B. took his shirt off, pulled down the brim of his LA Dodgers baseball cap, and opened the cooler full of beer. He popped three and passed them around.

Country thought it was pretty decent, being back in the South again. He hadn't realized he'd missed it so much.

"How many sailboats are out here, you think?" C.B. asked.

"Hell of a bunch of them," Pilo said, taking a long gulp from his can.

"Still, can't be that many."

There were. Country counted thirty-two before the sun went down, most of them headed in for a port. They continued to cruise up-coast for part of the night, then turned around and started south.

It was 11:30 the next day before Country, who was taking his turn with the binoculars, saw a single-masted, gaff-rigged sloop.

"Ten o'clock, Pilo. Maybe a couple miles away."

Pilo turned onto the new heading, and they approached the sailboat at about twenty-five miles per hour. Or knots, Pilo said. Whatever.

Country scanned the sea, looking for witnesses. A cruiser, three freighters, a couple more sailboats. All of them were miles away.

This one looked to be the right size, about thirty-six feet long.

Pilo came up to its rear, then swung into it.

"Name's right," C.B. said, looking at the gold letters on the stern.

As they came alongside, Pilo dragging the throttles back, the three men in the cockpit looked up at them. All of them were dressed like they ought to be playing tennis. They waved tentatively.

Back in the stern well, C.B. lit the gas-soaked rags in the vodka bottles with a butane lighter. He started tossing them.

"Hey, you son-of-a-bitchin' bastard—"

The first bottle broke on top of the cabin.

No real explosion. Blue-tinged flames spread rapidly over the cabin top and dribbled down the sides. Four more bottles.

Pilo backed away, and the three of them sat up on the flying bridge, drinking beer, and watching the three guys try to fight the fires. It was a losing proposition. The flames leaped upward, licking at the sails, which were supposed to be fire-retardant, but which burned anyway, if a little slowly.

The cabin got going pretty good, and the guys used up all of their fire extinguishers. When the heat got to be too much, the three men went into the water. They

tried to swim toward their attackers' boat but Pilo kept
steering it away from them. They looked pathetic out
there, bobbing around, yelling for help. Pilo kept reading
them their rights with a loud-hailer, but they didn't want
to listen.

Finally, when the gasoline-fed smoke rose high enough
and it looked like the cruiser off to the south might be
coming to help out, Country and C.B. popped the guys
with .22s, pulled them alongside with boat hooks, unfastened their life vests, and wrapped a few links of
logging chain around their necks.

The *Whisper* burned and sank eleven miles out of
Savannah, Georgia. The crew of three, who normally
lived in Washington, DC, was lost at sea.

By the time Taylor and Tuth parted company at LA
International, it was close to five o'clock. Taylor decided
to drive on to Van Nuys and check the receipts for the
day before going home. He still did not fully trust his
manager, though the man had been working for him for
nearly nine months.

He took the San Diego Freeway north. The Los Angeles Basin was filled with gray haze, but when he
reached the Valley, the sun was more visible. It was
warm and would have been a good day for skydiving.

He left the freeway at Roscoe Boulevard, driving west.
A lot of private pilots were taking advantage of the day,
and the airport was busy. When he saw the gray Chevy
sedan parked in front of Ride the Wind, his shop in the
general aviation section, his gut tightened up on him a
little. It was a typical cop car.

He was prepared for something official when he
opened the door, but not for the big black detective. The
guy was close to seven feet tall and probably tipped 275
pounds. A broad face with a mustache that looked a foot
wide. Dark brown, penetrating eyes. Wearing a tailored
blue suit. There would not be anything off the rack for
this guy. He held a folder that looked like a matchbook

in his big hand and, when he had Taylor's attention, flipped it open to the badge.

"Detective Sergeant Patrick Hogan, Los Angeles Police Department. You Frederick Taylor?"

Jesus Christ. True black Irish.

"Yes. How can I help you, Sergeant?"

"Gotta few questions for you."

"Sure thing. Let's go back to my office. Tim, you can go ahead and lock up," he said to the manager.

Taylor led the way to his office in the back of the showroom. It was small, and the detective dominated the room as well as the straight chair he straddled backwards. He rested his left hand, holding the notebook, on the back of the chair. He held what looked like a toothpick in his right hand, ready to make notes.

"What's this all about, Sergeant?"

"You know George Andropoulous?"

"Andy? Yeah, pretty well. We were in 'Nam together. I was sorry as hell to hear about what happened."

"You sorry 'bout Howard Pyle, too?"

"I can't figure out what Howie was up to."

"But you knew him?"

"Sure. Hey, the three of us jumped together. We were all in the same business."

"Get together often, did you?"

"When we first got out of the service, we did. But you know how it is? After a while, everybody kind of drifted apart. Andy got married, Howie moved down south somewhere. Maybe we'd see each other once a year."

"You didn't know what Andropoulous or Pyle were involved in?"

"Outside of the jump schools, you mean? No. Neither of them ever said a word about other interests. Our connection was skydiving."

Taylor's stomach relaxed. This was going pretty well.

"You remember where you were on the weekend of April eighth?"

"What? The eighth? Damn, I'd have to think some about that."

Those hard eyes poked at him. "Think 'bout it. Your manager—Tim, right?—says you own a Cessna 337."

"A Skymaster. That's right."

"That it out on the tarmac?"

"Yes."

"Log in it says you flew down to El Cajon that particular weekend."

Isn't he supposed to have a search warrant to go poking around in my airplane?

Taylor almost complained about it, but changed his mind when he took another look at those eyes. Hogan's whole demeanor suggested he wasn't receptive to questions or complaints.

"Oh, yeah. It must have slipped my mind. I spent the weekend with a friend. We played some poker." That was the alibi they had set up with Travis.

"Your friend's gotta name?"

"Will Travis."

Damn. He hadn't planned on giving that up so readily. Let the SOB work for it.

"What's he do?"

"Will has a skydiving school in El Cajon."

"He 'nother one of these guys you were in Vietnam with?"

"That's right."

"But you haven't drifted 'way from him?"

Hogan had big eyes, too, like saucers, and they didn't waver. Taylor felt less comfortable.

"We don't get together all that often," he said. "There's too much going on."

"Like what?"

"Like what?"

"What's going on?"

"Oh. Business. Social things."

"You married?"

What? "No, I'm not."

"Travis married?"

What the hell? "Yes. Her name is Doreen."

"Night of April twenty-first?"

Jesus. "What about it?"

"You recall where you were?" the sergeant asked.

This son of a bitch had already been through the plane's log. Taylor was having trouble remembering what the hell he had written in it.

"Let me think a minute. That was a Friday, right? I think that's the day I went over to Riverside."

"You meet some old buddy?"

"Yeah. Guy named Keck. Danny Keck."

The detective could sure write fast. He was flipping pages quickly in the small notebook, the pencil flying.

"Lemme guess. He's in the skydiving business, too?"

"As a matter of fact, he is."

"You got a lot of friends in the business, don't you, Mr. Taylor?"

"What do you expect? You have a lot of friends who are cops?"

Hogan grinned, his white teeth filling up the space below his mustache.

Taylor was beginning to think that all of the tight alibis were sounding thin.

"All of these guys—Andropoulous, Pyle, Keck, and Travis—were jumpers with you in Vietnam?"

"That's true."

"Anybody else you pal 'round with," Hogan asked, watching him closely.

Taylor felt a tic in his left cheek. "Nobody special that I can think of."

"You've gotta busy social life, you said."

"I have a lot of acquaintances." Taylor named a couple of neighbors and some people who'd been through his skydiving school.

"How 'bout more jumpers from 'Nam?"

"There were almost two hundred paratroopers in my company. I don't keep track of them."

"How 'bout the ones worked with you when you did the special jobs for the CIA?"

Goddamn. Somebody's getting awfully close.

"Boy, Sergeant, you'd have to check with Washington on that. As far as I know, it's still classified. I did what they told me to do then, and I've never been released from my oath to not talk about it." That sounded good to Taylor.

Not necessarily good to Hogan. He frowned, and it was like having the weather change abruptly.

The cop suddenly stood up, towering high over him. His head blotted out the overhead light.

"Appreciate it, Mr. Taylor. We'll be in touch. Count on it, in fact."

And then he was gone, and Taylor sat there wondering why his alibis sounded so lame now. And he had given up Country's and Brooklyn's names in the telling. And he didn't want to be in touch with this cop again, ever.

Patrick Hogan couldn't get in the telephone booth at the corner of the 7-Eleven without going through a lot of contortions. He stood outside it with the phone in his hand and watched a Jag convertible with a blonde in it waiting at the light on Sherman Way. She was wearing a mink jacket of some kind, long blonde hair spilled all over the collar. The sun's shining, the top's down, and she's wearing mink. Showing off the Jag and the jacket and the blonde. It was still close to eighty degrees out, and Hogan had trouble understanding some people.

"Pat? This is Luisa."

"Hey, babe. Talked to your man."

"And?" she asked.

"Got himself an alibi for both weekends."

"Damn it!" Rodriguez said. "I had some hopes there."

"But he's lying though his goddamned teeth," Hogan said. "I know it, and I think he knows I know it."

He turned away from the street as the Jag got the green.

His department car was parked at the side of the 7-Eleven store. Thirty feet away from him, two kids were hanging around by the store's front doorway, sitting on the hood of a fifteen-year-old Buick Riviera low rider.

Just hanging out.

"Are you sure?" she asked.

"Yeah. Don't know how we'll prove it, but the guy strikes me as thinking he's smarter than he is. There'll be some gaps somewhere. He gave me a couple names, his alibis, and says they're jumpers, too."

"All right! Let me get my list."

While he waited, he noted that there was another kid behind the wheel of the Riviera.

"Okay, got it."

"Danny Keck and Will Travis."

"Dah-dah-dah . . . dah, yeah, Pat, right here. Daniel Keck and Willard Travis."

"That help?"

"Immensely, *mi amigo*. You know what they do?"

"Run jump schools in Riverside and El Cajon."

"No lie?"

"No lie."

A middle-aged couple came out of the store, got into a Nova, and drove away.

"That adds up to a very big coincidence, *compadre*," Rodriguez told him. "Now we've got skydiving schools at San Luis Obispo, Orange County, Van Nuys, Riverside, and El Cajon."

"These guys only run into each other a couple times a year, Taylor tells me."

"Sure they do."

"I didn't believe him, either. Want me to drop in on Keck and Travis?"

"It's out of your way."

"Tomorrow's my day off."

The two kids slid off the Buick and sauntered into the store.

"Belinda will want you home."

"Belinda will understand 'bout it. I'll check out some of the other small airports in the area, too, see if we've got more skydiving outfits 'round."

"I'll owe you a big one, Pat."

"You wasn't married, I'd collect, Lu. Gotta go."

Hogan slapped the phone on its hook and wandered down toward the wide open doors of the 7-Eleven.

The kid behind the wheel of the Riviera looked up at him, stared a second, made a hasty decision, and tapped the horn.

Hogan stopped at the edge of the building's door, flipped his jacket skirt wide, and pulled the Colt .45 automatic. He carried the big pistol because anything else looked too puny in his hand.

The Buick's engine was running. He heard the change in the engine's tone as the kid pulled the shift lever into reverse.

He shot out the right front tire.

Another kid came running out of the store.

Hogan took one step with his left foot, then swung his right leg hard.

The kid saw it coming, tried to skid to a stop, bent over.

Hogan's steel-toed oxford caught the kid in the stomach, raised him three feet off the ground.

Ooomph.

It was going to take him two weeks to get his breath back.

"Po-lice, kid. Halt."

The third kid had gone to ground. Sprawled on the linoleum behind a comic book rack, holding a paper bag in one hand and a peashooter .22 in the other.

Looking up at the big bore of the .45.

"I trade you one of mine for one of yours," Hogan said.

Laid the .22 carefully on the floor.

"You guys have gone and spoiled my whole damned evening, you know that?" Hogan scolded.

* * *

It was nine o'clock in Santa Fe when Wayne called Boyles from Washington. He longed for the dry heat of the New Mexico high plains. He even missed yesterday's rain. DC was bright and hot today, dripping humidity.

"This's Boyles."

"Morning, Keith. How did it go in court?"

"Judge Oliver is not one to be hurried, Steve. I filed a motion to force the sheriff to pursue the cases and submitted my evidence. But Oliver won't make a decision until next week."

"I'll keep my fingers crossed."

"Yes. Me, too." Boyles paused. "Then, there's something you won't be too happy about, I think. Jerry and I went ahead and involved Janet Willow a bit more than we'd planned." He gave Wayne the gist of their luncheon conversation.

"I don't know; maybe it's a good idea. You guys know her better than I do."

"We made the decision primarily to add to the pressure on Blessing."

Wayne did not like having Willow know the whole story—leftover attitude about the press, but said, "Keep an eye on her."

"We will. How's the cap city?"

"The magnolias are dripping, along with myself. And I also have another body. I lost my contact." He relayed the events of the night before.

"Good God! You report it?"

"No. It was a hell of an ethical decision for me, Keith, and I might yet have to find a lawyer and go talk to the Bureau."

"Well, don't do anything before you talk to me. With some work, I can probably figure out a legal justification."

"I won't do anything rash. I got out fast, and as it happens, the news this morning reported the discovery of the body. Tentatively, it's a suicide. Sanders's bio is being hyped on all the TV channels this morning. 'The ultimate soldier,' 'the passionate patriot,' and 'the national hero' are frequent phrases of endearment. He was an ardent Soviet hater.''

"You didn't believe his reputation?''

"Maybe his sincerity, but not his zeal, not after the code names I heard on the phone. There is a high-level conspiracy of some kind going on, Keith, and it's linked to Taylor's commandos.''

"What was Sanders's job at the Pentagon?''

"Weapons procurement. Liaison with Capitol Hill, I gather. He spent most of his time lobbying and testifying before congressional committees. His frequent keynote was the disaster about to occur as the result of an underfunded military.''

"Speaking of which, I am reminded of Senator Ralph DeLamma.''

"DeLamma? That's right. He and Sanders would have been on opposite sides of the fence. Shit, you don't suppose . . .''

"It's a motive.''

"Who did the autopsy?''

"One of Jerry's assistants, I believe.''

"And where's the body?''

"At rest in his home state, I should think. Somewhere in Connecticut.''

"What's the chance of exhumation?''

"I'd need something really solid to add to this theory we're suddenly pushing. And we'd have to convince the US Attorney General.''

"Let me think about it,'' Wayne told him, but his mind was already turning.

"What are you going to do?''

"I've got a list of CIA people in Saigon at the time. I'm trying to pare it down. Luisa get anything from LA yet?''

"Damned right, she did. A shaky alibi for Fred Taylor and a couple more names, Keck and Travis. Then her man, a Sergeant Hogan, called back later and gave her another name, Carl Battey, who is also on the list. All of these people run skydiving clubs in the LA area. Luisa called Peter Conrad back and read him names from that platoon roster. Conrad thinks that Keck, Travis, and Battey might mean something in relation to the commando squad. Then, to top that off, Taylor owns himself a twin-engine Cessna. Luisa's out at the airport now, checking on whether or not it might have been in Santa Fe.''

Wayne felt it all closing in. ''Mr. DA, it may not be long now.''

''Only problem I see, Steve, is we may have spooked them before we have anything concrete enough to bring out the handcuffs. And these guys don't spook well.''

''Cottonmouth *did not* commit suicide,'' Rebel declared with a lot of heat in his voice.

''He had help,'' Boxer agreed.

''Shit! Why?'' Rebel had truly liked his friend. In a world where allegiances seemed to shift almost daily, Doug Sanders had been an unflappable ally.

Ellington often felt as if he had given his all, his whole being, to law enforcement. It had nearly cost him a family through divorce several times. Now, the kids were grown and gone, and Sandra had learned to live with his schedule. For so many years, he had poured fifteen- and sixteen-hour days into doing what was right. He fully believed in upholding the laws passed by Congress, in pursuing Justice Department cases with all of the vigor he could manage.

And all through his career, there had been those shrill voices off on the sidelines, chastising him for performing his job, for obeying the law of the land and the word of his superiors. The damned peaceniks parading through San Francisco and marching on the White House. The anarchists blowing up bridges and power plants and threatening the social fabric. Not a one of them had the maturity to understand how the real world operated. Even elected senators and representatives had devoted their beings to undermining what was good about America and what she represented.

Ellington did not make snap decisions. When Mayhew and Sanders had approached him with the plan to still some of those shrill voices that were undermining the nation's strength, it had taken him over two months to juggle the pros and cons before agreeing to the contract with the STRAC Unit. He remembered them from Vietnam, but he had not known that Mayhew was still using them.

"He was panicky, and Wayne had named him as a principal in the operation. I don't know how. He received a phone call from Wayne, and Wayne knew about Taylor's activities in 'Nam. Wayne also suggested Taylor's bunch was currently working for a government agency."

"I know all that. Cottonmouth called me before he met you. I didn't panic, damn it! Why did you?"

"I wouldn't call it panic," Boxer said.

"You killed a damned fine man! Did you do it yourself? Are you proud of it?"

"I'm not proud of it at all, Rebel. I did what had to be done."

Ellington felt a flood of nausea. "It's all falling apart."

"Not yet. Keep the faith."

"That damned Wayne's on a crusade." He should have seen that quality in Wayne's personnel file.

"You lost a good man when Wayne quit you."

Rebel's grip tightened on the phone. He had not known that Wayne was so persistent. The man did not give up. He began to worry in earnest about Wayne deducing his own role in a cover-up. And he was less assured of his earlier convictions that there were no solid ties between himself and the STRAC Unit.

"Wayne's working alone?" Boxer asked.

"As far as I can tell, he must be. It's been quiet in Santa Fe. Have you talked to STRAC?"

"Not answering the phone."

"We've got to call it off," Rebel said.

"Agreed. No more hits for now. I'll keep calling the unit."

"And when you get through, give them one more assignment," Rebel said reluctantly.

"Yes."

"I hate this."

"Got to be done, Rebel."

He abhorred the necessity of terminating one of his own, or formerly one of his own. The man was good, he was loyal, and he was almost as patriotic as Rebel himself.

"It's crap."

"I understand," said Boxer, "but it's necessary."

Taylor was no dummy.

He could tell by Boxer's tone that the Washington people were becoming unhinged.

He hung up before Boxer was through and lifted the chrome ball on his new teak rack. He let it go and watched the successive collisions of the three balls. *Click-click, click-click.*

No changing the momentum. Just have to wait until the inertia wanes and the action ends of its own accord.

He got up and wandered over to the bar and made himself a Manhattan.

The balls were slowing, the tiny collisions closer together. *Cli-click, cli-click.*

All right.

He would call off the rest of the operation. Sure as hell, though, Boxer would stick him for the balance of the contract. They had only received a half mil up front.

He wondered how Wayne had gotten to Sanders. Boxer said that the guy had resigned from the FBI and started off on some revenge campaign. He was going to take them all out, one by one, starting with Sanders.

Taylor had not talked to the old warrior in ten years, though he knew from his wire taps that the general had been Cottonmouth. And Dauntless Doug's philosophy would certainly have supported the STRAC Unit's activities. Hell, the old boy probably siphoned off some DOD money to pay the unit's contracts, finagling it back somehow through the agency's secret funds.

There was more. If Wayne had made Sanders, Taylor wondered how long he had before Wayne reached Boxer, or maybe Rebel. Taylor did not know who Rebel was, but suspected from the taped conversations that he was located somewhere in the Justice Department. All Wayne had to do was start looking for Sanders's very old and very patriotic friends, and he would soon have both Boxer and Rebel.

He was pretty sure Wayne would soon have his own name, along with Keck's and Travis's, if he had any connection at all with the big bastard Hogan.

Boxer was partially right. Wayne had to go, if only because he had blown such a great life. But Taylor thought there were some other self-protective measures that might also be taken.

He and Tuth would do Wayne, he decided. C.B. and Brooklyn would do the other job. He would make the calls and issue the orders to his troops, and then he would pack. Thinking about how things had successively deteriorated, and thinking about that big black detective, he thought it might be a good idea to take along his passport, his emergency cash, and a few tape cassettes.

The inertia balls still clicked away, making only tiny movements now.

"Hello, love," Wayne said.

"Where are you?"

"Still in Washington."

"When are you coming home? You left me a very short note."

"Sorry, I couldn't reach you. And I hope it won't be much longer. I've got a list I'm working on, and it's down to about thirty names."

"What kind of names?"

"CIA names." He told Cece about his list culled from Saigon directories, and he told her about Dauntless Doug Sanders. He had decided to not withhold anything from her.

She sighed. "When does it end, Steve?"

"It won't be much longer, I think, hon. Talking to Keith this morning, I see things falling together."

"What are they involved in?"

"I think I've got that figured out. It's the key to the whole scheme." Wayne had spent most of the afternoon in the library reading back-date newspapers. "Boyles mentioned Ralph DeLamma this morning, and that, along with Sanders's zealous background, gave me another idea. Besides calling to say I love you, I need a favor."

"I love you. Now, favor away."

"I can't reach either Keith or Janet Willow, and Jerry is in the middle of handling some traffic fatality. I've got a list of names to get to Janet."

"I'll do it."

Wayne had reservations about increasing the depth of Cece's involvement, but passing data to Willow was minor in nature.

"All right. She can't yet name names for all of the suspects, but there are five names that she can headline, if she wants to do it."

He gave Cece the names and the circumstances and a suggestion for how Willow should handle it. Not that the reporter was open to suggestions.

"You got all that, Danny?"

"Got it, Lew."

"You and C.B. can handle it?"

"No sweat. We can be on a plane inside a couple hours."

"Good. Take a risk if you need to; this has to be quick. After the hit, you hustle your butts back from

Washington, and then the whole Unit's going to lie low for a long time.''

"Sounds good to me, Lew."

Taylor had decided not to tell him about the black detective named Hogan. No sense worrying him.

"Hey, Lew?"

"Yeah?"

"I got hit up by an LAPD cop this morning."

"Big black guy named Hogan?"

"Yeah, that's the one. How'd you know?"

"I've already talked to him. Hell, Brooklyn, it was expected. You stick to what we worked out?"

"Sure I did. He didn't believe me, though."

Brooklyn was no actor. That was one of the problems. Taylor had to do everything for them.

"You don't think so? He say he didn't believe you?"

"No, but that's how I read him. Lew, I think I'm going to take a trip, after Washington."

"With Monica?"

"No. She's got her own thing going. And I'm going to tell Country, too."

"I'll call Country," Taylor told him.

Country had been acting a bit iffy, lately. Taylor didn't want him backing out too early. Or hauling Doreen along with him.

"Yeah, okay. Just so he knows. Maybe that cop's headed down there now?"

"Maybe." Taylor didn't think he'd bother Country with any of the small shit. Country had a job to do, covering for all of them.

"You got the contact number?"

"Memorized, Lew."

"If you need to use it, we'll meet up down south. Have us a ball in Rio or somewhere."

"Real good idea, Lew."

Willow ordered a wine cooler, and Carol Curtis ordered a glass of chilled Chablis.

The Naugahyde of the booth was a cool relief after the heat of the day, and the semidarkness of the lounge eased the eyes. It was still light enough to see each other.

Willow was thinking that the lady's breasts were too big for her. She was simply dressed in a light blue summer cotton dress that hinted but did not reveal cleavage, and she looked quietly elegant. Wonderful complexion. Light makeup, no jewelry. Willow felt downright oafish in her jeans and oversized checked blouse.

"I'm glad we could meet," Curtis said. "Steve has mentioned you before."

"In the same breath as a voodoo curse?"

"Occasionally. Well, frequently."

She grinned. At least the woman did not beat around the bush. "On the phone, you said Wayne had some information for me?"

"To add to what you've already gotten from Keith Boyles and Jerry Hayman."

Must be legit, if she knew that. "And he wants me to do something with it, no doubt."

"In tomorrow's paper."

Willow sat up. No more waiting.

"I'm supposed to clear this story with Boyles." She hated the admission. "It's a promise I made, and I keep my promises."

"Talk to him, and I'm sure he'll give you the go-ahead."

"So what have you got?" She dug for her notebook.

Wayne's girlfriend worked from memory. "First, the motive that you asked Sheriff Blessing about. There is a conspiracy among several men placed high in the federal government. These men are strong nationalists, supporters of a highly visible military and law enforcement stance for the United States. All of them have experience in Vietnam and are resentful of politicians and others they believe have betrayed the country. They have given a great deal for their country, and they are dismayed at the thought of soft-pedaling military defense and justice.

They see a real threat from the liberal opposition.''

"Hey, you sound like you're on their side."

"That's just how Steve gave it to me. The kind of tone he expressed."

Willow peered across the table at her. She was serious. Damn, this could hit the wires. "Can I quote him?"

"He said yes, but only as a private citizen. He is no longer with the FBI."

"Damn. When did that happen?"

"That's another story, Janet."

"All right. I'll follow up, though. How about names?"

"I'll give one of them to you now, but you can't use it yet."

Shit.

"But you can hint at, at the least, three men and their agencies."

All right! "Go on."

"Major General Douglas Sanders. Weapons procurement at the Pentagon."

"He died this morning. Suicide."

"Perhaps."

"Holy Christ! More?"

"There will be a person in the Central Intelligence Agency. Steve's certain of that, but doesn't yet have the name."

"Why CIA?"

"Because Sanders and a CIA contact made use of Frederick Taylor and his men in Vietnam. Boyles told you about them?"

"Yes." Willow wrote hurriedly in the light of the red candle. "Who else?"

"He is certain there is someone in the higher echelons of the FBI. He knows the name, but has no substantial evidence yet. He's hoping this story will force some mistakes."

Willow looked up from her pad. "That's it?"

"There are also the victims." Curtis gave her five names.

"Damn, oh, damn. I haven't heard of most of these people."

"They're important."

"He's sure about this?"

"He's sure, though the deaths of these people will have to be reexamined."

"What's the relationship, Carol? What are the first three conspiring to do?"

"To support the President's requests in regard to national defense, intelligence, and Justice Department funding and policies."

She threw her pen on the table. "For Christ's sake! There's no story in that!"

"By killing off the opposition voices. You take a close look at the victims, Janet. Then you'll see."

Scrambling for her pen, Janet knocked her drink over, spreading a thin rose stain across her notes.

EIGHTEEN

ANDY, SWEET, AND Lew moved into Santa Fe on Sunday; they were tourists, situated in three rooms in three different motels. Sweet and Lew flew in in Lew's Cessna, and Andy took a commercial flight. He had insisted on bringing Andrea along as part of his tourist cover, and Lew was pissed about it.

He hadn't made up his mind to tell Lew yet, but he figured he needed Andrea's strength behind him if he decided to go ahead with it.

The target, like the one three weeks before, was a confused man who was very influential and very much a threat to the national security. He was touring US defense installations, looking for places to cut into the very heart of America's might. That's the way Lew explained it to them. Sweet took it for gospel, but Andy wasn't so sure anymore.

Meeting in Lew's room in the Sheraton, Lew told them, "The guy's name is DeLamma. Senator Ralph DeLamma. As soon as he completes his tour of the Los Alamos Laboratories, he's going to have a heart attack."

Lew was good at selecting diseases.

Sweet grinned, but looked disappointed. Heart attacks were pretty mild for him. It was going to be a dull trip.

"Shit," he said. "I'm goin' out and look for some pussy. What's Andrea doin' now, Andy?"

Andy gave him the finger.

As soon as Sweet closed the door behind him, Andy jumped into it. "It's over for me, Lew."

"Over?"

"I want out. I'm not even going to do this one, Lew. I mean, hell, I'm getting too old for it. I've got the bicycle shops in addition to the jump center—all of them paid off, money in the bank, a good life. It's time to quit."

He was pretty certain Country was ready to quit, too.

"You been talking to anyone else, Andy?"

"Maybe."

"Who?"

"They'll tell you if they want to."

"And if I, as your commander, say no?"

"Then I'll say fuck you."

That was Andy's first mistake.

"I'm glad I caught you," Boyles said over the telephone.

"I was just going out the door," Wayne told him.

"How're you coming?"

"Slow, but this stuff always is. Nothing exciting in the investigations game. I'm trying to make appointments with several of the people who were in Vietnam in '70. How come you're glad you caught me?"

"Luisa flew to LA last night. She must have a lot of friends, because she's set up surveillance teams on Taylor, Keck, Travis, and Battey. She called Jerry this morning and reported that three of them didn't show up to teach their classes today. They've got substitutes teaching ground schools today."

"Who didn't show?"

"Taylor, Keck, and Battey. In fact, Keck and Battey left their businesses yesterday morning. Travis appeared on cue at the El Cajon airport, but went home early. Luisa's gone out to his place to watch him, just in case Travis is supposed to alibi the others."

Wayne did not like the chill in his spine. If Taylor,

Keck, and Battey were not at their businesses, then they were somewhere he did not want them to be.

"Anything else?"

"Taylor's plane is missing. Took off at four A.M., according to the Van Nuys operations people, but he didn't file a flight plan."

"Not good, Keith. Why don't you or Jerry spend the day with Janet Willow?"

"Superb idea! You see the story?"

"It missed the morning papers here, but all of the national TV networks are carrying it. There are some very agitated agency heads being dogged by the media. You can tell Janet they pronounced her name correctly."

"She'll be glad to hear that."

A SOURCE CLOSE TO THE FEDERAL GOVERNMENT HAS REVEALED THAT THE MURDERS OF ACTING SHERIFF CARLOS RIVERA OF SANTE FE AND HIS FAMILY AND THE MURDERS OF ANDREA AND GEORGE ANDROPOULOUS MAY BE RELATED TO THE RECENT DEATHS OF FIVE OUTSPOKEN MILITARY BUDGET CRITICS. THE DEATHS MAY IN FACT HAVE BEEN ORDERED BY PERSONS LOCATED HIGH IN FEDERAL GOVERNMENT AGENCIES.

THE SOURCE SAID THAT CARLOS RIVERA MIGHT HAVE BEEN KILLED BECAUSE HE WAS CLOSE TO DETERMINING THE IDENTITY OF THE KILLERS OF THE ANDROPOULOUS COUPLE.

GEORGE ANDROPOULOUS WAS ONCE PART OF A CLANDESTINE COMMANDO TEAM IN VIETNAM, AND MAY HAVE BEEN SUBSEQUENTLY INVOLVED IN SPECIAL OPERATIONS FOR THE CENTRAL INTELLIGENCE AGENCY. LOS ANGELES POLICE DETECTIVES HAVE BEGUN TO QUESTION OTHER FORMER MEMBERS OF THE COMMANDO TEAM, ALL OF WHOM LIVE IN THE SOUTHERN CALIFORNIA AREA.

WHAT DID SENATOR RALPH DELAMMA, REPRESENTATIVE ELROY SAVAGE, WILBUR KINCAID,

Walter Koenig, and Martin Dubose have in common? DeLamma and Savage served on the Appropriations committees of their respective legislative bodies. Kincaid was a respected counsel for the Senate Appropriations Committee. Koenig, a well-known economist, often provided consultative services to the House Appropriations and Armed Services committees, and Dubose frequently lambasted the Pentagon on wasteful spending in his syndicated column.

All five men were vocal in their opposition to requests for military funding, including appropriations for intelligence agencies. All five men have been critical of the administration's foreign, military, and justice policies for years.

An apparent heart attack, an apparent drowning, an apparent stroke from a drug overdose, an apparent mugging, and an apparent burglary that went awry have been listed as the causes of death for the five critics, all of whom died between November 21 and May 8.

In Santa Fe, District Attorney Keith Boyles said that information will soon be provided to the US Attorney General, seeking to reopen the investigations into the deaths and the relationships between former members of a 101st Airborne Division unit and high-ranked persons in the CIA, the FBI, and the Army. The source concluded by saying there may be grounds for bringing charges of suppression of evidence, malfeasance in office, and obstruction of justice at both national and local levels.

Locally, Santa Fe County Sheriff Del-

WIN BLESSING HAS ATTEMPTED TO CLOSE THE CASES
OF . . .

He forced himself to finish the article, then folded the
paper and dumped it in the wastebasket. He was going
to die. He knew that.

Delwin Blessing's heart beat in an irregular pattern
that seemed to pound in his ears. Something would happen soon, but he would not wait for it. He got up, put
on his new white Stetson hat, and walked into the outer
office. "Marilyn, I've got to run down to a meeting in
Albuquerque."

"How long will you be gone, Sheriff?"

"I don't know. I'll call you."

"And where can we reach you?"

"I don't know that yet, either."

The Four Seasons Motel. He would pick up Delores
and take her down there, and the two of them would wait
it out.

Like a second honeymoon.

Or something.

Willard Travis normally closed his school activities at
noon on Saturdays and left one of his assistants to help
any divers who came around to have chutes repacked.
He left at eleven that day because he was supposed to
go off to his cabin above Lake Henshaw, buy gas with
a credit card on the way—to establish time and place,
and stay by himself until the rest of them got back. He
would swear the others had been with him all weekend.
Lew always thought of everything.

He headed his four-wheel-drive Bronco east on Interstate 8 and was halfway to Pine Valley before he thought
that he might have a tail.

It was an older Cadillac convertible, maybe a '70, and
he was not likely to outrun it. It stayed back by half a
mile.

Travis slowed his speed to fifty.

The Cadillac slowed.

Reaching under his seat, he pulled the Browning automatic from its clip, checked the magazine, ran the slide back to inject a round into the chamber, then slipped it under his thigh.

He turned north at Pine Valley. The Cadillac followed obediently.

Where the hell was Lew when he needed him?

Highway 79 was a two-lane blacktop that wiggled through some deserted territory. Off on the right were the Vallecito Mountains.

"Don't like this shit, Lu."

"You mean, no traffic, no houses, no bars, no freaks?"

"Yeah. I'm a city boy."

Hogan handled the Cad with a decade's familiarity. He loved the car because it was big enough for him. The seat didn't put his butt on the floor, and he had nearly half an inch of headroom when the top was up.

The Bronco slowed again, then picked up speed.

"Hell, he knows we're on him," Hogan said.

"That's okay," Rodriguez said. "I'd just as soon he knew he wasn't getting away with anything."

"Just follow him to wherever it is he's going?"

"Unless you've got something better to do."

"Than cruising the countryside with a beautiful woman at my side? You gotta be kidding, Lu." He grinned.

Hogan had felt great affection for Luisa since she had first been assigned as his partner. She had been fearless and a little reckless. The scar on her cheek always reminded him of the night they had staked out a chop shop, standing in the darkness of an alley across from the chain link enclosed square block of wrecked automobile hulks. They did not even see the three Dobermans that had been released from the yard until they were in air. Hogan went flat on his back on the asphalt with two dogs scrambling for his throat. He heard the bark of Luisa's .38 when she killed the dog that attacked her. Then, blood dripping down her jaw and throat, she had walked over and calmly shot the two dogs on top of him. She had always been proud of the fact that she had not yet had to kill a human being.

She was Luisa Suarez back then, and it was a long time ago, but they stayed in touch. He and Belinda had been to Santa Fe half a dozen times, and Luisa and Jim stayed with the Hogans when they were in LA. Hogan liked the way she didn't let the job get to her. She was easygoing enough, but there was a core of toughness underneath.

They passed through Julian twenty-two miles north of Pine Valley, jogged over to Santa Ysabel on Highway 78, then turned north again. Hogan let Travis get almost a mile ahead.

They passed by a lake on the right. The pine forest thickened, closed in on him. The Bronco slowed for one of the many turnoffs to cabins, swerved, and disappeared from the highway.

Hogan slapped the accelerator down, then braked hard as he reached the intersection. He quickly spun the wheel and slewed the big car onto a dirt track. He drove until he reached a blind turn hidden by pines, slowed down again, and pulled into the curve.

The truck was broadsided across the narrow road. Travis was leaning against the door with his cowboy hat tilted back and a pistol hanging by his side.

"Probably thinks he looks menacing," Hogan said as he braked to a stop.

The right side of the Cad was angled toward the Bronco and its driver.

Luisa snapped the safety off on the Browning twelve-gauge resting against her knee, then rolled down the window. "What's going on?"

"Who're you?"

"My name's Rodriguez. Who're you?"

"You been following me."

The man's eyes widened a little. Asshole probably recognized her name from the papers.

"Who, me?" Luisa asked him.

"Yeah, you."

Hogan slipped the Colt from where he had pushed it between the seat cushions.

"We're sheriff's officers. We want to talk to you," Luisa said.

Travis swung his arm upward.

Not soon enough.

Too late he saw the snout of the shotgun lying on the car's window ledge. He may have heard the boom, the way he tried to throw his arm up to protect his face.

He was too late for that too.

Rebel told him, "You don't suppose Taylor would try to sever any connections that might lead to him?"

Boxer said, "Not even probable. The man's too greedy to want to cut off any future source of funds."

"I hope you're right," Rebel said. "The Director is getting intense pressure from the media and the White House, but I think I'll be able to stonewall him. I know I will."

"Same here," Boxer said and hung up.

Mayhew was not as certain as he had sounded, however. Ellington had raised a spectre that had been hovering in the back of his mind. Checking his calendar and noting that the rest of his afternoon was free, Mayhew went to his safe and got out his old Llama automatic. It was a copy of a Colt .45, made in Spain, but chambered for 9 millimeter. He had not carried a gun in ten years, but decided it would not hurt to have just a little insurance. He preferred the silenced Python he used to keep at home for its stopping power, but he had had to leave that with Doug's body.

It was getting to the stage where he was not certain he could contain it. The newspaper and TV people were hounding everyone. The DCI had ordered him to a meeting at ten in the morning. He would want answers. Like Ellington, Mayhew would plead ignorance. He might have to admit to using STRAC a few times in Africa and South America and the Middle East. Those were clean rationales though.

Mayhew was cleaning the gun and was half done when his intercom sounded, "Call on line two, Mr. Mayhew."

"Who is it?"

"A man named Wayne."

He sighed. It had been inevitable.

"I'll take it." He punched the button.

"Deputy Director Mayhew?"

"Yes."

"My name is Steve Wayne. I'm—"

"I know who you are. What do you want?"

"Well, sir, I wondered if I could make an appointment to speak to you."

"What's the subject?"

"You were in Saigon in 1970 when a 101st commando team was operating out of Phan Rang. I was hoping you could give me some background on their activities."

Unlikely as hell. But the media had been pushing the Director and Mayhew all day on the same questions. That bitchy little reporter in Santa Fe. And Wayne, of course, was her unnamed source.

"You want to come out here?"

"That would be fine with me, sir."

"No. The day's shot anyway. How about the Mayflower lounge? Forty-five minutes?"

"I'll be there, Mr. Mayhew."

The Deputy Director for Operations hung up and finished cleaning his pistol. He found the belt holster for it, clipped it on his belt on the left side, then donned his suit coat and told his secretary he was taking off for the day.

He left Langley in his own Pontiac, taking the George Washington Memorial Parkway south. Heat waves shimmered off the surface of the Potomac, interfering with his thoughts.

How had it come to this? It had been Sanders's idea in the first place, but hell, he and Ellington were believers also, and Mayhew happened to have the ideal team for the job. God, after the way the liberals had screwed up the Vietnam effort, taking out a few people in key legislative and staffing spots was a small price to pay in order to maintain a strong defensive posture for the nation. It was not as if he or Sanders or Ellington would benefit personally. Their target decisions had been made coldly and objectively, strictly in the national interest.

He had used the STRAC Unit for years, sometimes at Agency direction, and sometimes at his own. The Director was going to be highly unhappy if Taylor got cornered by some cop and spouted off about Agency contracts.

The ideal team.

Nothing was ideal, anymore.

Wayne was going to be tough to handle. The man obviously did not respond to pleas about national security. And Taylor had just as obviously not located Wayne yet. Sanders had thought the man was still in New Mexico from his phone conversation with him, but here he was, right on Mayhew's doorstep. He either thought he had evidence linking Mayhew to the STRAC Unit or he was fishing. It did not matter either way. If Taylor could not get the job done, Mayhew would have to do it himself.

Mayhew was considering the possibilities for getting Wayne away from the Mayflower when the first bullet shattered his door window. Glass shards stung his cheek.

Out of thirty years of training, he instinctively snatched the Llama from its holster, swerved the car to the right lane, and checked the lane next to him.

Directly beside him in the inside lane was a gray Mercury sedan with two men in the front seat. The passenger was less than six feet away from him, reaiming an automatic, and Mayhew shot him in the right eye, smashing his glasses. Blood, flesh, and gray matter erupted across the front seat, striking the driver.

Mayhew stomped his gas pedal, but the other man did also, keeping pace.

He eased toward the left lane, but the other driver would not give way.

The fenders tapped hard, metal buckling, and Mayhew pulled back to his own lane.

A car ahead of him drove off onto the shoulder, its brake lights flaring bright, and he raced by it, still increasing speed.

He laid his wrist across his left arm, aimed, and fired three shots. One found the mark.

The driver jerked, his eyes widened, and blood spurted from his throat. Mayhew grinned at him.

He gave Mayhew one glaring gaze of hatred and spun the steering wheel hard to the right. When the Mercury slammed into the side of his Pontiac, the steering wheel jerked out of his hand. Both cars left the parkway at seventy-five miles per hour.

Mayhew wondered what Alice was going to think about it.

The newspaper thumped against the door at 4:30, and Taylor cautiously opened the door, grabbed the paper, then shut the door. He took it to the living room and flopped on the sofa.

Tuth opened the refrigerator. "You wanna beer?"

"Sure."

Uncapping the bottles, Tuth asked, "Anythin' new in there?"

"No. Same shit as was on the TV."

"Gettin' tense, ain't it, Lew?"

"We're going to do this one, just for the satisfaction, Sweet, then head straight for Mexico."

With the way the news was erupting all around them, Taylor was glad he had brought along his passport, travel cash, and the insurance tapes. And Albuquerque was not far from Mexico.

He was going to miss the Malibu place though. If he thought about it hard enough, he might figure out a way to sell the house. From Costa Rica or somewhere.

"We could maybe go and get my boat?" Tuth asked, the anxiety evident in his voice.

"No. They'll be watching it."

"Damn," he whined, "I gotta lot invested in that boat, Lew."

"You've got a lot in your Cayman Island account, too."

Tuth frowned. "Maybe I ain't got as much as you think. I had expenses."

"I'll give you whatever you need for a new boat."

Tuth smiled at that, and the two of them sat on Wayne's couch and waited for the man to come home.

When they heard the key in the lock, they both scrambled for either side of the doorway. It was not Wayne.

But Taylor could tell that it was all right with Tuth.

Wayne waited in the lounge until 7:30, impatient and dragging out a Black Label and water. When Mayhew had not appeared an hour after their scheduled appointment, he threw a bill on the bar and went out to the lobby. A steady stream of patrons pushed through the hushed, thickly carpeted check-in area.

He took the end telephone booth, used his credit card, and called Cece in Albuquerque. A man answered his telephone.

"Who is this?" Wayne demanded.

"About time you called, Wayne. Your girlfriend told us you were in Washington."

"What the hell are you doing in my apartment?"

"Maybe we're playing footsie, who knows?"

Wayne could feel the pulse pounding in his throat. "Who are you?"

"My name's Taylor, and I've got two things for you

to do, Wayne. One, you keep your mouth shut, or your broad gets to know us better. Two, you catch the first plane you can get back here. We need to talk.''

Wayne clinched his eyes shut.

My God!

The images in his mind were all repetitions of photographs taken in a barn.

''I want to talk to Cece.''

Taylor spoke to someone else. ''Bring her over here!''

''Steve . . . oh, Steve . . .''

Her voice sounded weak, and it was quickly replaced by Taylor's. ''Better hurry, Stevie.''

NINETEEN

ANDY'S SECOND MISTAKE was to lie, and he knew it was a mistake almost as soon as he said it: "I've set aside some insurance for myself, Lew."

"What kind of insurance is that, Andy? Term? Whole Life?"

"You know the kind. If something happens to me, it all comes out. All the contracts, all the operations."

Lew did not say anything.

"My bank's got it, a package. I die anything other than a natural death, they ship it to the DA."

"I can't say as I believe you," Lew said.

"That's the way it is," Andy said, wishing he could sound more convincing.

"You don't put something like that in a bank. You got it stuffed in a wall in your house? In the garage?"

"You think I'd tell you?"

"I think you will."

"Damn it, Lew, the war's over."

It was over for Andy.

The Orange County Sheriff's Office was aware of the case, of course, because they had handled the investigation of Pyle's condo and cars. Santa Barbara and San Luis Obispo counties were also involved as a result of

Andropoulous's death and the discovery of Pyle's airplane at Santa Maria.

Now the San Diego County Sheriff's Department was on the scene, cleaning up what was left of Willard Travis. Fortunately, Detective Sergeant Patrick Hogan and Captain Luisa Rodriguez had checked in with San Diego before they started their surveillance of Travis.

Hogan made his statement to a homicide sergeant named Al Fender and waited in the Cadillac while Luisa made her statement. Finally, Fender and Luisa wandered back to the Cadillac, which had been moved back down the road around the curve, to allow an ambulance and a forensics van access to the Bronco.

Fender leaned against the Caddie's door, bent his head down to see through the window, and said, "I guess I believe you, Hogan."

"Hey, I'm happy."

Rodriguez looked less happy, but this was her first shooting. It was going to take her a while.

"You okay, Lu?"

She nodded, but her heart wasn't in it, and her eyes were cloudy.

"Going to be okay, kid, once we get a burrito and a beer in you."

"Now what?" Fender asked.

"Now, we need to see what's in Travis's house and maybe at his business," Luisa told him.

"Okay. You two follow me, and I'll radio ahead for search warrants."

They drove to Willard Travis's place in El Cajon, following Fender's unmarked Chevy Celebrity. The house was a sprawling ranch style, topped with curved red tiles. A Ford Taurus wagon was in the driveway, and a woman with cropped blond hair, a checked blouse, blue shorts, and plastic thongs met them at the door.

Al Fender explained the problem.

Doreen Travis went into hysterics, and Fender had to call her doctor.

They didn't find anything of evidential value in the house except for a blue book with several possible bank account numbers and a series of apparent balances.

Hogan said, "It does seem highly unlikely that Willard Travis was able to save himself nine hundred and twenty-four thousand dollars in his short lifetime. Not by jumping out of airplanes."

This was big-time stuff, not three freaks knocking over a convenience store.

Hogan said, "Glad you called me, babe. Maybe I'll get me a nice letter put in my folder."

"You can count on one from me, Pat."

"But speaking of airplanes . . ."

"Speaking of airplanes, Pat, we still don't know where Taylor's Cessna is."

"Could always put out an all points through the FAA, Lu. I wrote down the tail number here, somewhere. And how 'bout an APB for Frederick Taylor, at least for questioning?"

"Why don't we do that? At least we can cover the southwest and along the Mexican border. I'd like to know where Freddie is playing."

The six o'clock national news mentioned the accident on the George Washington Memorial Parkway which meant that it was important enough to merit announcement nationwide though no names were released at that time. Stay tuned.

At ten o'clock, the Albuquerque station repeated the item with more detail: "Harold Dixon Mayhew, the Deputy Director of Operations for the Central Intelligence Agency, died tonight when his car hit a concrete culvert after being forced off the road by another car. Virginia State Police stated that shots were apparently exchanged between the two vehicles before they left the highway at high speed. Two California men in the other vehicle died as a result of gunshot wounds. Their names have not been released pending notification of next of kin."

Tuth looked up from his examination of Carol Curtis's body. "What's that, again, Lew? I missed it."

Damn. It was really going to hell. Taylor said, "That was Brooklyn and C.B."

"Dead, they said?"

"That's what they said."

"No shit?"

"At least they got Mayhew." One more link snapped, but too late. They were not going to get to Rebel. Taylor did not know whether or not Rebel knew the names behind STRAC, but he had not planned on taking the chance.

"He was on the list, huh?"

"He was on the list." Taylor's list.

"Too bad about Brooklyn and C.B." There was not much remorse in Tuth's tone. And Tuth had been fighting shoulder to shoulder with Danny Keck and Carl Battey for twenty years.

Taylor didn't feel much, either. Though they had all been together for a long time, his role had been one of babying them through the crises, taking care of them. The commander's job was a lonely one, and now it would just be a little easier. Deep inside though, he knew he was going to miss having his team around.

He got up, went to the kitchen, and tried calling Country's cabin at Lake Henshaw once again. Still no answer. He tried the shop and the house without success. Doreen wasn't even home. Jesus! If he wasn't around to oversee every detail, nothing got done.

Walking back to the living room, he saw Tuth leaning over the woman on the floor with the scalpel. Tuth made one deft slice and the thin strap between her bra cups parted, allowing her breasts to spill out.

"Sweet!"

"Ah, Lew! Lookit this! Just a couple quickies?"

Carol Curtis was flat on her back on the carpet, her wrists bound to the legs of the sofa with some of Wayne's neckties. Her ankles were tied to the legs of two easy chairs. A wide strip of adhesive tape clamped her lips and now she wore only semitransparent panties through which the pubic patch could be seen. She had been tied there for almost five hours, and her eyes still rolled in fear. Her face was pale, and uncontrollable tremors raced down her body.

"How can I look at that stuff for so long and not get a goddamned hard-on?" Tuth was whining again.

She was nice enough looking that even Taylor was aroused, but he had other plans. "Not yet, damn it! I want Wayne to watch."

Taylor's hatred of Wayne had been growing steadily. If that first damned sheriff had not been in the one-oh-one, and if Wayne had kept his nose out of it, everything would still be lean and mean. STRAC. He wanted Wayne strapped in a chair, watching Tuth's handiwork.

Tuth reached out and fondled one of her breasts. Her face screwed up in revulsion and she tried to twist away.

"Not now, Sweet."

Tuth sighed and stood up. There was a mighty bulge in his crotch and Taylor was not certain how much longer he could hold him off. "Wayne'll be here in a couple hours, then you can have at it."

"Like Andy and Andrea?"

"Just like that."

Tuth smiled in anticipation, twisting the scalpel between his thumb and forefinger.

It was after midnight in Albuquerque when Wayne crawled into his Trans Am. He brought it to life and threw a twenty at the parking lot attendant as he gunned it out onto University Boulevard. At Cemetery, he cut over to the interstate and headed north.

He had had nearly six hours to devise a plan, and he had come up with nothing. Every time he had tried to concentrate, the pictures of Andrea interfered. Every thought of Cece was agony. If this, if that. He should

have, he should have not. The recriminations and sup-
positions tangled his mind.

He had been in hostage situations before, but now his
love for Cece twisted his ability to reason. All of his
training told him he should have called in others, should
have backup a block deep. Because of personal involvement, he should stay out of any rescue attempt
completely.

He'd make one quick call to Phil Norman. No. He did
not want anyone else screwing it up. He might already
be too late for Cece.

He could not give up hope. Taylor wanted Wayne,
and he would keep Cece safe until he had him.

That had to be the way they'd play it.

When Candelaria Road came up, he drifted onto the
off ramp at fifty miles an hour and squealed the tires
turning west through the red light. Then he forced himself
to slow down. He would have to be deliberate. And very
careful.

He parked a block away from his apartment building,
took the .38 out of the suitcase he had had to check
through baggage, and examined the load. He dropped
three quick-loaders in his pocket. He went around to the
back, opened the trunk, and found the vinyl bag he kept
for roadside emergencies. In it were flares, a tow rope,
jumper cables, some tools, and a first aid kit. He closed
the trunk quietly.

Walking on the parched grass and staying close to the
building fronts so he could not be seen from his top-story
windows, he began moving toward the entrance to his
building.

A second thought.

Taylor and whoever was with him—he figured there
was a least one more—must have a car. He turned into
the side street and went clear around the block before he
found it. It was a rental and it was empty. He looked
around to make certain he could not be seen from the
apartment, then tried the doors. They were unlocked,

and he let himself inside, then tried the glovebox door. The rental agreement was made out to Jeffrey Mars. There was a button for the trunk release, and Wayne punched it.

He went around to the trunk and found two suitcases.

He opened the suitcases. Two men. There were no weapons, but he did find two passports—Frederick Taylor and Ronald Tuth. Tuth's address was located in Santa Barbara. Inside Taylor's case, he found an oversized shaving kit, unzipped it, and dumped it. No toiletries, but there were banded sheaves of hundred-dollar bills. About a quarter million, he estimated. There were three tape cassettes. Wayne stuffed the bills and the cassettes into his vinyl tool bag.

In Tuth's suitcase, he found loose lining and another twenty-five thousand. He took that, also, then resettled the clothing, closed, and relatched the suitcases.

The interlude gave him a chance to reconsider his plan, but he did not see an alternative. There were two men, undoubtedly armed, and he would not have a chance going in the front door, the only door to his apartment. Cece would not have a chance.

Having seen the photos of Taylor's work in the barn, Wayne had no illusions about Cece's chances. Taylor or Tuth or someone else in the group was a madman. Maybe all of them. Surrounding the apartment with uniforms would trigger irrational action.

That was what he told himself.

Wayne left the rental car and went back down the side street to the alley, then followed it to the rear of his building. His key let him into a back corridor between the laundry room and the storage room. He took the stairs to the third floor, the top floor. The stairs did not go to the roof.

Pulling open the steel fire door, he could see obliquely across the hallway to his door. There were only two dim lights in the corridor, but it was bright enough that he could not tell whether or not light was showing under his door. He let the door close softly.

A steel-runged ladder was bolted into the wall of the stairwell, and he climbed it quickly, pushed open the trapdoor, and crawled out onto the roof. He closed the trapdoor as quietly as possible.

This time of year, he and Cece kept the windows closed because of the air-conditioning, but he could not remember whether he'd left them locked or not. He hoped he had not.

Wayne extracted the tow rope from the vinyl bag, rezipped the bag, and placed it behind the roof-mounted air-conditioning condenser. Finding a steel ventilation vent near the corner over the bedroom, Wayne wrapped the tow rope around it and slipped the hook over the rope. He moved to the edge, found the back window of the bedroom, sat on the parapet, and swung his legs over. There was no light on in the bedroom. Doubling the other end of the rope, he made a loop, pressed his instep into it, and pushed it taut. He gripped the two strands of the rope tightly and slid off the parapet. By releasing the pressure of his hands, the free end of the rope slid through them slowly, letting him descend.

He went down eight feet, until his free toe found the top edge of the window. His palms burned. His right hand bled where the skin had been lacerated. Letting himself down another four feet, he got a foot on the window ledge just as the tow hook reached his hand.

Wayne used the rope to steady himself, got his right foot out of the loop and onto the ledge, and bent to peer in the window.

The drapes were closed.

The window was closed, but not locked. He got it started with his fingertips at the top, then grabbed the bottom and slowly pulled it up. It squeaked several times, though not loudly.

When it was open, he waited. He heard the TV going at low volume. An unintelligible voice. Gingerly, he slid inside and rested on his buttocks on the windowsill behind the drapes, parting them slightly. The door was half closed and there were lights on in the living room. He could see a back corner of the couch, the flicker of light from the TV screen.

Moving to his right, he looked further into the living room and saw the shoulder and elbow of a man peering through the curtains in the other room. Wayne eased the .38 from its holster, stepped from behind the drapes, and crossed the carpet to the edge of the doorway. He leaned around the jamb.

It might be Taylor at the window. He could not see Tuth.

He saw Cece's lower torso, spread flat on the floor. Her ankles were tied to chairs and she had panties on. The sofa blocked out the rest of her.

His heartbeat increased and the adrenaline pumped. He felt as if his vision were tunneling. Her right knee moved, trembled.

Hope.

The refrigerator door slammed. "Sure you don't wanna have one, Lew?"

Taylor turned around toward the room, so he could see into the kitchen. "No. And you've had enough, too. We've got work to do."

Tuth gave him a dirty look, but put the can down on the counter, then sat at the kitchen table. "You think he'll be here soon?"

"It's only a four-hour flight."

"Maybe he could'n getta ticket."

"He'd have called if that happened," Taylor assured.

"Maybe he's roundin' up a bunch of cops?"

"No. He won't want to risk the bitch."

"Hey, Lew, lemme have one shot at her before he comes. I'm gettin' pretty horny."

"He's got to watch," Taylor insisted.

But his plans had changed since the news bulletin at

midnight. They had been watching the Late Night Show when suddenly, unbelievably, there was a picture of Frederick Taylor of Lubbock, Texas, on the screen. Wanted for questioning in the murders of George and Andrea Andropoulous in Santa Fe.

Sweet was amazed. He had had no idea they were getting that close. Sweet spent half his life amazed. But Taylor had never gotten him to read newspapers or watch the news shows.

No goddamned doubt, though. It was getting late, and this was the wrong place to be. They might have to truss up the broad and move to another location.

Taylor paced. He was irritated, getting impatient, getting just a little scared, maybe. The fear did not bother him. There was always fear in an operation. It was a good high.

He walked toward the kitchen, and from the corner of his eye, saw movement by the half-closed door of the bedroom. He stopped, turned, and went back to kneel beside the woman. Her wide eyes followed every move he made.

Slipping the Beretta from the pocket of his sport coat, he held the muzzle against her temple.

"Wayne! Come out of there, and your hands better be empty!"

Quiet.

Tuth got up from the kitchen table.

"Now, Wayne!" shouted Taylor.

The Fed pulled open the door and stepped out of the bedroom, his hands held out in front of him. His face was pale as death.

Good.

"Hot damn!" Tuth said. "Now?"

"Not now. We've got to move."

"Ah, but shit, Lew—"

"We don't know who he's got on the way."

"Hey, you said—"

"Get the needles, Sweet. Do it now."

* * *

At 2:10 in the morning, Albuquerque air control radioed, ''Cessna four-six, you are cleared for takeoff.''

''Albuquerque, four-six. Roger, cleared for takeoff.''

Taylor advanced the throttles, and the Cessna Skymaster rolled forward, picking up speed quickly. The airframe shuddered as the two 210-horsepower engines—one pulling prop forward and one pushing prop at the rear between the two tail booms—climbed through the RPMs.

The lights along Runway 27 picked up momentum, flashing by, and halfway along the length, the yoke lightened as the airspeed reached eighty miles per hour. Taylor eased the yoke back, and the Skymaster took to the air. Over the outer marker, he retracted the flaps and landing gear. The speed picked up quickly, and Taylor eased the throttles back a couple notches when he reached a cruise speed of 180 miles per hour at five thousand feet.

He picked up the mike from where he had dropped it in his lap. ''Albuquerque Air, this is Cessna four-six.''

''Go ahead, four-six.''

''Albuquerque, four-six. Requesting VFR for Yuma, Arizona, at twelve thousand, heading two-seven-zero.''

''Cessna four-six, you are cleared to twelve thousand, heading two-seven-zero.''

''Albuquerque, four-six out.''

Taylor increased power to 80 percent for the climb, then finally relaxed. At 12,000 feet, he engaged the automatic pilot. It was strange, flying the plane from the right seat.

They had put Wayne in the lefthand seat, and he was limp against the side of the cockpit, his head lolled back against the window. His mouth sagged open, and his breathing was raspy, but unheard under the steady drone of the engines. His hands were bound with a necktie.

Tuth and the woman were in the back. The Skymaster could handle six seats, but the four in the rear had been

removed and replaced with a cushioned mat for jumpers
to sit on with their gear. The woman was sprawled out
along the left side, also out of it from the heavy dose of
sedative Taylor had injected, good for close to two hours.
They had had to dress her again, in slacks and blouse,
in order to transfer her to the car, then to the plane. Tuth
had bitched and damned near cried putting clothes back
on her.

Tuth sat on the floor next to her, leaning back against
the parachutes, and every once in a while, he would
reach out and caress her.

It was difficult to talk over the roar of the engines,
and Taylor did not bother to try.

An hour out of Albuquerque, when he saw the lights
of Springerville, Arizona, on his right, Taylor retrimmed
the autopilot. The plane started to lose altitude gradually
as it changed course to 190 degrees. Taylor advanced
the throttles until the airspeed indicator was showing 195.
He switched the radio to Tucson's frequency, just in case
there was a weather report he should know about. By
the time he reached the Mexican border, east of Nogales,
he wanted to be flying low enough to make radar tracking
in the mountains difficult.

In another hour, they would reach the border. It would
be close to first light, but still murky enough if there
were border patrol or DEA planes in the area.

He checked the back, and saw Tuth starting to stretch
out, rubbing up against the woman.

"Goddamn it, Sweet!"

"Goddamn it, yourself!"

"Jesus, man. She's out cold."

"That's okay. Just once? Before we toss 'em out?"
It was Tuth's idea to drop them from around fifteen
thousand feet on the other side of the border. He wanted
them conscious and alert, so they could think about it
all the way down into some deserted arroyo.

"Oh, hell. Go ahead."

But Tuth hesitated when the radio speaker overhead

crackled, "Cessna four-six, this is Tucson air control."

Taylor did not answer the call.

"Cessna four-six, Albuquerque air passed you to us. Four-six, respond please."

His fingers twitched, but he left the mike alone.

"Cessna four-six, are you on the air? We're showing an IFF for you."

Taylor's eyes shot to the radio stack. The Identify Friend or Foe, or "Squawk-Ident" to civilians, which tagged his particular blip on a radar screen, was still transmitting. He had forgotten to shut the damned thing down.

"Goddamn, Lew!" Tuth crawled forward on his knees until he was behind the seat.

"Cessna four-six, Tucson Air. The FAA is requesting your cooperation. Can you respond, please?"

Damn it, they were looking for the plane.

Wayne's arm jumped, his head jerked against the window, and then he slumped again.

Taylor reached forward and flipped the toggle for the IFF. He cut off the autopilot and eased into a shallow dive.

"Cessna four-six! I am notifying Mexican authorities and requesting that F–15s from Davis-Monthan search for you. By authority of the Federal Aviation Administration, you are ordered to land at Tucson."

Taylor shut off the radio.

"Jeez, Lew! What're we gonna do?"

"Shut up, I'm thinking."

Taylor shoved the throttles in until the Skymaster was maxing at around 205.

They crossed over Interstate 10 at four thousand feet, dodging the 6700-foot Lime Peak on its left. Benson, Arizona, was lit up to the west.

Speaking above the roar of the engines, Taylor said, "Saddle up, Sweet."

"What?"

"As soon as we cross the border, we're getting out. We'll let somebody chase the plane."

Looking back, he saw Sweet grinning at him. "Good damned idea, Lew."

Wayne was coming around, but still groggy. Taylor reached over, took the tail of the necktie, and tied it to his belt so he could not move his hands around.

Ten minutes more. He put the plane in a shallow climb and engaged the autopilot.

Maybe some Mexican fighter pilot would shoot it down, maybe Wayne and the woman would have themselves a crash.

Wayne's head hurt like hell, throbbed to a slow beat of his heart, and when he opened his eyes, he saw dials and buttons.

Why dials and buttons? Airplane yoke right in front of him. What the hell? Slowly, he became aware of the engine noise, the sway and bump of a small plane. The sun was rising on his left, still low. Ahead, in vague light, he saw endless, choppy darkened earth.

He shook his head. He looked to the seat on his right. It was empty. He was all alone.

Why am I here?

He tried to move his hands, but could not. Looking down, he saw that they were tied to his belt.

"Hurry up, Sweet!"

Wayne spun his head around, the headache lancing against the back of his eyes.

Two men in the back, the shorter, ugly one buckling straps for the other.

My God! Cece! Was she dead? Her chest moved. Breathing. Was she moaning? Snoring? He could not hear over the engine noise.

"Hey, Wayne! Glad you could join us!" The man had a white scar on his forehead, a broken nose. The same as the fake agent named . . . something. Sidney Gregg. Taylor. He was smiling broadly.

The big smile. The needle.

Wayne's mouth was dry. His voice croaked. "What the hell do—"

"I'm sorry we can't hang around, Wayne. I hope you'll have a good flight."

"What'sa altitude, Lew?"

Glancing at the instrument panel, Taylor said, "Fourteen-five."

"Good. Nice long drop."

Taylor shoved the seat back forward, released the door catch, and shoved the wide door open. The wind was a loud shriek. On his knees, Taylor worked himself into the doorway dragging a suitcase, set his feet, gripped the bag in his arms, and then he was gone.

The other man waddled on his knees to the door, grinning at Wayne. "You gonna miss that pussy, fed man. Not for long, though."

He got his feet under him, shoved the door wide, and leaped out with his own suitcase. The door slammed back into place.

Frantically, Wayne worked at his belt buckle. When it released, his hands were free, though still bound. He looked back at Cece. Moaning? God, her face was so pale.

He looked at all the controls. He had never flown an airplane before, but he had watched the pilots of small craft he had chartered many times. Autopilot. He reached out with both hands and clicked the toggle to the Off position. He felt the plane sag a trifle as he put his hands on the yoke and his feet on the rudder pedals. Airspeed over two hundred. Climbing now with the loss of the autopilot and the weight of the two men.

He moved his hands to retard the throttles, then brought them back to the yoke as the plane tilted to the left. He panicked for a moment, then added left rudder. The plane started a turn to the left.

The airplane felt like it was skidding.

He eased in some right rudder, and it felt better.

Shove the yoke forward. Too much, back a little.

Compass? There.

The nose dropped as the plane came around 180 degrees.

He straightened out. Rudder and yoke centered. Turn-and-bank indicator level, nose below the horizon.

Cece was moaning. Louder, over the roar of the engines.

Plural. There were two engines. Twin set of engine gauges. It was one of those strange Cessnas.

He peered through the windshield.

There. Way below him, the morning sun reflected off two parachute canopies, maybe a half mile apart and a couple miles ahead of him. The far one was much lower.

Cece yelled.

He looked back.

Her blouse was stained red, and he saw the scalpel protruding from her chest, just below the breastbone. She struggled, then fell back.

Wayne would remember later that he screamed.

He shoved the yoke forward, and the plane dove.

A little left rudder and aileron.

He lined up the plane on the parachute. Bring the nose up a little. The face seemed so clear in the morning light. So damned ugly.

The head turned to look at him, and the mouth opened wide in a silent scream.

The plane hit high on the the canopy, the prop shredding it.

He tilted the nose down. Taylor was lower. Too far. Back with the yoke.

Taylor's face became distinct in the windscreen. Genuine surprise. He dropped his suitcase, and it spun away toward the ground. The propeller caught him at about his waist. A thump shook the airframe. Shredded flesh, gore, and blood splattered the windshield.

The airplane began to vibrate badly.

Wayne felt dazed.

It took him a few seconds to realize he had a bent propeller. The shaking increased violently.

He leveled off, then moved his hands to the throttles, found the one for the forward engine, and pulled it all the way back. Below the throttle were controls marked Ignition and Feather, and he shifted both to new positions. The engine died and the propeller wound down to a stop.

The vibration disappeared, but he saw that his speed was coming down fast. The earth appeared awfully close.

He looked back at Cece, saw the tremors in her bound hands and her lips as she struggled with consciousness.

Sleep, baby.

Wayne struggled with the binding that was wrapped around his hands, but could not loosen the tie. His eyes found the radios, searched their faces, and spotted the power switch. He turned it on.

Picking up the microphone resting on the floor by its coiled cord, Wayne depressed the transmit button and held it close to his mouth.

"Is somebody on this channel? I've got an emergency."

"This is Tucson Air Control. Who is this, please?"

"My name is Steve Wayne, F . . . ex-FBI. I'm aboard a . . . Cessna owned by Frederick Taylor, and I don't have a pilot."

"Tucson Air to all aircraft. We have an emergency. All aircraft go to alternate frequencies. Wayne, are you straight and level?"

"Yes. Losing a little altitude, altimeter shows six-six-hundred. I've shut down one engine."

"All right, Wayne, or Steve. How's Steve? Let's you and me be calm. We're going to talk you down."

"Get to it, damn it. I've got a wounded woman on board."

Cece was crying, calling his name.

Four minutes later, an F–15 Eagle went by, but the pilot could not fly slow enough to stay with him.

Three minutes after that, a twin-engine Beechcraft pulled up on his wing, and somebody named George started talking to him. George told him what to do with his flaps and landing gear.

Tucson, when it came up, had never looked so good to him.

Cece had stopped crying.

TWENTY

DELWIN BLESSING HAD disappeared for several days, but he was in his office on Monday, full of good cheer, when Willow walked in unannounced with Keith Boyles and Jerry Hayman. Janet was wearing a new yellow sundress, and she felt fresh.

He smiled broadly at them. "Well, hel-lo, citizens! Come in. Have a seat."

They did not sit.

Hayman lowered his voice and said, "You look fit, Del, ol' boy. Feeling good?"

Blessing frowned, and Janet knew he was remembering who else had called him "ol' boy." One of the tapes Wayne had acquired somewhere made extensive use of the phrase. He said, "Of course. It's a beautiful day."

Boyles was not in a similar mood. "It's a nice day to resign, Del."

Blessing came out of his chair. "What are you talking about?"

"Janet?"

She laid a copy of the cassette on the desk. She was halfway sorry she had decided not to make a story of it. It was one of two major decisions. She had received four employment offers, from Alburquerque to LA, and she had decided to forgo them, too. She was a Santa

Fe girl, and she had to help Luisa get elected. Which should not be too difficult, after the news stories out of San Diego.

"I don't know whether or not you ever got your copy of this," she said. "We've got several, so you can keep this one."

Blessing's face paled and his eyes narrowed. "What is it?" he squeaked.

"I think you know."

"That's . . . that's blackmail."

"That's a pretty mild accusation," Boyles said. "All you have to do is go back to the practice of law."

"You weren't cut out for this, anyway, Del, ol' boy," Hayman concluded.

Wayne tried the same tactic with information he had gathered from the other tapes, which had mentioned the four code names of STRAC, Boxer, Rebel, and Cottonmouth.

He called the familiar number in Washington.

It was not the private number, and he had to go through several secretaries.

"Hello?"

"Rebel, this is Boxer."

"Wh . . . what?"

"It might as well be Boxer. Taylor had lots of information on tape."

"What are you talking about? Who is this? Wayne?"

There was some growing hysteria in the voice, Wayne thought.

"There's probably not enough to convict, Ellington, and I didn't have a search warrant when I picked up the cassettes, but it's damned sure your voice—we can voice-print it, and there's enough to ruin a career. I'd like to see you sitting in the electric chair, but I'll settle for your resignation. By five o'clock, your time."

Wayne hung up.

Mark Ellington did not resign by five o'clock, but he blew his brains all over his office in time to make the six o'clock news.

There was also a human interest story on the same telecast. Some benefactor had mailed a box of cash to the American Red Cross. It came out right at $275,000.

Wayne spread a blanket on the cedar planks of the deck and settled down onto it. The lights of Santa Fe were a pale white blush to the south. The stars above appeared exceptionally clear.

The dark expanse of manzanita snuggling up to the deck seemed comfortable and secure, rather than menacing. He could smell the aroma of wildflowers. Someday, he would have to learn to identify them.

Cece lowered herself to the blanket beside him, bracing herself on his upraised arm. She was still sore from the surgery.

Her mind was becoming more flexible though, after talking about her fear and anger with the psychiatrists. These feelings would always be with her, but she had told Wayne she would try to control it.

"Someday," she said, "we'll have to get furniture."

"No hurry."

"No, there's not."

"I got you something."

He pulled the box from his pocket and opened it. In the dark, the stone did not twinkle like a star, but she knew what it was when he slipped it on her finger.

"It's about time, lover," she said.

"Sorry. I got sidetracked."

"Coincidence, though. I got you a little something."

Retrieving a package wrapped in white tissue paper from her purse, she handed it to him.

Wayne ripped the paper free and discovered a hammer.

"You want to get started?" she asked.

"Can it wait until morning?"

"Sure."

They sat in the dark and held hands and watched Carlos Rivera's stars go by.

GRITTY, SUSPENSEFUL NOVELS
BY MASTER STORYTELLERS
FROM AVON BOOKS

OUT ON THE CUTTING EDGE
by Lawrence Block
70993-7/$4.95 US/$5.95 Can

"Exceptional...A whale of a knockout punch to the solar plexu[s]"
New York Daily Ne[ws]

FORCE OF NATURE
by Stephen Solomita
70949-X/$4.95 US/$5.95 Can

"Powerful and relentlessly engaging...Tension at a rive[ting]
peak" *Publishers Weekly*

A TWIST OF THE KNIFE
by Stephen Solomita
70997-X/$4.95 US/$5.95 Can

"A sizzler...Wambaugh and Caunitz had better look out"
Associated P[ress]

BLACK CHERRY BLUES
by James Lee Burke
71204-0/$4.95 US/$5.95 Can

"Remarkable...A terrific story...The plot crackles with eve[nts]
and suspense...Not to be missed!"
Los Angeles Times Book Rev[iew]